ROCKY MOUNTAIN
WATERSHED

ROCKY MOUNTAIN
WATERSHED

ITS RIVER – ITS PEOPLE

BILL BURCH

iUniverse, Inc.
Bloomington

Rocky Mountain Watershed
Its River—Its People

Maps researched and drawn by Towne's Elementary students

Author's Photograph: Sharon Burch

iUniverse books may be ordered through booksellers or by contacting:

iUniverse
1663 Liberty Drive
Bloomington, IN 47403
www.iuniverse.com
1-800-Authors (1-800-288-4677)

ISBN: 978-1-4502-7148-6 (sc)
ISBN: 978-1-4502-7149-3 (dj)
ISBN: 978-1-4502-7150-9 (ebk)

Printed in the United States of America
iUniverse rev. date: 12/28/2010

Dedicated to my wife Sharon and our daughters Pam and Kelly.

Thanks to Char and Bruce Turner for their computer expertise, patience and encouragement.

Special thanks to Linda Kimble for her editing skill and unique insight.

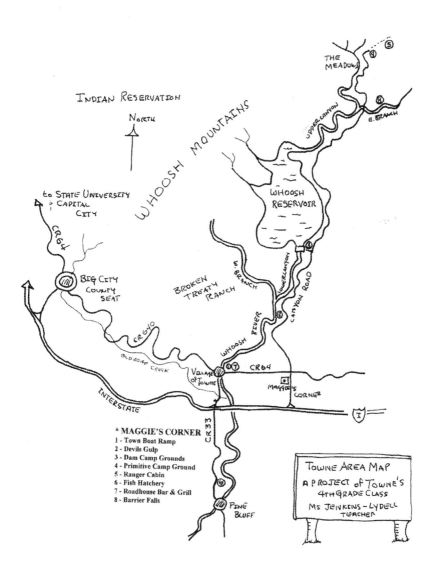

INDIAN RESERVATION

North

WHOOSH MOUNTAINS

THE MEADOWS

E. BRANCH

UPPER CANYON

WHOOSH RESERVOIR

to STATE UNIVERSITY & CAPITAL CITY

CR64

BIG CITY COUNTY SEAT

LOWER CANYON

CANYON ROAD

BROKEN TREATY RANCH

E. BRANCH

WHOOSH RIVER

CR40

OLD ROAD CREEK

VILLAGE OF TOWNE

CR64

MAGGIE'S CORNER

INTERSTATE

I

CR33

PINE BLUFF

* MAGGIE'S CORNER
1 - Town Boat Ramp
2 - Devils Gulp
3 - Dam Camp Grounds
4 - Primitive Camp Ground
5 - Ranger Cabin
6 - Fish Hatchery
7 - Roadhouse Bar & Grill
8 - Barrier Falls

TOWNE AREA MAP
A PROJECT of TOWNE'S 4TH GRADE CLASS
MS JENKINS-LYDELL TEACHER

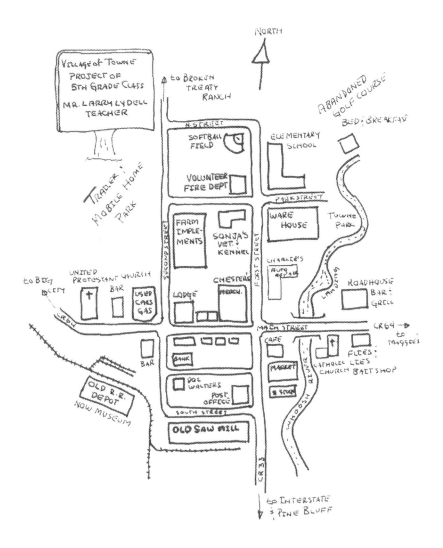

PROLOGUE

◗◀

North America's last Ice Age did not extend far enough south to engulf the area of *The River*, but the melting of billions of tons of frozen snow did create torrents of raging water and glacial rubble that molded it en route south to form one of several huge pre-historic lakes. Though shifts in the earth's crust would occasionally alter *The River's* path, 10,000 years of erosion was mainly responsible for its present course, even as the great lakes slowly evaporated and eventually disappeared.

Theory holds that the first humans to reach the area came across the now submerged Beringia plains. They were hunters following the Woolly Mammoth into North America long before the ice cap receded. Stone projectile points associated with the Clovis, Folsom and Plano cultures have been discovered throughout the area. Archeological evidence of the adventurous Wooly Mammoth have been found in the watershed, though it is believed that the animal was doomed before the present cut of *The River* was scoured. Whether it was the change in climate, some meteorite explosion in the atmosphere, the hunters themselves, or a combination of factors that drove the Wooly Mammoth to extinction, the creature was gone long before the first white man appeared.

American Indian tribes greeted the earliest fur traders, explorers, adventurers, and fugitives with differing degrees of hospitality. Time and conflict sorted out claims of sovereignty over the lands. When Chester Ratzigg built the first permanent home on *The River* only one tribe remained. Fortunately, it was friendly. Well, friendly for the most part. Indians called the waterway many things, some even charitable, but it was Chester who gave the river its first English name.

◄━

Watershed tells the stories of several individuals who, over many years, followed Chester Ratzigg to the Whoosh River Watershed. Some reside there today. This book is about relationships and the struggle to endure in a high Rocky Mountain community.

Watershed is about the successes and failures, loves, ambitions, obsessions, the hopes and fears of people who face important personal decisions—decisions with deep and permanent effects. However, the one common thread that inevitably binds them all together, *The River*, will be little changed by their choices—not if viewed in the context of a total geological time scale.

WATERSHED

An area of land that drains down slope
to the lowest point. The water moves
through a network of drainage pathways,
both underground and on the surface.
These pathways converge into streams
and rivers, which become progressively
larger as the water moves on downstream,
eventually reaching an estuary and the ocean.

CHAPTER 1: Maggie's Corner

L aura crested the last foothill out of the mountains, a route filled with hairpin curves and abyss-like drop offs, the danger exaggerated even more by the oncoming darkness. Ahead she saw headlights moving along the Interstate and an exit ramp less than a mile away. A lone billboard promised services ahead. There it was. A gas station nestled just below, an oasis of sorts, ablaze in electric light. With lots of luck it would be a full-service garage. With just a little luck there would be a tow truck.

Pushing the hazard light button, Laura shifted into neutral and shut off the engine of her pickup. As a result, she also stopped the rhythmic banging under the hood, along with the power steering and power brakes. With all the strength she could muster, she aimed for the side of the building, away from the fuel pumps. Cranking the steering wheel, while standing on the brake pedal, she sent a spray of loose gravel bouncing off the vinyl siding like a machine gun's report. With flashing amber hazard lights reflecting back into the cab, the truck came to a stop inches short of the shiny free air and vacuum tanks.

Taking a deep gasp of late evening air, Laura wiped her sweaty palms on her pant legs and climbed out of the truck, slamming the door with a sense of relief and disgust. Unfair, with all the scrapes she and her truck had been through, she had no right to be angry at the vehicle. She glanced down at her dust-covered bumper sticker:

*THIS IS **NOT** MY
BOYFRIEND'S PICKUP!*

Right now she wished she had a boyfriend—a boyfriend that was a mechanic. "Thanks, truck. You certainly know how to make a grand entrance." She patted the back bumper and headed for the front of the convenience store.

Laura stopped a second to get her bearings. She noticed the fueling area in the front was equipped with the newest self-service equipment for autos, with diesel pumps for semis in the back. Brilliant lights on tall poles illuminated the entire area. The building itself could have been mistaken for new until you noticed that it was a timeworn, two-story structure, recently covered with pure-white vinyl siding. An old, unlit neon FUEL sign topped the second story. In the brilliance of modern lighting and cheap plastic, hung another sign announcing:

MAGGIE'S CORNER

Laura stood for a moment peering through the double glass doors, took another deep breath, and shoved her way inside. A glance around showed a pre-WWII patterned-tin ceiling and a well-worn plank floor. Side walls were lined by modern head-high coolers with thick sliding glass doors. Three aisles of shelving were stacked with food products and assorted items for kitchen or camp. A fourth row contained fishing gear and small repair items plus rows of motor oil cans. Against the back wall was a second entrance from the diesel area. A rack of magazines, mostly aimed at the hunter or fisherman, stood in the corner.

Enough, you've been in a truck stop before.

Laura slid a cooler door aside. The cold blast of refrigerated air sent a shiver up her spine. Resisting the wine, she picked up a single can of Pepsi, popped the top, and walked over to the cashier's counter. Registers, credit card machines, and a surveillance monitor were surrounded by open boxes of candy bars and cheap lighters covered with pictures of leaping trout. Racks behind the checkout held assorted packs of cigarettes, and round tins and pouches of chewing tobacco, along with a modest offering of hard liquors.

Behind the counter, studying a pile of invoices, stood a small woman of forty-five or maybe even fifty-five. She wore jeans, a plaid shirt, and well-scuffed leather cowboy boots. Her graying black hair was pulled back into a pony tail.

"Heard you slide in. Brake problem?" the woman asked with the warmest smile Laura had seen since leaving her home state of Wisconsin. She had discovered that most people 'out here' in the Rockies generally ignored you. The ones that didn't went out of their way to be rude. Of course, there was the occasional exception when someone seemed ready to adopt you on the spot, listen to your life story, and then offer you a home-cooked meal. Sometimes it was better to be ignored.

"No, my motor…er, engine, has been banging for the last ten miles and I just shut it off at the top of the hill. Forgot how hard it was to handle a truck without power breaks or steering. Almost came through your building. Guess I nicked up your siding a little. Sorry."

"Forget it," the woman said, continuing to smile. "It's not like I've got real wood siding."

"Well, thanks. But now I have to do something about getting my truck fixed. Can I have it hauled somewhere?" Laura asked, without much hope.

"Unless you've got twenty-four hour road service, you're stranded until tomorrow. It's Sunday night. Even if you did get a tow, nobody would check it out until morning."

"Do you know anyone close by who would take a look at it? I'm due back in Madison…Madison, Wisconsin on Thursday. Guess that's out," Laura sighed.

"Something important?"

"Going back to school. I came out here with a bachelor's degree looking for work…a job with pay. Apparently, unless you have a Master's, or are willing to be a volunteer, you're out of luck. I've been offered room and board for forty hours of work a week. I really have to do better than that. So my job search became a three month fishing trip…which isn't all bad." For the first time a genuine smile crossed Laura's face.

"Well, let's see if we can get you back on the road real soon," Maggie said. "I've got a cousin, Charlie…lives in Towne. He's the best mechanic hereabouts. Better than anybody in Big City. And he won't cheat you…at least he won't cheat you if I send you. Look, I've got a guy going by there tonight after we close. Shoot, I'll send him home early. He lives in an apartment near Charlie's. I'll have him load your truck onto our flatbed.

"George," she hollered, belying her small stature. "Charlie's garage is only six miles from here, and by ten tomorrow morning he should know what's wrong with your truck and how long it will take to fix it."

"And how much," Laura muttered to herself. "Looks like I have no choice. I'm at your mercy." She shrugged and tried to return the older woman's smile.

"I'm Laura, Laura Menard." She stuck out her hand. Eventually, everyone who came to know her closely would call her Laurie, but she saw herself as Laura. One day, coming home from junior high, she had announced: "Hence forth, I will no longer answer to the name Laurie, only Laura." And yes, she did indeed say *hence forth*.

"I'm Maggie, just like the sign says. I'm the Maggie of Maggie's Corner." And the two women shook hands.

"George!" This time it was more of a bellow than a holler.

George appeared from the back storeroom. He was a short, stocky man dressed in caramel-colored bib overalls, clean-shaven with a military haircut.

"Take a look at this young lady's pickup. The one nosed up to the air pumps." She winked at Laura.

"Keys in it?" Maggie asked. Laura handed them to George. Without acknowledging her, he took them and exited with a noticeable limp.

"Old war wound. What war? I'm not sure. Not sure if he really knows. George came back to Towne just out of the Army with his head all scrambled. He looks a little scary, but since he got out of the Veterans Administration Hospital in Big City, he hasn't hurt anybody. And he does have a heart of gold. If George likes you, he likes you. Really don't know how I ever got along without him."

Laura nodded. Not knowing what to say, she changed the subject. "Do you have a place where I could set up my tent... somewhere I'll be out of the way?"

"Nonsense, I've got a vacant cabin out back. Who am I kidding? I have six cabins and five of them are vacant. The old guy in Cabin #6 rents every summer from the end of the snow runoff through September. He uses it as a base camp for his fishing trips.

The rest of the time he wanders around the area with a notebook in his hand, just scribbling away and asking questions of the local folks. Not sure if he writes down his thoughts or what folks tell him…maybe both. He's a little eccentric and harmless enough… really quite nice.

"Anyway, we'll get you settled in Cabin #1 until we get your truck fixed. Cabin's clean, with a hot-water shower, and I just changed the bedding. There's heat, air, a refrigerator, an old gas stove, and a new microwave oven, although you won't need the air until July." Laura forced a smile. "Don't laugh now, you might like it well enough around here to stay awhile. Winters aren't all that bad. Well, some years they aren't," she amended. "Come to think of it, nobody has ever called this the Banana Belt of the Rockies."

Laura attempted another smile but didn't quite pull it off. "I'm sorry. I really can't pay you for much more than a campsite. I could give you my credit card, but it's over the limit. I'll probably have to call home for money," she whispered more to herself than to Maggie. She reached for her wallet to pay for her Pepsi.

"Not to worry. We'll figure it out later and the soda pop is on me."

The sound of Laura's crippled pickup starting and quickly shutting off preceded George through the back doors.

One shake of his head said it all. As if he were reading Maggie's mind, he said, "I'll load it up and haul it to Charlie's. Be back before you close."

"Slow down George. I'd like you to officially meet Laura Menard." George nodded his head and Laura returned the greeting. "Help Laura get her stuff out of the truck before you leave. Take it to Cabin #1. After you drop her truck at Charlie's, get some sleep. Don't you dare come back here tonight. I'll call Charlie early in the morning and let him know what's going on.

You come in anytime. We'll have the usual Monday deliveries to put away."

Maggie turned to Laura, "If you like to fish and have a rod and reel in your truck, grab it before he leaves. You may have some time to kill." She flipped the cabin key to George. "Use the dead bolt when you get settled, Laura. If you need anything tonight, just come up the side stairs and bang on my door. I live in the upstairs apartment. I'm a light sleeper. Have to be in this business."

"I can't thank you enough," Laura said, slight apprehension in her voice.

"Shush. Go take a hot shower and get to bed. I'll see you in the morning."

George dumped Laura's *stuff* on the front porch of the small cabin, turned the lock, and handed her the key. He left without a word. Laura watched as he crossed the pavement and loaded her Dodge Dakota onto the flatbed. He climbed into the cab, did a one-eighty and headed toward Towne.

Laura repressed a smile then laughed out loud. "What have I gotten myself into now?" Other than the problem with her truck, she didn't see a downside to the situation. Not yet, anyway. Oh sure, the expense, but that's a given with an old truck, especially after tearing it up in the mountains. She had certainly gotten her money's worth and she could always register a few days late for grad school.

She opened the door to Cabin #1 and felt for a wall switch. A ceiling fixture in the kitchen area flooded the modest but extremely clean cabin with fluorescent light. Four ladder-back chairs surrounded a kitchen table covered with a red and white-checkered oilcloth, reminding her of her grandmother's kitchen. An overstuffed chair and small sofa faced the television. A tiny antique desk and chair filled another corner. A paneled door led to the bedroom where a wicker chair sat next to a queen-sized bed covered with an authentic Amish quilt. The walk-in closet and cedar chest of drawers crowded the rest of the room. Another door led to the bathroom that held a small stand-up shower.

Laura tried the heat first. The blower kicked on and in seconds warm air poured out of the vents. She pushed the lever over to air conditioning. It worked. Now, for the supreme test—Laura held her hand under the showerhead and felt a powerful burst of cold, then warm, then hot water. It was apparent that someone took great pride in these cabins.

"I've hit the mother lode," she proclaimed to a porcelain ballerina on top of the chest. For almost three months she had lived out of the back of her pickup and slept in a mountain tent. Yes, this *was* the mother lode.

After a very long and hot shower, she found some Myers's Rum stashed in her backpack and poured it into the now half-empty Pepsi can. She took a swallow and began examining books on the shelves under the TV. There was the obligatory bible (surprisingly, it looked like it had been read before), a Pat McManus book, and an Ernest Hemingway volume of *Nick Adam's Stories*, two dated fly-fishing magazines, and a large ledger where fishermen had recorded their *fish stories*. Most of the entries, some dating as far back as the 1930s, were signed. She thumbed through the pages and had a feeling that there was more useful information contained on these yellowing pages than there was in all the modern fishing magazines put together. Of course, you couldn't believe all the handwritten entries anymore than you could believe the stories in the glossy-covered periodicals.

By the time she finished her drink, Laura had crashed on the bed, out for the night.

><

There was a kicking on the cabin door just as Laura had finished dressing from her morning shower. Two showers in twelve hours, it was heaven. She opened the door to find George standing on the porch with a loaf of bread, carton of eggs, slab of bacon and a tub of oleo all balanced in one arm. In his other hand, he gripped a steaming pot of coffee. Mumbling "good morning," George pushed past her to the kitchen, put the food in the refrigerator, set the bread on the table, and lit the stove for the coffee.

"Frying pan and toaster in the cupboard. Dishes too. Coffee pot is mine."

Laura watched him go down the stairs. "George." He stopped and half turned. "Thank you very much." He gave a half wave and headed toward the store.

"I think he kind of likes me," Laura smiled to herself. "How could I tell him I really need cream for my coffee?"

God, how she loved bacon and eggs—death-on-a-platter.

After finishing breakfast she washed the dishes, rinsed the coffee pot and walked over to the store, pot in hand. Maggie was behind the counter, as if she had been there all night.

"Just set the pot on the counter. Did you sleep, Laura?"

"Like a hibernating old bear. Thank you so much."

"Good news and bad news about your pickup. Charlie said it wasn't all that serious, but it will take a few days to fix. He doesn't stock many parts...has to send to Big City for most of them. Take my Blazer and go talk to him."

"No thanks, I'll just have to trust him. I couldn't come up

with anything intelligent to ask him anyway. Not about trucks. Would you please call him and tell him to go ahead and do whatever it takes to fix it. Well, within reason. Then maybe I'll go for a hike." Laura hesitated, "Is there anything I can help you with around here, Maggie?"

"Tell you what," Maggie said, "Why don't you run the Blazer up to the dam and do a little fishing? That rust bucket should be good for one more trip. God, I've put a ton of money into that piece of...," she trailed off.

"You were probably too worried to notice last evening, but you came right past the cutoff to the reservoir. It's a great tail-water fishery and there won't be many fishermen around. Probably none," Maggie amended. "Judging by what George lugged over to the cabin, you're a fly fisherman. It should be fun for you and it may be your last chance."

"Why's that," Laura asked.

"Well, there's some talk about removing the dam. Got the tree huggers...er, environmentalists pushing the Bureau of Land Management to take out the dam but there are rumors that some big East Coast money wants to lease land from the government and build a private resort with an 18-hole golf course over looking the water. Some claim it's actually Hollywood money. If true, that could mean jobs and a boost to our economy. Drain the reservoir and they'll have a view of a canyon, not a lake. It's a beautiful view but I don't think that's what those folks have in mind."

"Pebble Beach North?" Laura asked.

"That's good," Maggie laughed. "And then there's the Indian uprising."

"The what?" Laura asked.

"Just kidding. Our local tribe has hired a bunch of lawyers to break the treaty that exchanged territory along the river for their present reservation. That was signed in the late 1800s long before the dam was built. The Indian Council claims the white man took advantage of them...they probably did at that...probably no question about it. Seems the tribe wants back enough land above the dam to build a gambling casino. A casino-hotel complex, complete with the obligatory culture center. Managed right, it could bring in millions.

"Besides all that, taking out the dam could mean the end of our little community, but the greeners have some powerful friends in Washington."

"Greeners?" Laura asked.

"Greeners, Greenies, Environmentalists...whatever. Those who pride themselves as politically correct think environmentalists sounds better than tree huggers.

"Anyway, this whole thing has got everybody's shorts in a knot.

"Oh my, I'm sorry, Laura. Your eyes are starting to glaze over. Please forgive me, you've got your truck to worry about, not our problems here in Towne."

"Not really. Dam removal does seem to be the new national debate. I've certainly heard a lot of talk about it on campus and from my professors...much of it uninformed, if not completely wrong." Laura smiled.

"Just like around here." Maggie laughed. "Tell you what, you go fishing today. Forget all this. Tomorrow you can help me around here, if you don't mind. As much as I hate Big City, I usually go there for a few hours every Tuesday, do my banking, and buy store supplies and personal things."

"Sounds more than fair, but I don't know anything about running a truck stop."

"Nonsense, I'll show you how to operate the cash register

and you'll know as much as I do in ten minutes. You can make change, can't you?"

Laura grinned. "Sure, I worked at a McDonald's one summer. I showed up two days in a row and they made me an assistant-manager."

"Great. I have a couple of high school kids working for me part-time and George will be around if you need him. I think he kind of likes you."

◆

Well, that's how Laura Menard ended up at Maggie's Corner. With a degree in zoology and a major in ichthyology, she was hoping for a research job that would involve fish and allow her to be outside; outside any office, outside any lab, just outside. No luck on that account, so she was headed home to pursue a master's degree when her truck broke down. It's been almost three years now and she's still here.

Oh, she did catch four very large rainbow trout that first day. She caught them on dry flies. Maybe that's one of the reasons she stayed. Well, it's as good a reason as any.

What kind of dry flies was she using? Come on out and do your own experimenting. Say, why don't you hire a fishing guide? Help the local economy. Lord knows, it could use some help.

CHAPTER 2: George Otis

George Otis resembled a fifty-five gallon oil drum with stubby limbs, one shorter than the other causing a noticeable limp.

Sometime between Vietnam and Desert Storm, George fought in an obscure war. The official record of the conflict was erased with the assistance of a Fellows paper shredder, Ollie North-Model 1986. George might mention the battle in the most abstract way, but only after a few beers, which wasn't often.

"It happened. I know. I was there. No newspaper covered it. If it isn't in print it never happened, right? Well, it happened." Rarely did George utter more than one or two of these statements at a time.

When Maggie helped George move out of the Veterans Administration Hospital in Big City to a small apartment in Towne, she came across a tin box of medals and battle ribbons stuffed beneath his underwear. Maggie had seen discharge papers when she agreed to be responsible for George or at least look out for him. His DD Form 214 showed no mention of awards. The chronological section was covered with whiteout.

Maggie and George had known each other *forever*. Growing

up in Towne, they went through elementary school there and high school in Big City. Learning didn't come easy for George, but with an enormous amount of work and determination, he graduated in the top ten percent of the class. Three days later he enlisted in the army. Occasionally rumors circulated about George and years went by before Maggie received a call from the V.A. asking for help. She never learned how her name came up and she never questioned it.

Yes, she would help George Otis. "Of course, I will," she had replied.

After Maggie got George settled into a furnished apartment in Towne, she helped him obtain his driver's license. It was restricted to work-related activities. Maggie's cousin Charlie found George a used pickup truck. Probably over-priced, but it came with Maggie's one condition that, if it broke, Charlie would fix it. Maggie immediately gave George a job at the Corner, a twelve mile round trip. As the odometer showed, he only used his truck to travel back and forth to work. The rest of the time he rode an old bike with no gears, a handlebar basket, and foot brakes.

Every Wednesday, on George's day off, he was seen first at the bank, where he cashed his paycheck, and then at the Towne supermarket. After dropping groceries at his apartment, George headed for the Roadhouse Bar & Grill. He'd park his bike, go in the front door, turn right toward the bar section, and sit down on *his* stool at exactly four in the afternoon. You could make book on it.

How long George sat there and sipped draft beer was in direct relationship to how long it took the locals to start making fun of him. Anywhere from two to eight unemployed ne'er-do-wells, in their early twenties, started drinking beer around noon when the bar opened. County Commissioner Fred Barnes' two sons were always the first to arrive and usually the last to leave.

Mike Tapio, the bartender, had cautioned the troublemakers to be careful how far they pushed George. Mike wasn't worried about George, and he didn't really care what happened to the local riffraff, but he would hate to see his side of the Roadhouse torn up. Should a confrontation occur, Mike was pretty certain he could predict the outcome. He once watched George lift the back end of a Chevy Suburban off the ground while someone pulled a puppy to safety. The dog didn't live, but George's reputation certainly grew. That incident, plus stories that had followed George from the VA Hospital, had convinced Mike there would be little left of the locals and probably less of the bar should a scuffle take place.

Mike's warnings were ignored. Each week the harassment continued until George would eventually slip off his bar stool, and with a mock grin forcing his lips tight, he would hand Mike a crisp twenty-dollar bill, raising his palm to indicate that Mike should keep the change. Then George would turn and make his way past the tormentors. Not surprisingly, each of the hecklers would suddenly find something to inspect at the bottom of his beer glass. Not one, count 'um, not one returned George's grin.

Finally, he would turn and walk out of the bar, his limp barely noticeable. Each Wednesday the mystery surrounding him swelled as he climbed on his bicycle and pedaled home. Old Western legends were built around far lesser men than George Otis.

Hard to guess how long before somebody, with alcohol-fueled stupidity, would take up George Otis' silent challenge, but Mike knew there would be a day when someone would be drunk enough to make that mistake—possibly a fatal mistake.

CHAPTER 3: Richard Whendelstat – Flies & Lies Shop

"Hung over…you're always hung over, Brad! When are you not hung over? What's so different about today?" Richard Whendelstat demanded. He was admittedly upset, but restrained from using vulgar language. He halted his trembling hand short of slamming the phone into its cradle. He prided himself on his self-control, a practiced skill from his years at a Wall Street brokerage. It hadn't been easy working all those years on *The Street*, but after owning a fly shop for ten years in the Rockies, he felt it was a piece of cake *back there* in New York City compared to *out here* in Towne.

It was late in the trout season and he had allowed two of his guides to go fishing in Oregon in pursuit of some anadromous species of fish—not that he could have stopped them. Richard had no illusions about controlling his fishing guides. Independence was a main factor in choosing the occupation. He only hoped the two wouldn't wander off to Alaska and not bother to return in the spring. He was left with only one guide, the one who just called in hung over.

Richard had cultivated a list of potential trout fishermen from his old financial clientele. Most of them were what he called BS-

FOE, Big Spenders From Out East. Two of them were due in his shop in two hours, promised the fishing trip of their lives.

It wasn't that difficult to deliver on a promise of a great experience, a Rocky Mountain fishing experience. Even if the size or number of fish wasn't always predictable, at least the scenery, the float down the majestic river, and a fabulous shore lunch helped ease the pain.

He had no option but to take the men out himself. Not after they flew in from Boston. Not with the referrals they might give, or not give. Business was good, but he had to continue to deliver.

><

When he lived on the east coast, Richard Whendelstat had been a fair trout fisherman, some say very good. He had lived within driving distance of the Battenkill, the Delaware, the Connecticut, and the Housatonic. He had always fished those rivers with waders and boots. In the Rockies, he was forced to adapt his fishing skills to a new environment. He now fished from a drift boat that he wasn't all that adept at handling. Richard lettered in crew at Harvard but, other than developing muscles, it was little help on a roaring freestone river. It was much like flying a glider and then moving into a stunt plane. It just wasn't the same.

With fishing clients, running the river safely and finding fish is only half the job. A good guide must be aware of the season, weather conditions, water temperature and how each of these elements affects hundreds of insect species and their life cycles. This knowledge is crucial in order to tie on the right artificial fly. You do have to fool the fish. Plus, unless your clients are seasoned anglers, you will have to tie on their leaders and flies. And if they hook a fish be required to net, land, photograph, unhook and release the catch. While doing all this, you are expected to describe the flora and fauna along the river and explain the region's geology. Historical facts are important too, especially if there were rumors of an Indian massacre. It doesn't matter if the victims were Indians or white men, as long as the narrative is bloody enough. Naturally you have to smile, compliment the clients on their angling skills, and tell a joke or two.

"Too bad, guys, you should have been here yesterday."

While a reluctant guide is not a good guide, Richard couldn't afford to blow this booking. Then he remembered Laura Menard who lived out at Maggie's. Laura had become an excellent guide in a very short time and occasionally filled in for Richard. She knew trout and where to catch them. She knew how to handle clients and she knew how to control a drift boat. She was good. Damn good. And she wasn't afraid to call an asshole an asshole, even before the client had calculated her tip. Richard secretly admired that, as long as it wasn't one of *his* clients. He reached for the phone before realizing it was Tuesday, the only day of the week that Maggie left her store with Laura in charge. As conscientious as Laura was, she wouldn't stiff Maggie, even if it might be her last chance to guide this season.

When Richard first met Laura he wasn't thinking of her as a fishing guide. He had come close to making a complete fool of himself. Young enough to be his daughter, if he had one, she said she was more than flattered by his attention, but she gave the impression that she really preferred another gender. He later learned that was a complete fabrication. There was that biologist-ranger with the U.S. Forest Service, Ted something or other. He rarely came out of the field, but when he did, Laura always seemed to be at his side.

He never held Laura's rejection against her. In fact, he later offered her a job as a full-time guide. "If that's not enough, take a partnership then, a co-ownership, anything, just help me out," he had pleaded. Richard was not usually known for pleading.

She shot him down in the nicest way, saying that if she did stay out West, it would be with Maggie. Maybe they would add a sports shop of their own. "Just a little friendly competition," she smiled at him. That's all Richard needed, more competition, friendly or not.

Okay, he'd have to play guide today. He dialed Shirley Wheeler's number and asked her to come in. When Sam Wheeler died of lung cancer, his wife Shirley couldn't run the shop alone, so she sold it to him. She was, however, always eager to help out when he was short-handed. Wages were fair and when the counter was slow she would hand tie trout flies for a little extra income.

How did Richard Whendelstat get hooked on fly-fishing? His father, a very rich and influential man, had fished with the likes of Nick Lyons and Joan Wulff. He had told his son about the old time great fishermen like Theodore Gordon and Art Flick and introduced him to John Gierach and A.K. Best. They generously shared their knowledge and encouraged Richard to become a fly fisherman with a passion for trout.

The first real fishing trip Richard remembered was when he was about ten years old. His father took him into Maine country, gave him an old bamboo fly rod and reel, some leaders, an assortment of dry flies and pretty much said; "Here you go son, have at it. Oh, and don't let the black flies carry you away."

Richard didn't hook many brook trout that trip, but was certainly hooked on fly fishing. Throughout high school, college, and graduate school his love was trout fishing. He dreamed of retiring at forty-five to head west and buy a fishing business with enough guides and clerks to allow him to fish as much as he wanted. Dream on.

The first part of his dream came true. At forty-four, he had his secretary transfer his well-worn Rolodex to a CD, told his boss to kiss off, and headed west.

"YOU'RE LEAVING US?! We were about to offer you a partnership."

"Yeah, right." Richard caught the next plane out of LaGuardia.

Scott Waldie wrote a trilogy about the fictional town of Travers Corners which, writer Jerry Kustich claims in his book, *A Wisp in the Wind,* is in reality Twin Bridges, Montana. A small laid back community where neighbors not only knew each other, but also were indeed neighborly. Where people had time to fish, attend Little League baseball games and hang out at the local coffee shop every morning and listen to local gossip revolving mainly around trout fishing. Richard was hoping for a village where one could make a living renting drift boats, tying flies, or crafting bamboo rods by hand—a place where you could run a business and make enough money to survive, if not prosper. Waldie's vision had smoldered in Richard's chest long before he published his trilogy or Richard had heard of Twin Bridges.

After *only* three airline changes, his plane landed in Big City. A real estate agent met him in front of the field hanger which served as waiting room, repair shop, and ticket office.

An elderly grey-haired man, dressed in a plaid sports coat and tie that almost matched, introduced himself. "Mr. Whendelstat? I understand you are looking to buy a business, a fly fishing shop."

"That's right," Richard shook the man's hand. "Are there any on the market?"

"Well sir, I doubt there's a fly shop west of the Mississippi that's not for sale. Not all of them are listed, and some may come a little expensive, but I'd say they are all very much for sale." A lupine grin crossed the agent's face. Maybe he should have been a used car salesman or, better yet, a snake oil salesman in another century. How about a politician?

After two days checking out available businesses, Richard and the agent stopped by the Flies & Lies Shop, a name admittedly stolen from a store in Deckers on the South Platte. They talked with Shirley Wheeler, toured Towne and checked out the river. Luckily for Shirley, all her fishing guides were out with chartered clients and unavailable for input. They struck a deal. No financing was necessary. Richard returned to Big City, made a few phone calls and finished the day by presenting the agent a cashier's check for the total price, back taxes and all.

Richard Whendelstat was in the trout business—up to his wader tops.

━━◄

The phone rang again. Maybe Brad had sobered up. Maybe Laura was looking for extra work. Maybe the day would turn out okay. Maybe…

No, it was his father calling from the Poconos.

"Hello, son."

"Dad, how are you?" His father was just shy of eighty and mentally as sharp as ever. His only physical problem had been taken care of with the operation du jour—his prostate had been removed.

"Good. We just closed up the summer home…headed back to New York City. Your fish business still afloat?" Richard ignored the pun.

"Yeah, we've broke even the last few years so at least it's not eating up anymore of my retirement fund."

"To the point." His father never took long to get to the *point*. "I'm hearing they're about to take out that old dam on the Whoosh. You know anything about that?"

"Just rumors. The pressure is building to rip it out. If it's approved, everything out here will change…everything. What's your interest?" Richard could be blunt himself.

"I've put together financing for a private golf club. Several retired CEOs, living off their Golden Parachutes, came to me with the idea. The money is available and all the proper administrators have been paid off." Talk about blunt. "Problem is the bastards are starting to renege. What with elections coming in a few weeks, their political bosses are getting cold feet. We had a rider all ready to attach to an appropriation bill that should pass almost unanimously. It allowed us to lease 500 acres of Federal land and stop any attempt at removal of the dam…until the lease runs out. A few days ago some of the environmentalist groups were tipped off about the rider, probably by a Senate staffer, and now nobody has balls enough to do anything until after the election. By then the dam removal could be approved. If that happens, our investors will bail."

"What do you want from me," Richard asked?

"Son, if that dam goes out you'll have more to lose then anybody…just giving you a heads-up."

"Thanks. I'm aware of the consequences," he knew that was not why his father had called.

"So, do you know anybody out there with any influence we can get to...er, that I could contact?"

"Aw, the bottom line. No, I don't know anyone important, not on the Federal or State level...no one that could do you any good. There are so many overlapping jurisdictions out here that very little ever gets done...quickly, anyway. As I understand it, the Bureau of Land Management makes the recommendation for dam removal but the final decision rests with the U.S. Department of the Interior."

"Son, we are well aware of the process...believe me. What we need to do is get to somebody who's in on the decision process... somebody out there close to the situation...somebody with authority."

Richard thought a second, "Well, the reservoir is in Whoosh County...Commissioner Fred Barnes seems to have his fingers into everything that goes on. I don't know if he would be any help but he probably knows people up the line that might. The County Clerk should have his private phone number...if you can talk her out of it."

"Thanks, son," and the line to the Pocono Mountains went dead.

"Some days you really shouldn't answer the phone," Richard muttered.

◗◄

That evening, high in the foot hills overlooking Big City, County Commissioner Fred Barnes sat on a deck attached to his spacious ranch home. The sun had just dropped below the mountain range behind him and lights began to illuminate the city in valley to the east. It was a beautiful evening—too beautiful to last. His cordless phone began to ring. The non-informative caller ID claimed an *out of area number.* His wife, who was vacationing in Europe, was certainly out of the area, but she would never call, not unless she had lost her American Express card. The Sheriff's number was *in the area* but it was far too early for the department to inform him that his sons were in trouble again. Very few people had his unlisted home number. One way to find out…

"Yo."

"You Fred Barnes?"

"Yeah."

"Whendelstat here. I believe you know my son Richard… Richard Whendelstat. He owns the Flies & Lies shop in Towne… stupid name for a city, Towne. Not as stupid as Big City, though."

"It's a long story," Barnes replied, a little defensively.

"Forget it. Name your cities whatever you damn well choose. Look, I'm working on a project…big money project. Richard said you might be interested…it could benefit us both."

"How'd you get this number?" Fred had been taken completely off guard and he didn't like it.

"Doesn't matter. Look, I'll be in Denver Friday around noon. I've arranged for a direct flight for you from Capital City to Denver International. All you have to do is get to the Capital City Airport and pick up the ticket."

"Slow down. Interested in what?"

"Not over the phone. I have a two-hour layover in Denver. I'll explain everything then. Think about it. One of my associates will call within the hour. He'll have your flight information and my gate number. Use it or not use it…up to you."

"Hold on." Barnes was regaining his footing. "If I do come, how will I recognize you?"

"No problem. I'll know you. Look, I realize this is sudden… right out of the box, but it will be well worth it. It won't take much of your time or effort. You have until Friday to decide. Check us out…Whendelstat Investment Group." With that, the line went dead.

"What the hell was that all about?" Barnes mumbled. He reached across the arm of his chair, set the phone down, picked up his bourbon Manhattan and relaxed back into his lounge chair.

"No harm in taking a free flight to Denver and meeting with this Whendelstat. You bet I'll check you out, Mr. Whendelstat. If you're on the *Fortune 500* list, I'll give you twenty minutes… tops," he laughed out loud, startling an Evening Grosbeak off the bird feeder. "Then I'll catch a cab to the Brown Palace Hotel," he mused. "Could be the Denver Broncos are in town for a football game this weekend." County Commissioner Fred Barnes took a long drag of his drink.

"This could be a fun weekend," he grinned, "maybe even profitable."

CHAPTER 4: Bradley Hawkins – River Guide

◄●

"What happened last night?" Brad questioned his pillow. "Oh, yeah."

From his bed he could see a certified envelope anchored by several empty beer bottles. Divorce papers from his wife's attorney had arrived late the day before. Rather than read them, Brad had headed straight for the Roadhouse Bar & Grill, nearly crashing into George Otis, who was exiting the bar with that stupid smirk of his. Brad just wanted to get stupid, forget the smirk.

◄●

Brad rolled over in bed and groaned. Now that he had called in and totally irritated his boss, Richard Whendelstat, he had to make a decision. If he tried to sleep, his headache would keep him awake. If he got up for three or four aspirin (he was trying to cut back) he wouldn't be able to fall back asleep. Ah, life's little dilemmas. He looked at his pillow for understanding—nothing. He heaved his non-conversant pile of feathers across the room and watched it bounce into a dusty corner. He gulped down some pills, took a long shower, and drove his ancient pickup to the Roadhouse. It was too early for the bar to be open, so he slipped into the first booth on the restaurant side. Deloris Jankowski, the only waitress on duty, was either preoccupied or ignoring him.

"Del, can I get some coffee and a large tomato juice?" Brad's request seemed to startle her.

"Oh. Sorry, Brad. Didn't see you come in. A little early for you, isn't it?"

"Don't you start on me, I feel bad enough. Got the news from my soon-to-be ex-wife…she wants a divorce."

"Yeah, I heard about it from you, here at the Roadhouse last night. Brad, why don't you just pack up and go back home? At least see her and talk face-to-face. Get out of this godforsaken country. It's ruining you."

"I don't know, Del. I think it's too late for that. Maybe the wife's finally had enough of me. She's having a hard time raising the kids. I send her all the money I can. What I don't spend in here, that is." He waved his arm around the restaurant. Deloris pointed toward the bar.

"I know…you're right. I drink too much, way too much…got nothing to show for it. If I went home I'm sure I could get my teaching job back, at least as a substitute. Guess it would be a start, a restart. Maybe she'd go for that. I don't know. But, I love these mountains, this country…your *godforsaken country*. I'm not sure I could live anywhere else…not anymore. I'm afraid it's too late." He gazed out the window for a few seconds.

"Anyway, how's your life going?" Brad asked, sounding genuinely concerned.

"Oh, you know. My daughter, Penny, she's…well, you know what she is," Deloris trailed off.

"Want me to talk to her? I was a high school counselor, besides teaching math, and coaching the win-at-all-costs football team. I was a better counselor than teacher. Certainly a better counselor than coach…the gentler side of Bradley Hawkins." He tried to make Deloris smile and failed.

"Thanks a lot, Brad, but no. Things are moving along. I would change things if I could, but I can't. Don't have any choice. I'll get your juice and coffee." She turned and disappeared into the kitchen.

Brad stared out the window toward Main Street. How in the world had he ended up in Towne? He had gone from high school to Ohio State University on a football scholarship intending to major in engineering, make the All-American Football Team and win a National Championship for the Buckeyes. He always had speed and dexterity, but in his freshman year the coach redshirted him in hopes that Brad would build some bulk and strength. Then in the third game of his second year, he blew out a knee. Even with advances in surgery and rehab, he lost mobility and most of his speed. Coach called him into his office and told him that he had no choice but to list him as the fourth outside linebacker on the depth chart with a chance at a regular spot on the specialty teams. That was the best he could expect. Brad transferred to a Mid-American Conference school and finished a mediocre career on a mediocre team in a mediocre conference. His aspirations of All-American died, along with his ambition to be an engineer. He had spent far too much time on football and not enough on his studies.

Weeks after he graduated, Brad married his college sweetheart and took a job teaching math at the local high school, with the provision that he coach the varsity football's defensive team. They had two kids before he took a Rocky Mountain fishing trip with three of his old college buddies. His friends returned home. Brad never went back. He brought his wife and children out for a year to live in his single-wide while he basically ignored them, continuing to fish and ski even on his days off. Finally, his wife had enough. She loaded the kids up and flew home to be near her family and went to work as the city librarian. That's how the situation more or less stayed until *those papers* arrived.

Brad finished his juice and coffee. He didn't see Mike moving around in the bar yet, so he walked out onto Main Street and headed west across the bridge spanning the Whoosh River. The water level was low, but it was the end of the season. Late autumn clouds were building, hopefully an omen of heavy snow in the mountains, snow that would continue all winter.

Drought conditions didn't benefit anyone. Well, maybe they gave the global warming freaks something to gloat about, or are they now called climate-change alarmists? After four years of less than normal precipitation, it was near panic time for fishing guides, ski and golf resort owners, farmers, ranchers and city folk who wanted to fill their pools and water their lawns. Hopefully it was just another weather cycle that would run its course. Nature has a timetable that doesn't always coincide with the desires of humans or, for that matter, doomsday advocates.

Brad walked on the north side of Main Street passing Chester's Mercantile and several vacant building fronts that matched those directly across the street. When he passed the Lodge, he saw a notice for the Friday night fish fry taped to the front door. Maybe he'd go, he thought—probably not.

Continuing west, Brad crossed the street to the gas station and used car lot, taking a second to check out a newly arrived Jeep Wagoneer. The arrival was new, not the Jeep. He figured his rusty

old beater still had more miles left than the Jeep being offered as
The Steal of the Week.

Past the car lot was the I Dare Ya Bar and the United Protestant
Church. He cut diagonally back across the street to the front door
of the What Are You Lookin' At Saloon and walked through the
swinging doors. Two old ranchers sat by the front window with
a cribbage board between them. Neither one bothered to look
up. Four unemployed oil field workers were in heated debate over
what their local union had, or had not, done for them before and
after their layoffs. On a bar stool, a middle-aged woman stared
into her beer mug, oblivious to anything but her own problems.
Zeke Astor, with an empty wine glass in his hand, was flipping
through the jukebox sections hoping to find something other than
country-western music.

The only distinguishing feature in the saloon was the long
cherrywood back bar, which allegedly came from France through
Chicago. It was only half as big as Edna's in Cody, Wyoming, but
just as elegant. Well, it was elegant at one time. The saloon owners
had let it deteriorate. Even the mirrors were cracked, but grease and
dust obscured the flaw lines so it really made little difference.

Brad ordered a large coke, much to the bartender's amazement,
while two local businessmen, deep in conversation, entered, and
poured themselves coffee from a self-serve Bunn. They sat down
at a table across from Brad.

"It's just not right, Randy. That dam is part of this town.
Taking it out would be a disaster." The older man took a sip of
his coffee, grimaced, and went on. "How many businesses around
here would be hurt?"

"Jerry, you know there are *not* many businesses around here
to begin with," the younger man replied. "Me? I'd just move if
the worst happened."

"Yeah, if the worst happened. If they don't have a controlled take down of that dam the whole area could be flooded. With its history around here, do you trust the Army Corps of Engineers to do it right?" Randy just shrugged. "What about the sludge behind it? It has to be toxic. There used to be a smelter operation up stream... copper ore. You can see some of the old cement foundations where the East Branch runs into the Whoosh. That was a Canadian operation. They ran it for a few years after the dam was built until World War II ended...wasn't very profitable. They dumped everything in the river, tore down the buildings and hauled the lumber away...left all those slag piles and then declared bankruptcy. Seems the government neglected to have them post a bond for clean up, if one was even required back then. Anyway, do you know what kind of chemicals they use to extract copper from that ore?"

"No, do you?" Randy asked.

"No, but I'd bet it had something to do with sulfuric acid. You want that washing downstream through Towne and Pine Bluff? You know whatever they used it had to be toxic and it ended up behind the dam as sludge."

"Well, it's possible to dredge."

"Safely? My God, how much would that cost and who the hell pays? Where would you dump that shit? Even if it isn't toxic you couldn't possibly dredge all the silt...it's been building up for years. What they didn't get out would wash down river and fill in the natural holding holes. Guess where the water goes then. Up over the streets of Towne, don't you suppose?"

"Maybe, but in a few years the current will clear that all out and the river will be back to its original channel...the way it was before the dam."

"A few years? What happens to the fishing in the mean time? You're taking out a great tail water fishery. You watch, there'll be nothing but carp and suckers in the canyon with a few monster pike eating all the trout. Reservoir fishing? There won't be any reservoir fishing because there won't be any reservoir." The men were quiet for a few minutes as Randy tried to choke down more coffee and Jerry tried to cool down.

"Look Randy, I'm sorry. I get a little hot when the subject comes up," Jerry, the defender of the status quo, said. "I know you're a member of Trout Unlimited and they're one of those organizations pushing it. They've done a lot of good over the years but tell me again...what's the up side of taking out the dam?"

"Don't apologize, Jerry," Randy smiled. They had obviously been friends for a long time. "Let me run down TU's talking points real quick."

"Talking points...do you mean propaganda?"

Randy laughed. "Yeah, you're right. It's pretty one sided... can't say I agree with it all myself."

"Well, at least you're honest."

Now they both smiled. Randy went on, "TU wants the Whoosh opened all the way to the Pacific Ocean. That would give the salmon a clear path upstream to spawn. I know there are two other dams downstream. They'd have to put in fish ladders. It's a pretty ambitious plan," he ended weakly.

"Yeah, great. They get fish ladders and we lose our dam. You know there has never been a history of salmon up the Whoosh River. What the hell are they talking about?"

><

Brad finished his coke and got up to leave. He had heard it all. It was the constant chatter around the watershed; on the street, on the river, in the newspapers, at church, and in every bar for miles.

For Brad, it wasn't all that important. He could always get another job as a licensed guide in another town on another river.

"Got to get out of here," he said to a yellowing autographed picture of Teddy Roosevelt, dated 1903, hanging by the door. The President was straddling a bar stool, not a horse. Story has it that Teddy visited the tavern on one of his adventures to Yellowstone. The photo might better hang in the Township Museum rather than a smoky old saloon.

Brad went outside where he took a deep breath of mountain air. He walked past Doc Walters' office, swung back east and then north to check out the ads in the Towne Super Market windows. Back on Main Street he swung right crossing the Whoosh again before he passed the Catholic Church, avoiding his workplace, before jaywalking to the Roadhouse. He had toured most of Towne except for the residential district, the city park, and the abandoned railroad yards, and an old sawmill. His timing was right. Mike had just unlocked the bar and was turning on the overhead lights that would be dimmed around eight that evening. Ambiance, you know, or was it ambivalence?

"Aren't you supposed to be on the river today?"

Brad grunted.

"Seems like that was the last coherent thing I heard out of you last night," Mike interjected, being far more critical than usual. Brad settled down on his favorite stool.

"Yeah, I messed up. Poor Richard's going to see how the working class lives...at least for one day. He'll have to take his clients out on the river himself." Mike drew Brad a small draft beer. The jukebox pumped out Tom Petty's "Into the Great Wide Open." The lyrics didn't much apply to Brad, but the one line, *rebel without a clue,* had always haunted him.

"Where in the whole wide world can you walk into a bar

at noon and hear Tom Petty?" he asked. Mike shrugged and continued rinsing glasses.

Brad's stroll had resulted in no insight about what to do with his life, but he had clarified his options. Usually, he had to be on a trout stream for any revelation, useful or not. Today his mini-tour of the village would have to suffice.

He had saved enough money to keep himself alive until the ski resorts reopened and he knew he could get a ski-patrol job at any of three or four resorts. Actually, he was now a certified ski instructor, bum knee and all, and that would get him to the opening of trout season in the spring, which would put him right back at the Roadhouse one year to the day, probably listening to that same Tom Petty song.

As he told Deloris, he could head to Ohio, get his teaching job back, and try to patch things up with his wife and family. "She must still love me. It's just my lifestyle," he laughed. The real question was: Did he miss his kids and wife enough to dump his mountain man life? Apparently his wife didn't miss him enough to move back west. But, why should she? She had the kids and her parents, his parents too for that matter, all back home. He had basically ignored them when they were out west. No, he couldn't blame her at all. The one thing Brad couldn't face was the fact that his wife had probably met somebody else—another man with *his* wife—another man bringing up *his* kids.

><

Then there was Rhonda. Rhonda came west two summers ago for her bachelorette party—by herself. She hired Brad as a fishing guide and after two bends in the river the rest was inevitable. For three weeks there wasn't a pull-off or backwater pool on the whole

Whoosh River where they didn't make love. Sometimes it was in the drift boat, sometimes under it, sometimes on shore, sometimes in the water, sometimes high on a cliff overlooking the river. For three weeks Brad was in paradise. He had a woman to love, a woman who could double haul her fly line better than any man he had ever guided. Both knew the party had to end. Rhonda was due in Chicago to marry, as she put it, an asshole doctor. Brad assumed she meant a proctologist, but never did learn if she was referring to the guy's profession or his personality.

Rhonda married and moved into a condo on Lake Shore Drive with a view of the West Michigan shoreline. Well, on a clear day anyway. Occasionally a humorous greeting card would arrive at his trailer, with the simple message:

> *"Brad – Come see me!*
> *I miss you – Ronda"*

From the jukebox, a Cole Porter song, "Just One of Those Things," interrupted Brad's melancholy.

"Who the hell picks the songs around here?" Brad grumbled. Mike shrugged and went on cleaning the bar.

As Brad studied his empty glass, he weighed his options once again. One; he could stay out West and *things* would continue as is, year after year. Two; he could go home and try to make *things* occur the way they once did. Three; he could see if Rhonda could make him forget all those reoccurring *things*.

Brad decided that for the moment the more important decision was whether to have another draft beer or have another draft beer with a shot of whiskey?

A major dilemma. Does the future really turn on such choices? God help us all.

CHAPTER 5: Sheriff Oscar Cowdrey

Sheriff Oscar Cowdrey pulled his Ford Bronco into Maggie's side parking lot, away from the fuel pumps. Setting the emergency brake, he eased his dilapidated body out of the front seat. Maybe dilapidated is a little cruel. How about obese? You'd never know he had been a star athlete at Big City High School. Oscar was the *golden boy*, achieving all-state status as a football player and favorable recognition for his exploits on the baseball field and basketball court. Years behind an office desk and in a county patrol car took a huge toll on his once impressive physique and good looks. Only with a creative imagination could one visualize him as a jock.

By the time Oscar made it to the front door of Maggie's, sweat beaded on his forehead. It wasn't all that warm so early in the morning, but Oscar always broke out in a sweat whenever he met with Maggie on official business and this was official business. Very few people actually intimidated Oscar. Maggie was one of them.

Oscar had known Maggie since first grade, but had never felt comfortable around her. She was never impressed with Oscar's athletic accomplishments or his appearance. She apparently saw right through the macho veneer that hid his insecurity.

More importantly, Oscar was afraid Maggie knew about his shady little deals made possible by his position as County Sherriff. Come to think of it, some of those deals weren't so little. She never confronted or accused him of anything and he had never heard of her talking behind his back. Truth was, while not supporting his four consecutive elections publicly, she had generously contributed to each of his campaign fund-raisers. "Protection money," she proclaimed as she signed a check for his re-election committee. Oscar never was quite sure if Maggie was serious or not but, with what he thought she knew, she'd always be protected by his department.

Delaying the inevitable, Oscar turned from the front door and walked slowly past the pumps to the edge of the road. Across the pavement he saw a few wisps of smoke drifting up and away from the burned out motel. Two days before, on Saturday night, the old rotten building disappeared in minutes, long before the volunteer fire department could get its act together. The attached restaurant burned even quicker, aided by years of rancid bacon grease that coated the walls and vents.

Both buildings had been abandoned for years. The owners hadn't bothered to declare bankruptcy or even put them up for sale. They just left early one morning and headed for Texas. Surprisingly, the taxes and the two remaining employees had been paid in full. With no reason to track down the owners, the county took possession and listed the property with a realtor in Big City. Given economic conditions in the area, it had only been shown once or twice, and no serious offer was ever made. So the buildings sat silent and slowly went to hell.

Oscar heard about the fire long before he answered the *official* call from the Fire Chief. On Sunday afternoon the Chief told Oscar there was no doubt it was arson. Oscar wasn't so sure. Was it really arson, or some damn fool kids burning an old building down because they had nothing better to do on a Saturday night? Forgive him; he's just thinking like a bleeding-heart liberal judge. That's a first! While Oscar was unsure of the legal definition of arson, he was pretty sure he knew who torched the place. Now he had to find out if anybody else knew, which led him to Maggie's Corner.

Oscar mopped his face with the arm of his khaki shirt, turned with a sigh, and walked towards the front door.

"Morning, Mags." Oscar had always called her Mags, presuming a familiarity that didn't exist.

"Morning, Sheriff." Since his first election, Maggie had always called him Sheriff. She wanted nothing to do with familiarity. "Grab a brew," she offered.

"Mags, you know I don't drink on duty."

"Of course you don't, silly. I was offering you an iced-tea. It's hot out there." Maggie gave him a shy grin. "Have a Red Bull."

"Damn," the Sheriff muttered to himself. Snatching a regular cola from the cooler, he jumped right in. "You see anything unusual last Saturday night? Likely closed early, I bet...probably over to the Roadhouse at the time of the fire?" His leading questions went unanswered.

"No Sheriff. I was open pretty late. Saturday night is always busy. You know...last minute six-packs and lotto tickets? Never did make it to the Roadhouse."

"Did you see anything out of the ordinary?"

"Are you asking if I saw who burned down the motel? Yes, Sheriff, I did." Sometimes Maggie could be as direct as a pissed off rattlesnake, other times as wary as a brown trout looking for its evening supper.

"That's what I was afraid of," he mumbled to himself. "Could you identify them?"

"Absolutely."

With that, the investigation was closed. Well, actually there never was an official investigation; no report, no call to the district attorney, no reporter from the *Buzz* nosing around. No, the only call Sheriff Cowdrey made was to County Commissioner Fred Barnes.

Fred Barnes had, over the last three decades, turned the part-time, no-pay job of County Commissioner, into a lucrative occupation. The problem for Cowdrey was not that he knew all about Barnes' profitable arrangements. No, the problem was that he was in on most of them. The conversation between the two *public servants* was short.

"Fred? Oscar here. That incident Saturday night…I know who was involved. Didn't think you'd want me to pursue it, your boys being on probation and all. We'll blame it on faulty wiring. Funny, the electricity was never shut off. Mice, maybe squirrels, could have eaten through the wires. Anything like that is always possible in those old abandoned buildings."

"Thanks Sheriff." Barnes replied. "I will take care of it."

The connection went dead and Commissioner Fred Barnes did indeed take care of it.

That very afternoon County Road Commission trucks, a front loader, and a grader, showed up across from Maggie's. By four o'clock there were no signs of fire, motel, or restaurant. A large, gravel-covered parking lot replaced the smoldering buildings.

The next day the County Clerk, Stella Hemlock, called Maggie and offered the property to her for one hundred dollars. Maggie's momentary hesitation was misinterpreted as a negotiation ploy. Quickly Stella added a stipulation that Maggie would not be obligated for any property taxes as long as she held title to the land, and then the county clerk dropped the price to one dollar.

"What the hell," Maggie thought to herself. "Guess this makes me as crooked as the rest of that bunch."

"You'd be doing the county a great service," the clerk continued. "Maybe you could build a retail strip mall. Or, we really need a new restaurant at your Interstate exit. How about *Maggie's Kitchen?*" The silence was deafening. Stella plunged on. "At any rate, whatever you did with the property would be a lot better than that old eyesore of a motel. If you took the land it would certainly put an end to the county's problems," she lamely concluded.

"And an end to Commissioner Barnes' present problems," Maggie mused aloud.

"I'm sorry, I didn't catch that."

"Send the papers out. Can't say what I'll do with the land, but I'll be glad to do the county a *great service,*" Maggie sighed.

With that transaction, the county's problem was solved, as was Fred Barnes' immediate problem. Other problems with Fred's two sons would probably never be solved. Thanks in large part to Sheriff Oscar Cowdrey that is how Maggie came to own a piece of property that eventually became known as Maggie's Over-Da-Hill Clunker Lot.

CHAPTER 6: Professor Leonard Russell

Professor Leonard M. C. Russell hung up his desk phone. He had been talking to the Registrar at the University of Wisconsin who promised to fax Laura Menard's college transcript to him at Big City Community College, maybe yet that afternoon. He wasn't sure why he felt it necessary to verify Ms. Menard's undergraduate record. On his desk was a transcript the young woman had handed him. She had received a BS in Zoology, with a minor in ichthyology. Her grade point average was 3.98, with a 4.00 in fish studies. Amazingly, her only B was in a required humanities course. What, she wasn't human enough? Did she argue a conservative point of view too successfully, too convincingly for a liberal professor to handle, at a liberal university?

Maybe Leonard needed the official transcript to prove that, while he felt he was being somewhat impulsive, he was correct in his personal evaluation of this woman—a person he had never met before, a person who had walked into his office without an appointment. Then again, maybe he wanted time to collect his thoughts regarding Laura.

You want honesty? Maybe it was love at first sight.

One thing was certain; before he had verified anything, he

had offered her a teaching job at the college and booked a fishing trip down the Whoosh River with her as his guide.

Professor Russell was not only a professor of whatever class or subject needed an instructor at the time; he was the acting president of the Big City Community College. That might give you some idea how small BCCC really was.

Its size and remote location made it extremely difficult to hire qualified teachers, which in turn, made it increasingly difficult to keep accreditation. Without accreditation, funds would evaporate along with the flow of incoming students. That would be the end of the school and the Professor's job, forcing him to return to California where he could take a position as a professor of English Literature at some private school, teaching long-dead classics to rich students in freshly starched uniforms.

Leonard knew if he didn't upgrade things soon his personal *Rocky Mountain Experience* would be over.

Leonard met his wife, Jennifer, at Berkley. She was born and raised on a small buffalo ranch south of Missoula, Montana, on the Bitterroot River. She went to California for a taste of its culture and lifestyle. With an education, she planned to return home, but things didn't work out exactly that way. When the two graduated and married, they settled in Berkley, and had two daughters. It wasn't until they learned that Jennifer had cancer that Leonard agreed to her plea; "Len, please, let's just go home."

Home was somewhere, anywhere, in the Rockies where they could bring up their children away from the *Left Coast*. Jenny promised him she would beat the cancer and "we'll live happily ever after." She believed it, and he *had* to believe it. Just as his appreciation of the mountains, its culture, and the people his wife loved so dearly began to seep into his own being, Jenny broke her promise—she died.

Leonard vowed to find a way to fulfill Jenny's wish of raising the kids *back home*, even if it meant painting houses with college students during the summer months, teaching U.S. citizenship classes to legal immigrants, or English classes to undocumented aliens. Len was determined to stay in the mountains—somehow.

Laura Menard came to Professor Russell's office to inquire about courses at BCCC. She wanted to earn credits that she could eventually transfer to State University toward a master's degree in ichthyology. The community college didn't offer graduate coursework. The best the Professor could do would be to aid her in establishing an Internet program with the University. Laura thought it might be better to just move to Capital City, where the University was located, and work directly with the professors. She sincerely thanked Professor Russell, and said she would consider his Internet idea.

Before Laura could leave, Professor Russell made her an offer; a job teaching Chemistry 101, Biology 101, or Algebra 101, her choice. Actually, he needed her to teach all three, but didn't want to appear that desperate. The only stipulation was that she would take some credits toward a teaching degree. If she decided to join the staff, she could start immediately. The college would provide necessary teaching aids and class syllabi. She could even start midterm.

During Laura's undergraduate days at Wisconsin, the possibility of a teaching position never crossed her mind. She asked the Professor for time to consider his generous offer. Her smile grew as she rose to leave.

In an effort to prolong their time together, Professor Russell asked Laura, "What brought you *out here*, from the Midwest?" She explained she had come to the mountains to camp and fish with an eye toward finding employment. Then her truck broke down and she had coasted into Maggie's Corner. She fell in love with the country and became a licensed fishing guide on the Whoosh River Watershed. Go figure.

Leonard told her that he had always wanted to raft the river with his two daughters, but not to fish. He stressed that he wasn't a fisherman and added that it had become extremely difficult to find things that interested his girls anymore—at least things that involved their father. It was harder still, since their mother had died.

Laura immediately offered, not a raft float, but a McKenzie drift boat trip with enough fishing equipment for Leonard and the girls.

"I won't promise you'll catch anything, but it will be a great time. It will be fun for your girls…I do promise that. No charge for the first excursion." When Leonard protested she told him: "The first trip is free. It's just a way to get you involved, a come-on. If you go again, we'll set the hook, so to speak," she grinned. "That's when we hit you up for the big bucks." He didn't know if he believed her but, oh Lord, that smile of hers.

◄●◄

Professor Russell sat at his desk mulling his sixty-minute meeting with Laura Menard. He wondered if he was hoping to become involved with this woman for the sake of BCCC, for his children's sake, or because he was just lonesome? Who was he kidding? Yes, he was lonely, but it took two people for an involvement. Was that why Laura Menard had come in looking for classes and left with a customer for Maggie's Corner and a potential career in academia?

One thing was certain, the college would benefit from her expertise and the fishing trip might be something his girls would enjoy. Besides, was it really necessary to feel guilty every time he thought about another woman? He had no feelings for any of his female colleagues or Jennifer's old friends. He certainly had no interest in the coeds at BCCC. Were they even old enough to be in college? Maybe it was time to start thinking more about himself than the school, or even his own kids.

Naturally, this triggered a rush of guilty feelings, which ultimately led to the same reoccurring dream. For no apparent reason his wife would desert him and he would desperately search for her. He had to know why she left him. He needed her back, but his search was always fruitless and seemed to take hours. Then he would awaken in a cold sweat long before his alarm went off, long before he remembered that Jenny was dead. He felt empty, so God-awful empty.

Suddenly his mind returned to the clanging fax machine, as Laura's transcript spit out. Not surprisingly, the record was an exact duplicate of the one on his desk.

CHAPTER 7: Cat

◂●◂

Buckheart Beastley was making his mid-morning rounds of Towne. It was always worth a daytime look at his domain, a shorter trip than his nightly sojourn. As unofficial mayor of the village, he considered these patrols part of his duty to the village. Bucky, as most of the citizens called him, was a totally black, twenty-two pound alley cat—er, mixed breed, male feline. His weight varied depending on the kindness of the people on his route and the severity of the winter at hand. Regardless, he was one big dude.

Bucky's lineage can be traced to his grandfather, about fifteen generations removed, who jumped off a covered wagon headed toward Oregon. While checking out the back of Chester Ratzigg's store, the wagon pulled away without Grandpa. His descendents have been in the Whoosh River area ever since.

Bucky's evening patrol usually ended around two in the morning. He'd slip into the Roadhouse Bar & Grill before closing to sleep in his favorite cushioned booth. Mike Tapio, the bartender, always had something from the kitchen set out for him, with any luck, fish.

Bucky was pretty beat up for his age. Most of one ear was

chewed off in an altercation with a raccoon. His noticeable limp was the result of a wrestling match with an enormous jackrabbit that had catapulted both of them into a deep ravine. After doing the rabbit in, Bucky dragged himself up the steep grade, regained his dignity, and finished rounds on his three good legs. He also had puncture wounds, now healed and hidden, where a weasel had gone for his jugular and missed. Bucky feared nothing, although he no longer went out of his way to challenge the local dogs. He was top cat, alpha male. He was head honcho and the cats and dogs in Towne knew it.

Bucky began his early patrol one Friday on a typical Rocky Mountain, mid-summer day. The morning began with an absolutely crystal clear sky followed by an afternoon accumulation of clouds, then a short wind-driven shower and finally a perfectly calm, clear sunset behind the hazy blue mountains of the western range.

Bucky's first stop was always The Café. Greta Heinzel, the owner, was known for fresh fish on Friday. Some suspected that her fresh catch was illegally netted rainbow trout from somewhere in the Whoosh River Watershed. Bucky had no qualms against eating fish—legal or not. Who could tell the difference?

After a swing past the Super Market and the Dollar Store, Bucky strolled down the alley that ran behind the post office, state offices and the bank. Ignoring any traffic, he arrogantly crossed the street to the Lodge before checking for any new critters in the vacant warehouse.

Down the street was old Doc Swensen's veterinary barn. Empty paddocks once housed large animals—horses, cows, and an occasional injured elk or mule deer. Doc's widow, Sonja, now in her 80s, still administered to small cats and dogs in the weather-beaten, two-and-a-half story home. Sonja had no formal education, but after working with her husband for fifty years, she really didn't need one. She knew all that was necessary to tend to the local pets. Owners of large animals were forced to drive to Big City or, if they could afford it, have the vet drive out to care for their animals.

Mrs. Swensen didn't have a license, but then she didn't charge for her services either. Although she wasn't above taking staples for her kitchen, or having her lawn mowed, or driveway plowed, she never accepted cash. Apparently the medical suppliers didn't realize her husband had died, or just ignored the fact. They continued to fill Mrs. Swensen's orders.

Bucky always avoided the Swensen's place. He couldn't remember exactly what had happened to him there, but it was enough to steer him away—posttraumatic stress disorder? Maybe he was just being prudent.

After leaving the warehouse, Bucky swung around behind Chester's Mercantile to peruse the loading dock. He always stopped back at The Café for any goodies Greta had left him and then would dash across the bridge back to the Roadhouse for a long afternoon nap, thereby avoiding any afternoon rainstorms.

Bucky's evening route was more extensive and, because it was dark, far more interesting.

CHAPTER 8: History of the Whoosh River Dam

><

The Army Corps of Engineers, with a history dating to 1775, held the mistaken notion they were the invincible, all-knowing masters of Mother Nature and perhaps in their minds, the entire universe. In a few cases they were right. In some cases, they were right for a period of time. In most cases, they weren't even close. Some would say they weren't even in the ball park.

In 1932, the Corps held a public hearing in Big City. The meeting was not to ask the good citizens for their input, but to inform them that they were constructing a new dam on the Whoosh River. The Corps explained what glorious benefits the behemoth would bring to the region. Rancher and farmer alike would benefit from irrigation. They claimed tourism would flourish with a multitude of recreational possibilities, including all-water sports. There would be new ski resorts, with water for snowmaking machinery, and water enough to spray on golf courses. Water would even be made available for mining and petroleum exploration and development. The Corps predicted unprecedented prosperity and growth for the valley with skyrocketing employment opportunities. The Great Depression would end and all for the loss of a stretch of *worthless* canyon river and a few thousand acres of barren rangeland.

"Oh, Hallelujah, we're out of the depression!"

"Let the good times roll!"

The entire Whoosh River Watershed was caught up by the hustler's hype. Developers bought land options near the proposed dam site. Real estate signs spread like locusts across the valley. Commercial banks stopped trying to dump repossessed ranches at ten-cents-on-the-dollar and went looking for speculators, calling for insightful investors, people willing to catch the next tidal wave to prosperity and independence.

An arch-style dam was built in record time and not necessarily by the lowest bidders or the best contractors. Maybe you had to know somebody.

After the dam was completed, postwar prosperity brought some tourists who fished and water-skied behind the new structure. Eventually they left for more popular locations with plush hotels and Olympic-sized pools, casinos with entertainment, and towns that sponsored big dollar bass fishing tournaments.

New tourist cabins and one-story motels, so popular after World War II soon stood vacant in the Whoosh River Watershed. The ski resort never materialized and the thirty-six-hole golf course is now overrun by wild grasses and Canadian Geese.

Even with irrigation, soil was not rich enough for cash crops. Only a few Amish families made a living and they were doing that long before the dam was ever built.

Production of electricity became a subsidized commodity, as the area never had enough customers to make it profitable.

Oil exploration required very little water—there was very little oil.

Mining and smelting operations on the East Branch vanished

immediately after World War II. While there was copper ore in the ground, it was far too deep to be profitable.

On the positive side, logging occurred only on a selective basis rather than the clear cutting method. The land was never subjected to deep open-pit coal mining as there was no coal.

What the dam did produce was a reservoir where trout could live and flourish. Even that didn't last long. Some moron at the Department of Wildlife thought pike and bass would make better game fish and attract more anglers to the reservoir than trout. As it turned out, the pike and bass grew to enormous size, devouring the trout.

The state record for the largest northern pike still belongs to the Whoosh River Reservoir, but a problem occurred. The water was too cold for the bass to reproduce naturally and the reservoir lacked shoreline marshes and wetlands for northern pike to spawn. Then funds ran out for dumping hatchery fish into the dam's backwater and eventually the transplanted fish died of old age. While some trout did return down from the headwaters, only a few ever grew to the size of previous generations.

Fishing below the dam was another story. Water, released from the bottom of the dam, created a tailwater, which produced a year-round water temperature between 50 and 56 degrees, perfect for aquatic plants. In turn, aquatic insects prospered by feeding off the plants, which meant rainbow and brown trout and an occasional mountain whitefish survived and prospered by eating those insects and fry of other fish, occasionally even indulging on their own offspring.

The Whoosh River tailwater fishery never received the publicity of the San Juan in New Mexico, Bull Shoals in Arkansas, the Cheeseman tailwater on the South Platte in Colorado, or even Wyoming's Miracle Mile. Truth be told, the fishing was not quite as good as those famous, now over-crowded stretches. However, there was another problem. It seemed that whenever a reporter from one of those glossy fly-fishing magazines showed up, the fishing was lousy, or so they wrote. Actually, the fishing wasn't that bad. Trouble was that when those freeloading correspondents came to check out the area there was no one to greet them, take them fishing, or give them free lodging at a posh resort. In other words: wine and dine them. A shunned reporter can be very vindictive, just ask any career politician.

So, for better or worse, the Whoosh River went mainly unnoticed. Those willing to accept recommendations from locals were usually rewarded.

Naturally, the Corps of Engineers took credit for the success of the tailwater fishery. It was obviously the result of their *visionary thinking.* In reality, it was as much a surprise to them as it was to their ever-growing number of critics.

Population in the village of Towne eventually dropped to its pre-dam total. However, based solely on the Corps rosy predictions, the municipality of Big City benefited when voters prematurely elected to move the county seat there. Those still alive who voted against the move loudly proclaim, with a grin, "…that dam was a damn silly idea."

CHAPTER 9: Horse

Horse knew that after Ranger Ted Miller's slap he would be rid of the saddle and reins, and soon he'd be rid of Ted. It was a friendly slap, so Horse would play out the little game. When Ted's hand landed on his rump, Horse would sprint into the meadow, do two twisting bucks, and turn to watch Ted fire up the Jeep.

Horse loved his freedom, but whenever Ted was gone he missed the occasional apple or carrot. Well, maybe he missed Ted.

Horse came to the U.S. Forestry Service via Sonja Swensen, Towne's de facto veterinarian. As a colt, Horse was left with Sonja as payment of sorts. She had patched up a rodeo circuit rider's dog and had done a little work on the cowboy himself. Before she realized what had happened, the cowboy, his dog, his pickup and trailer had all pulled out of the driveway leaving Horse tethered to a gatepost. Sonja sold Horse to the Forestry Service. The government, like all bureaucracies, requested documentation. Sonja had no bill of sale or other proof of ownership or origin, but the government had her sign paperwork in triplicate before awarding a payment of fifty dollars. She could have gotten more from the glue factory in Big City with absolutely no paper work involved. Anyway, Horse became the property of the U.S. Government.

Sonja never had the chance to question the cowboy about Horse. General consensus was that his sire was Buckskin and his mother was half Buckskin and half Quarter Horse. From the Buckskin breed, Horse got his strength, stamina and large size. At the withers (the ridge between shoulder blades and the ground) he stood over sixteen hands or sixty-five inches. How's that for horse terminology? And no, the Buckskin is not a mere color. The Buckskin horse is thought to have originated from the Spanish Sorraia and the color is an indication of the genetic heritage they possess.

From the Quarter Horse side of the equation, Horse got his speed and dexterity, though not the usual docile temperament. No way. Horse's lousy disposition may have been a result of his treatment as a colt rather than a genetic glitz.

His coat was a grayish yellow color (buckskin), with one patch of white high on his snout. People swore it was the perfect outline of a skull and cross bones. Hair above all four hoofs was as white as his patch. The mane and tail were a pure "Satan Black." That's right—Satan, not satin.

Horse never understood his feelings toward Ranger Miller. Maybe he viewed Ted as a fellow loner. He was assigned to other rangers before Ted, but it had never worked out. Horse was spirited. Some called him stubborn. They also called him a lot of other things; SOB, God-Damned Horse, Jackass, Dog-Food-Walking, Mule Breath and on and on. Ted just called him Horse. Ted had no special talent. He was certainly no *horse whisperer*, but he had never hit the animal, never jerked him around or otherwise abused him. They had hung out together in the meadows for two weeks before Ted even threw up a saddle.

Horse and Ted made a good team. Whenever Ted was out of the saddle and doing whatever it was he did, he would let Horse roam free. The shrill sound of Ted's whistle would bring them back together. At night, Horse was not tethered, even back at the Ranger's cabin. Ted would lead him to the dilapidated, slant-roofed structure behind the cabin and release him. Actually, the weather-beaten grey cabin wasn't in much better shape than the shed. Horse could use the building for cover from the elements, or in the event some rogue bear or passing cougar made a visit, he was free to defend himself or flee, though Ted doubted there was much *flee* in the animal.

＊

Horse watched as Ted drove over a gentle rise into a blur of dust, then out of sight. Oh well, he was never gone for very long. When he came back maybe he would bring that woman, Laura, with him. Horse liked Laura. Hey, speaking of women, Horse had heard rumors of a family of wild horses finding their way down from the Pryor Mountains. He bucked twice more, threw in a third just for fun, and was off to check them out.

CHAPTER 10: Ranger Miller

><

ed Miller had been working in the Whoosh River meadows, high above the canyon, watching beaver build a lodge behind an already established dam. He had wandered over to his horse to scrounge lunch from his saddlebags. Normally he didn't check his cell phone until evening. Cell phone calls were hit or miss in the meadows. It was three in the afternoon and Ted wished he had held to form and checked his calls later.

"Bad news, Ted. Your father died. Sorry. Take all the time you need. Call when you get back and fix your damn radio. Burg."

His supervisor, Sidney Rosenburg, was sincere enough—he just didn't waste words, whatever the situation. His lack of tact, or political savvy, had dead-ended his career. Everybody knew Sid would never advance beyond District Ranger.

Forgetting lunch, Ted closed his notebook, mounted his horse, and headed for the ranger cabin—an old abandoned trapper's lodge originally built by Chester Ratzigg and now used by anyone who needed it. Ted took the saddle and reins off his horse and flung them through the open door of the cabin along with a weather-faded blanket and tattered saddlebags. Taking a pen from his shirt pocket, he scribbled a note and pinned it to the outside bulletin board bolted between the window and door. The only other posting was a warning of black bear in the area.

Ted crossed over to Horse and gave him a swat on the hindquarter. Horse pranced off a few paces, bucked twice, snickered at Ted, and headed for the high country.

Climbing into the Forest Service Jeep, Ted half hoped it wouldn't start. It did and he was off, paralleling a nearly invisible hiking trail which led to a primitive camping area, then on down to an old logging road. Eventually the two-rutter connected with Canyon Road and a treacherous downhill vault before crossing the dilapidated steel bridge that spanned a ravine holding the East Branch some hundred feet below. He passed the reservoir, and headed towards Maggie's Corner. A right turn, where County Road 64 intersected, led him to Towne and his trailer. Another twenty miles and he'd be at the Big City Airport.

Following the funeral, Ted rented a van, and packed up the last of his father's possessions. Really only the old fishing gear had interested Ted. Before the service, he had rummaged through his dad's paraphernalia hoping that any grieving process would be short and soon forgotten.

Somewhere west of Kearney, Nebraska, Ted Miller sped along Interstate 80. Ted knew he was in Nebraska. He could prove it. Every 500-watt local radio station along the way had three things to broadcast; the girls' high school volleyball results, the commodities report, and the constant chatter about Husker "Big Red" Football.

He had left Michigan in the predawn darkness and crossed the Indiana-Illinois line before the sun appeared in his rearview mirror. It chased him across Iowa and was about to overtake him before shining through his front windshield. Ted reached for his clip-on sunglasses. Talk about nerdy. Not cool. Unfortunately, he had left his prescription sunglasses on his bedroom bureau in the rush to get to the airport.

━◄

Ted's head jerked. He must have nodded off—dangerous at those speeds. He was still on I-80 this side of Paxon. From a billboard beside the highway, a large polar bear promoted Ole's Big Game Steakhouse and Lounge. To his right, behind the highway fence, was a large farm pond, maybe ten to twelve acres, its surface a large jigsaw puzzle of floating blue hues mingled together by a slight breeze. Colors ranged from cobalt, to navy, to midnight, to nearly black. Transplanted cottonwood trees, uniformly placed around the water, betrayed the fact that it was not a natural farm pond, but once a productive gravel pit, made to appear as if nature had done the excavation. The water level was the same as the Platte River off to the north.

Ahead a bright green highway sign announced that the next exit had: NO SERVICES.

Ted coasted up the ramp and stopped while a huge John Deere tractor, complete with air-conditioned cab, crept by dragging a trailer stacked with freshly-baled hay. The driver's head was hidden by large earphones and a bright green baseball cap, the same green as the tractor. The aroma of hay lingered long after the rig disappeared north into a cloud of white dust.

Ted pulled out and took an immediate right heading east over a gravel road pounded into shape by years of heavy truck traffic. After a half mile, he turned north onto a driveway leading to a sturdy looking farmhouse painted entirely white with a contrasting black roof. It was a home straight out of Northern Indiana Amish country. Except for the electric cable and phone lines running to the house and barn, and the enormous satellite disc aimed to the southwest. You would expect Rachel Yoder to greet you from her copious flower garden, wearing a long black dress and bonnet and a cautious, yet friendly smile on her broad face. Ted missed the mailbox with *Miller* stenciled on both sides.

He parked by the open barn doors that were mitered and pinned in place with wood dowels and bracing. A silver galvanized roof covered the rustic hand-sawn lumber of the post and beam building. The most unique feature, the silo, was built of wood, not the usual clay tile or concrete.

Ted entered the barn. In sharp contrast to the timeworn barn, an enormous brand new Massey Ferguson four-wheeled tractor with a Sisu Tier III, six-cylinder, diesel engine rested on the wood planked floor. "Awesome," thought Ted.

Seeing no signs of life, he carefully closed the barn doors and walked over to the house. A collie-husky mix lay on a rag rug next to an empty rocking chair on the long front porch. He, maybe she, lifted its head off its front paws, opened one eye and snorted.

"Anybody home, old boy?"

The dog looked at Ted as if to say: "You see anybody home, dummy? And who are you calling old?"

"You're absolutely right. Nobody is home, and you really don't give a rip do you?" The dog rested its head back on its paws closing one eye as he watched the intruder with the other. Ted reached for the note pad and pen, which were always in his pocket protector, a gift from his grandfather when he was five. It was probably the only object he still owned that had belonged to his father's father. The ink was partially worn off, but you could still make out the advertising for a local hardware store. It was another thing people told him was nerdy, but he couldn't seem to break the habit. He printed a note asking permission to fish the pond. Folding it with a ten-dollar bill, Ted stuffed it between the screen door and jam.

He complemented the dog on what a great security guard he was and drove off. The dog closed his other eye, snorted once more, and was fast asleep.

Approaching the pond from the west, Ted could see late afternoon shadows from the cottonwood trees spreading across the near-side water. He parked, got out and walked around to the back of the vehicle. Lifting the back door of the van, he rummaged through his father's rusty three-tiered tackle box. He found a few flat fish and buzz baits. From a large assortment of red and white Dardevles he selected the largest one. Taking a closed-face reel from a Ziploc bag, he slipped an old spinning rod out of a length of PCV pipe, and hooked it all together.

To his left a cottonwood had fallen, its roots tenaciously holding on to the bank. The trunk, just six inches below the surface, had several leafless branches extending at various angles up and out of the water. If there were any bass in the pond, the biggest would be hiding under that sunken tree.

The reel, rusty as it was, sent the red and white lure sailing toward the far end of the submerged tree. Ted quickly cranked the monofilament line in, wondering how strong it could be after all those years wrapped around the spool. He also wondered what the authorities would do if they caught him without a Nebraska fishing license. After all he worked for the Federal Government, not the State of Nebraska. Hopefully, there wasn't too much animosity between wildlife agencies in the area, and they would extend professional courtesy. Certainly he could plead.

"Don't give me a ticket, officer. We're all in this together, right?"

Ted again flipped his lure to the fallen tree and thought he saw a rippling of water just before an explosion. The reel sung as the monofilament line ripped off the spool. Ted fumbled with the drag, slowing the fish only slightly. Just as he was about to run out of line, a huge bass catapulted into the air, did a three-second tail dance through the spray and slammed back into the water, sending a shower of droplets high overhead. The struggle engaged for more than ten minutes before Ted became impatient.

"Don't horse him. You'll lose him for sure." A familiar voice came from over his shoulder. "That gear hasn't been used in years."

The placid instructions didn't startle Ted. In fact, they had a calming effect as he brought in the large mouth bass—an enormous fish. Ted was mainly a trout fisherman, but he knew enough to believe this would set a record in Nebraska. It wasn't big enough for Georgia, or Texas, but certainly for Nebraska. The monster hybrids in California were in a class of their own.

"Nice fish, son," the voice said. "Guess all this pond needed was some cover. If I can ever get the water cold enough, maybe I'll try planting some trout. What do you think, maybe some German browns? Of course, they couldn't reproduce, but they sure could get big and fat. The gravel company scraped all the sand and gravel out down to the layer of muck then abandoned the pit. I threw in some crawdads…did they ever take hold. Bass do love those crawdaddies for supper. If the browns got big enough, fast enough, maybe they could both survive…brown and large mouth in there together. What do you think?"

With a quick twist of the treble hook, Ted released the fish without taking him out of the water. With a three-sixty swirl the fish was gone. Aided by years of corrosion, two of the three barbs had broken off in the battle. Ted slowly rose, stretched his still road-weary body, turned and saw his father. He was dressed in blue denim bib-overalls, a short-sleeved cotton shirt, ankle high boots, and a slightly soiled straw Panama hat. Obviously he had not been working in the fields, as he was smooth-shaven with that familiar smell of Aqua Velva after-shave lotion.

"Got your note. The ten wasn't necessary, but I'll hang onto it. You never know…"

"What are you doing in Nebraska, Dad?" It didn't seem to phase Ted that he was talking to the man he had just buried.

"Well, you know, I always wanted to be a gentleman farmer… at least got it half right…the farmer part." His smile broke into a full-blown grin. "Living in Detroit didn't give me much chance to be either farmer or gentleman."

"Dad, you never lived in Detroit. We lived in Grosse Pointe Shores by the golf course. And you were a gentleman."

"You're right about Grosse Pointe, but sometimes it's easier to deal with people if they think you're from Detroit. Then there are others who would rather believe you're from some rich suburb. You've got to read your customer, son."

"You were good at that."

"I suppose…anyway, I'm glad you're doing well. Really haven't gotten to see you very much over the last few years. Not throwin' a guilt trip on you or anything, but your mother sure has missed you."

"Mom's here too?"

"You bet. She had the place all fixed up for me when I got here. Did you see her garden when you drove up? Sure is proud of that. She'll be sorry she missed you. Would liked to have shown you around, but she had to run one of her casseroles over to the church. They're big on casseroles around here, even bigger on churches. Did you see my tractor? Must have. Thanks for closing the barn doors."

"Dad, that tractor is big enough to work Nebraska and half of Kansas."

"Yeah, I got carried away...over-the-top for our spread, but I did get a good deal," his smile grew even wider. His father loved a good deal.

"Suppose you met Lucky on the porch," he went on. "You were pretty young when he passed. Not sure he was too happy when you were born....a little jealous, maybe. Still and all, he always was a good dog...so protective of you when strangers were around. Rest of the time, he pretty much ignored you. Don't remember him being so darned lazy, though. Guess he figures he's got a lot of catching up to do."

"About mom, I really don't know what to say, I...," Ted trailed off.

"Hey, you loved your mother. We both know that. You were never really big on communication. Just remember, your mom and I understood.

"We're really happy here. Sure was glad to see her when I woke up...figured she'd think forty-five years together was enough.

"Say, that little gal, Laura...you start paying a lot more attention to her. *She's a keeper.*" His father chuckled at his fish analogy.

"You know, we could use some grandchildren to look over? What are you now, thirty-two or so?" He slapped Ted on the shoulder. "Life is short. Trust me, on that one, son."

◄►

With his father's friendly back slap, Ted Miller was on I-80 again, headed west toward Towne. After several miles of reflection, he realized that a mourning period wouldn't be necessary. He had just experienced something far more reassuring, something far more profound. Maybe his father was right—he should pay more attention to Laura, instead of researching beaver.

"Damn-da-dam beaver." Tired old pun. Must have heard it from his father, maybe his grandfather.

Ted Miller had been intrigued with beaver since he read the R. D. Lawrence book, *Patty.* Lawrence's expansive, tedious, sometimes even torturous explanations and descriptions of an orphaned beaver and its habitat surprisingly did not deter a young Ted from reading the entire book—three times. Ted wrote his master's thesis on the North American beaver, *Castor Canadensis,* and had enough original research for a doctorate, but he was tired of formal schooling. He could just self-publish and move to another subject. Wasn't there some sort of vanity press where you paid your own publishing fees? Can you imagine?

Another area of study perhaps. How about chronic wasting disease in deer? Nah, Ted had little interest in animal diseases unless, and until, they showed up in his beloved beaver. Giardiasis…there's a thought. He could research *beaver fever.* Or the new threat to the West, the blue stain fungus, carried by the Mountain Pine Bark beetle, that was slowly and methodically wiping out huge stands of the Rocky Mountain pine. Ted knew virtually nothing about trees.

Rumors were spreading that a population of yellowfin cutthroat, thought to be extinct, had been found in Colorado. That would be more in Laura's field of expertise, but not his.

After graduation, Ted went to work for the United States Fish and Wildlife Service in Michigan and eventually was transferred to the Rocky Mountains, his first assignment, a backcountry ranger. He shared jurisdiction of two parcels—over two million acres of federal land with the Bureau of Land Management (BLM) and a small slice of a National Park with the National

Park Service. With an area nearly as big as Yellowstone National Park and twice the size of Rhode Island, there was rarely any dispute over who had first priority. The three agencies, along with state's Department of Natural Resources, worked together for the *greater good,* as it was so snidely called. The only friction came when somebody screwed up. Then came official reviews, reports to write and file, responsibility denied or passed down the line, and finally, reprimands when necessary. Within days things would return to normal with few, if any, long lasting grudges. But, when the Federal Bureau of Investigation intervened, it was best to just step aside and let them grab the headlines. Of course, they only took credit for *good* news. The FBI was long gone if the news was *bad.*

The Rocky Mountain area abutted an Indian Reservation. Every agency was careful not to step on the toes of the tribal police force or the grounds designated as sovereign. Federal and state officers intervened only when asked. And, of course, there was the local sheriff's department, headed by one Oscar Cowdrey and friends.

Severe federal cutbacks meant Ted also trained as a law enforcement officer with duties to chase down poachers, check hunting and fishing licenses, and assist in rescue missions, human or animal.

A recent trend toward big game trophy poaching proved little concern to Ted, as the area's animal life ran on the diminutive side, falling far short of ever being listed in any *Boon and Crockett* record book. Ted's biggest problem with poachers was their use of trout lines, also known as trotlines, for big rainbows and browns. Poachers would attach a main cord (with several sinking lines running from it) across the width of a placid run and connect it to large floats making it impossible for a fish to pass without coming near one of the many treble-hooks baited with exotic enticements. After leaving their rig, poachers returned later to reap a harvest. The only more efficient method of catching trout was dynamite, if you didn't care how messy the fillets looked. Two restaurants, a grocery store, and one lodge in Towne would be forced to look elsewhere for new suppliers if Ted ever succeeded in shutting down the illegal fishing operation.

A more hideous threat was aimed at the black bear population, not because of their size but because their parts could be sold on the black market for lucrative profits. Paws, organs, and claws were in great demand by Asian communities. Even many in North America were willing to pay enormous sums of money. Probably the most insidious torture imaginable is trapping a bear, immobilizing the animal, and then implanting a crude catheter in the stomach to drain bile from its gall bladder. The liquid, ursodeoxycholic acid or UDCA for short is commonly called *junbu*. Supposedly this cure-all can even improve your sex life. It certainly improves the financial situations of its predators. Scum bags, if you will. Ted fantasized public executions of these entrepreneurs. Every Memorial Day they would be paraded out onto the Yankee Stadium infield just before the baseball game and summarily shot. Maybe summarily is too harsh. As Hangin' Judge Roy Bean might have said; "Give the bastards a fair trial and then hang 'em." Judge Bean was alleged to have kept a pet bear in his saloon—er, courtroom.

Unscrupulous butchers had not yet tapped into the Whoosh area, but it was only a matter of time. When that happened, Ted would need help, available funds or not.

As long as he submitted his findings, accounted for his hours, and didn't run up an expense account, any spare time Ted spent acting as a biologist in the field received tacit approval by his boss.

Ted even had full use of the Forest Service Jeep and Rosenburg trusted him to not abuse the privilege.

"Just remember to change the oil," Ted heard his boss admonish him on several occasions.

Other than his rent on a doublewide trailer, which he split with another ranger, Ted's living expenses were few. Most of his paycheck went to his financial advisor, an old college friend who majored in economics. He had done *very* well for Ted. With a decent wage, plus his family's more-than-modest estate, Ted would soon become financially independent. Money would never be a concern, not as long as he kept his present lifestyle and his financial advisor stayed honest. Is that too much to ask?

Ted considered requesting a transfer to the Northwest to study salmon spawning runs, or the effects of dam removal on resident fish, or even—"What's the difference between a steelhead and a rainbow?" Now with the possibility of the dam being removed, he might have the same options without leaving.

Then he met Laura Menard.

On their first trip to the Whoosh meadows together, she asked him why the Whoosh River strain of rainbow was resistant to the whirling disease that had devastated so many other western rainbow stocks. He gave her the standard line about how the Whoosh River Fish Hatchery, at Pine Bluff, was so much cleaner than other hatcheries where the disease had taken hold.

"Oh, come on, you don't really believe that do you?" was her response. Ted's first reaction to her statement-question was anger. Then he saw she was actually grinning at him.

"Gawd, what a beautiful smile, what a beautiful woman." He almost said it aloud.

He remembered making some dumb comment like, "Good thing you smiled when you said that, stranger." Or maybe it was,

"That's my theory and I'm stuck with it." Whatever he said, it was stupid, and they both laughed. He went on to explain the introduction of a breed of rainbow, Hofer, which was far more resistant to the crippling bacteria. And yes, a clean fish hatchery was a large part of that theory.

From that day forward, Ted thought he was in love. Hell, he knew he was in love. He enjoyed how easy it was to be with Laura. He was sure that Horse felt the same, not that Ted needed his approval. Maybe Horse wasn't in love, exactly, but Laura always stowed a handful of carrots in her backpack.

Until the dam issue was settled, staying in the Watershed to study the problem of whirling disease seemed a reasonable option to Ted. He knew Sid would delight in reading a research paper on something other than beaver. And Laura's knowledge could be a big help to him. "Yeah, maybe she can type," he said aloud. "Just kidding, just kidding," he hurriedly amended in case anybody might be hiding in the van racing across Nebraska.

He flipped open his cell phone to see that Laura had called three times.

"Ted, so very, very sorry. Laura." She had apparently heard about his dad's death. There was no message with her second or third calls.

Ted punched Laura's number on the speed dial and waited for the connection. If she was working at Maggie's, she would pick up, but if she was guiding on the river, he'd have to wait until she had finished. For the first time, Ranger Miller was really concerned she might not call back. His dad was right—she was a keeper.

"Pick up, Laura. Damn it, pick up."

CHAPTER 11: Mike Tapio - Gangster

Mike Tapio eased his weary body onto the middle stool in front of the long cherrywood bar, reached across the polished surface and grabbed a glass. Backhanded, he poured himself a draft beer. Mike had just sent his last patron home with a deputy sheriff and turned off the lights. Only the glow from the juke box and several muted beer signs illuminated the empty room.

Another long day, he wondered if his anonymous life style was worth it. He had never worked this hard—ever. Noon to close, six days a week with only Mondays off. Big deal, Mondays off, as long as his manager, Freda Morrison, knew where to reach him. Of course, it was Freda that made it possible for him to stay in Towne and hold a forty-nine percent stake in the Roadhouse Bar and Grill, while knowing absolutely nothing about the *adult beverage* business.

Mike was flown into Big City in a private jet and chauffeured to Towne in a nondescript automobile with the windows tinted nearly black.

When he reached the Roadhouse, Mike was introduced to Freda and given an account number at the only bank in the village.

Independent Beneficiaries would make an electronic deposit each month in his name. He was given the key to a safety deposit box which contained instructions on how to contact the Feds, but he was highly encouraged not to.

Mike moved into the modest apartment above the Roadhouse. For nearly two years Freda instructed him, first in the basics, then in the intricacies of the bar business, constantly reminding him that the most important thing for his own safety was silence about his personal life.

"Listen, sure…but keep your mouth shut," she constantly implored. Mike learned to deflect personal questions with minimal effort, while gaining the confidence of his customers. He pretended to be concerned about their woes and their lies about the huge trout caught or almost caught. He acted as if he cared about the destiny of the Whoosh Dam. Mike knew nothing about dam removal and cared even less. He passed along big fish stories to his patrons, but never their petty stories of grief and misfortune.

"What do these clowns know about grief and misfortune?" he often asked himself.

Like any good bartender, he never took sides in a discussion, unless it involved the bar itself. He didn't care about the people, the area, the climate, or the possibility the dam would be removed, and he certainly had no interest in the trout. How could people talk endlessly about a stupid fish? What, they have a brain the size of a pea?

After only two weeks he had seen enough of the West. His heart remained in the big cities of the East Coast. But, if he hadn't made the move, Mike could picture life in a federal penitentiary or lying in some alley with a bullet in the back of his skull—executed gangster-style. Fact was he wouldn't have lived long in prison either. You don't skim from the mob and run to the Feds. Well, he didn't actually run to the Feds. They picked him up on three or four minor charges. As one FBI agent expressed it, "Together it's enough to put you away for a very long time."

Without trust in any attorney, he refused to talk. After several days in confinement, the Feds informed Mike they had arranged for a judge to hear his case—a judge with no qualms about sending him to a hard-core prison, with no special protection. Word would be spread to his fellow inmates that he was a prolific child molester. As he agonized, a pretty female FBI agent (wasn't she once with the X-files?) showed up and explained the Federal Witness Protection Program, WITSEC. Mike spilled his guts. Told it all. They couldn't shut him up.

To the surprise of most, indictments were issued and charges brought. Mike testified and the jury convicted half the defendants on half the charges. Mike's problem wasn't the half that was serving time, but the half that had beaten the rap and were now looking to beat him.

The Feds met their part of the bargain by constructing a phony personal history, which Mike was to memorize. They gave him a new name, Tapio. It was an East Finnish name meaning "forest spirit". Then they asked him where he wanted to relocate.

"Guess I always wanted to see the mountains." Mike now considered that his biggest mistake. "What in God's name was I thinking, the mountains?"

Does anybody know the East Finnish name for a "mountain spirit," or better yet, the East Finnish name for "stupid?"

"I should'a picked L.A. to hide out," he constantly complained to Freda.

To help avoid discovery, Mike was expected to sever ties with all former acquaintances, including family members. If the

Feds discovered him communicating with any of those people, the deal was off—the government would be absolved of further responsibility.

"No problem," Mike assured them. "I ain't got no family and now I ain't got no friends. Rita will get along fine without me." Rita was his last girlfriend. "It'll take that bitch about ten minutes to latch on to some other poor slob." Freda Morrison's top priority was to clean up Mike's language.

❧

Now, as he drank his second cold beer, Mike began to wonder about Rita.

"Maybe she's not a bitch. She's just trying to survive, like everybody else.

"Survive, how do you do that? You cover your own ass, that's how.

"Besides, maybe she misses me and wants me to contact her. Maybe, I should call her…see if things have cooled off.

"It's been two years." Mike was talking to the town cat, Bucky, who had just settled into his favorite booth.

"Damn, I miss all the action. I'm a fish out of water." He smiled, a fish out of water, indeed. "Maybe I'll turn things over to Freda for a few weeks and kinda slip back home and see what's comin' down. What do you think, cat?"

Bucky stretched and yawned, "We're going to miss you, boy. We are really going to miss you," and he curled up, yawned again, closed his eyes, and immediately fell asleep.

CHAPTER 12: Rufus - Rancher

Rufus Jefferson III threw down a shot of whiskey, set the glass carefully on the bar, picked up a draft beer and drained it. He slid the beer mug next to the shot glass and Mike Tapio refilled both. Rufus studied the glasses for a moment and repeated the impressive show. Mike refilled them again. This time Rufus pushed back his sweat-stained cowboy hat to reveal a tan line, unusual for such a dark, African-American. What was really unusual was seeing a black person in the village of Towne. Actually Rufus' ancestors were settlers, some say squatters, as far back as the late 1860s.

Rufus had just come from the County Clerk's office in Big City with clear title to his ranch clutched firmly in hand. Being Wednesday, he was waiting for his friend, George Otis.

Rufus and his family worked over twenty thousand acres northeast of Towne and northwest of Maggie's Corner, roughly a five-by-six mile spread. It was dubbed the Broken Treaty Ranch, BTR for short and operated as a combined ranch, farm and hunting preserve. The farm produced much of the food for the Jefferson clan and grain for their cattle. Rufus' eldest son and his brother-in-law packed hunters, on horseback, to the outer reaches of the ranch in search of elk and mule deer, sometimes far exceeding the Jefferson property line.

For diversion Rufus operated a woodworking shop. He built quality toys, bird houses, rocking chairs, and picnic tables. Maggie sold many of the items at the Corner. The extra money helped supplement Rufus' income when beef prices were low or when drought or harsh winters thinned his herd and killed off the game. He was so good at his craft that Town's all-white school board arranged for an annual field trip to expose students to something other than chasing trout or herding cows. A busload of sixth graders was carted to Rufus' ranch and shown around the workshop. Rufus demonstrated machinery and donated several hand-tooled bats to the baseball and softball teams. Some cynics, Zeke Astor among them, thought the idea was for the children to be exposed to the area's only African-American family. Nonsense, the existence of the Jefferson family, living peacefully in the Whoosh River School District, was "a tribute to the area's diversity and tolerance."

"The Lord be praised."

The ballplayers wished Rufus had gone into metalwork since they preferred aluminum bats.

◄━

After recently returning from a double tour of the Middle East, Rufus, a member of the Army National Reserves, walked into the County Clerk's office in Big City with a pile of legal-looking papers and asked for clear title to the Broken Treaty Ranch. Around the Whoosh River Watershed there was no animosity toward the military. Oh, some folks had seriously questioned the Korean and Vietnam wars being run out of Washington DC by politicians, but they certainly held nothing against any of their residents who fought in those conflicts, least of all Rufus Jefferson.

"Morning, Mr. Jefferson." Stella Hemlock, the County Clerk, and great-great-grand niece of Towne's first elected Clerk cheerfully greeted Rufus. She was a shining example that not all small town nepotism is bad. "What's all that legal looking stuff under your arm?"

Rufus carefully laid the papers on the counter and tried to straighten them. "I'm filing for a deed to our property. I'd tell you we lost it somewhere but that ain't the truth…as far as I know there's never been one."

"Why Rufus, that land has been in your family forever…from the Civil War time and everybody knows that."

"True enough…true enough, but I want to make it all legal… don't want no White Man takin' away my place and moving us all out to some reservation."

Stella looked stunned until a shy grin crossed Rufus' face.

"I'm just foolin' with ya, Stella. All I want to do is make sure everything is legal. Hired a lawyer in Capital City to write it all up. There's as much historical junk there as we could find; newspaper articles, correspondence, whatever. The Jefferson clan seems to hold on to everything…that's why I can't tell ya we lost the deed. Besides, we're just plain honest folks," the grin grew bigger.

"I'm sure…," Stella hesitated. "I'm almost certain there won't be a problem. Give me a few days. I'll check with our lawyers, and the commissioners, and call you. Is that okay with you?"

Rufus nodded and headed for the door, stopped, turned and smiled. "Thank you. Oh, if I didn't mention it, I've got duplicates of all that." He pointed at the stack of papers and left the office.

As it turned out, not only did Rufus want clear title to the land, but also entitlement to water from the West Fork of the Whoosh River, mineral and oil rights to the entire property (oil shale included), and year-round hunting privileges.

●◄

Exactly one week later, Stella had organized and indexed Rufus' papers, and placed them squarely on the County Commission's *conference table* at the I Dare Ya Bar. The Commission liked to pick up a little travel expense money and make an appearance throughout the entire voting area. They figured it didn't hurt at election time. Besides, if they planned it right, they could adjourn just as happy hour began.

Without even looking at the stack of papers, they unanimously agreed to deed the property, the water allotment, and the oil, mineral and hunting rights to Rufus. They felt good about their act of generosity and charity, especially to a black man. Besides, nobody else could make a living on that God-awful waste land west of the reservoir.

Rufus needed water to operate his ranch, so the Commission gave him water. Geologists from around the world had proven over and over again that there was no amount of oil or mineral worth extracting from that piece of land. So why not give him the rights to it? Finally, who cared about a few mangy elk and undersized mule deer? Let Rufus hunt all year. He probably did, anyway.

Zeke Astor, the unofficial curmudgeon of Towne, sat in a corner booth, musing: "Above and beyond all that balderdash, won't Rufus be surprised when he receives his first property tax notice?" Zeke doubled as the village misanthropist. It's a tiny village.

It was four o'clock when George Otis walked into the Roadhouse and saw Rufus at the end of the bar. Rufus' self-satisfied grin told it all.

"You got it." It was a statement, not a question. "Good. It always belonged to your family." George eased himself onto a bar stool next to Rufus, as Mike set a draft beer in front of him.

It amused Mike that when George and Rufus sat together at the bar, not one derisive comment came from the table of local misfits. The usual verbal abuse showered on George, when he sat alone, was so apparently missing that it created an eerie silence. Those locals may not have been as dumb as they appeared. Well, maybe not.

George and Rufus never talked much, but when George was ready to head home, Rufus would always shake his hand and offer him a job at the Broken Treaty Ranch.

"I can't work for you, Rufus…I don't know how to ride a horse." George would grin and, in return, offer Rufus a job at Maggie's Corner.

"You'd be great pumping gas." Rufus would just shake his head as George threw a couple bills on the bar and left.

"How can you live in this country and not know how to ride a horse?" Rufus questioned Mike. Mike was the last person to ask about horseback riding in any country.

CHAPTER 13: Doc Walters, M.D.

◂━▸

The examination door slammed shut. Doctor Walters released a long sigh, more from sorrow than pain. Without standing, he rolled his stool over to the window and turned the blinds open. He watched Deloris Jankowski, head waitress from the Roadhouse Bar and Grill, and her daughter, Peggy, pull away in their pickup truck. Deloris was visibly angry, Peggy not so visibly pregnant. Doc closed the blinds, shutting out the impossible blue of a glorious Rocky Mountain day. In no mood for a glorious day, Doc removed his worn stethoscope and laid it gently on the examination table. It seemed as if he had owned it forever. A brand new electronic model was lost in one of his medicine cabinets. It was unopened, unused, unappreciated. It was a gift from a well meaning colleague.

"That's it, I'm done," he stated aloud and then silently to himself, "I can't do this anymore. I'm tired, I'm so God-awful tired."

Deloris and her daughter had come to find an abortionist. Doc Walters had delivered Deloris, and Peggy, and was not about to help them abort a healthy baby—not the beginning of a third generation. He suggested they call Phoebe McMillan in Big City.

Doc Walters and Phoebe McMillan went through undergraduate school together. They had as close to a *thing* going as that era allowed. Doc Walters went on to medical school. After graduation he returned to practice in his hometown and married a local gal, Millie. Phoebe entered a prestigious law school and stayed on in Washington D.C., where, she claimed, "the action is."

Phoebe became a national advocate in the Maryland and Virginia area for the pro-life movement. She attained notoriety and even some success. Many felt she should be credited with the slogan; *It's a Baby, Not a Choice.* Phoebe retired, much like Doc Walters, worn out—spent. She came home to the Whoosh River Watershed to recoup and tried to forget the names she had been called and the threats that had been made against her, all in the name of pro-choice. Phoebe wasn't retired long, and soon she was promoting adoption, serving as liaison between community hospitals, foster homes, agencies, churches and pregnant women.

Over the years Doc Walters and Phoebe had communicated occasionally. Phoebe wanted medical advice to back her position on abortion and Doc Walters enjoyed Phoebe's insights into a world he neither knew nor understood. They remained friends via the U.S. Mail and later the Internet.

When Deloris had walked into Doc Walters' office she was hoping he would take care of Peggy's *problem,* but was well aware that Doc wouldn't perform that type of *procedure.* Deloris wanted nothing to do with adoption. Doc questioned her and Peggy about how the father of the unborn baby felt, which only elicited a snort of disdain from the elder Jankowski and a flood of tears from the younger.

"If you won't give me a doctor's name, at least give me the number…the number of Planned Parenthood…somewhere close," Deloris had demanded.

Doc Walters realized that he wasn't going to change Deloris' mind. Maybe Planned Parenthood would do, at least in his way of thinking, the right thing. He took one of Phoebe's cards and wrote the Planned Parenthood number on the back. He handed it to Deloris and turned away. It occurred to him that he had lost his professionalism. He was becoming too involved, too judgmental. Then he remembered the young couple that he had counseled just before Deloris and Peggy.

Down near Pine Bluff, Jim and Paula Ketchum managed and operated a modest-sized ranch for an absentee landowner. After five miscarriages, the report from University Hospital in Capital City said they had no other suggestions for Doc's patients. He should in effect, tell them to "give it up."

They took the news stoically, too stoically. They simply thanked him and told him to send them the bill. But, he saw the hurt and desolation in their faces. As they left, he palmed one of Phoebe McMillan's business cards into Jim Ketchum's hand. This was no time to hit Mrs. Ketchum with the idea of adoption.

❧

Doc Walters had arrived early that morning, long before Helen, his girl Friday. He was greeted by an unfamiliar young couple sitting on the sidewalk bench next to the front door. Between them sat a 6-year-old boy who had obviously broken his arm. In the olden days Doc would have set the arm, put on a cast, taken two-dozen eggs for payment, and sent the family on their way.

Not in today's world.

First, he checked the child for signs of abuse. Thankfully, there were none. He had never seen these people before, so had no prior knowledge or record of mistreatment. He accepted their story that the boy had fallen out of a tree house. The child actually seemed rather proud of his *accident.*

Doc stabilized the arm with splints and gently tied the arm tight to the child's body before calling County Hospital in Big City and arranging for an x-ray and a waiting physician. The possibility of a malpractice suit sent the family on a forty mile round trip.

"I'm just into protecting my own butt. What was life like before lawyers? Have they been around long enough to lay claim to the world's second oldest profession?" Doctor Walters pondered under his breath.

"Excuse me?" Mr. Ketchum asked.

"Nothing…nothing, just an old man talking to himself."

Finally, in lieu of two-dozen eggs, he slid a plastic card, from an unfamiliar downstate insurance company, through a scanning device. He would have told the couple to forget about payment, but for his own safety, he needed a paper trail.

It had not been a good day for Doc Walters—not good at all.

❮❮◄

If you can envision a Norman Rockwell painting of an elderly, grey-haired, country doctor, you've pictured Doc Walters. You'd probably have to add a touch of cynicism to his smile and a look of weariness around his eyes, but you would be close. At one time he made house calls working out of a large, black medical bag. Sonja Swensen tells about her husband, Doc Swensen the veterinarian, and Doc Walters making their rounds together to save on gasoline. She didn't mention if they ever traveled by horse and carriage, but an old buckboard still resides in Sonja's barn cloaked in cobweb and shrouded in mystery.

❧

Doc Walters rolled his stool to the door and opened it calling to Helen his R.N., secretary, accountant, friend of forty years and, yes, his girl Friday.

"Please phone Doctor Brandon and ask him to call me when he gets a chance. It will only take a couple minutes of his time."

"Certainly." Helen knew it was over. The sadness in Doc's voice told her all she needed to know. He had had enough.

Doctor Walters met Doctor Tim Brandon during a medical convention at State University. Tim represented a group of doctors from Big City. Doc Walters was immediately impressed with the earnest young physician. On the last evening of the convention, a social hour was scheduled. To tell the truth, a social hour was scheduled every evening. Over cocktails, Doc Walters suggested that Tim's group might consider opening an office in Towne, even if it were only for one or two days a week. Doc Walters willingly admitted that Towne could use another physician. He couldn't take on any more patients and hated to keep sending them all the way to Big City. Besides, he was considering retiring and would gladly turn over his patient's medical files with their permission.

With Doc Walters' encouragement, Tim's group did eventually rent and remodel a vacant building in Towne. They sent a doctor, usually Tim, and a registered nurse down every Monday and Thursday. Business was slow at first until the community realized that Doc Walters had given his full blessing to the new practice. Loyalty isn't all bad.

⋘

"Excuse me, Doctor." Helen entered the examination room. Doc was staring at a Trout Unlimited calendar hanging behind his desk. "Doctor Brandon is on line one." Doc came to with a jolt, a gentle smile crossing his face, the first in months. He had tied into one big rainbow trout somewhere on the Snake River in Wyoming.

"Thanks, Helen. Thanks for everything." He picked up the phone. "Doctor Brandon? Doc Walters, here. How are you doing?"

"I'm fine, Doctor. The question is: How are you doing?"

"Fine. Fine. Today, I retire. Today I did retire. I'll have Helen start calling our patients and advise them that we will be transferring their files to your office. If any of them would rather have a different physician, please see that the chart is sent on. I would bet an easy hundred percent will stick with you. I know your landlord. I'll get the key and have somebody haul the files over to your office this weekend. Now you'll just have to be open all week…24/7 as I heard someone say. They're all good people… my patients." He hesitated, "Well, most of them are good people. Please, treat them well…I know you will," he ended weakly.

"Of course we will," Doctor Brandon assured him. "I can't thank you enough. Not exactly sure about the 24/7," he laughed, "but we'll take care of all we can. Will we be seeing you around much, Doctor?" he asked.

"You bet you will. You have my home phone number. If I

don't answer, call Helen. She'll know where to find me. I feel bad for her. She will be lost without a job."

"Maybe we can work something out. We certainly could use her help…for awhile, anyway. Why don't you mention it and I'll give her a call myself?"

"I will. She would like that, she truly would. She's a good woman." Doc Walters paused for several seconds as if lost in thought and then continued. "I do intend to travel some. My wife, Millie, wants to go visit her sister, Sharon Mai. She's been in a nursing home in Wheat Ridge, Colorado. That will make a nice little road trip for us…haven't done that in a long time. Seems I spend all my free time stalking fish on the Whoosh. I think Millie would enjoy a little vacation. It would be a chance for her to be with her sister for awhile…if she can put up with me that long," Doc Walters chuckled.

"You know what? I could drop Millie off and drive down to Spinney Mountain Reservoir, rent a boat, and catch some trout. I've heard you can catch big ones in that lake. All that heavy wading on the river has finally gotten to me. I'll just sit in the boat, soak up some sun and cast bead-headed nymphs to monster fish. Might even drink a cold one or two," his chuckle turned to laughter. His weariness was gone. He had a plan. He had a goal. "If I get bored with the boat, somebody told me Eleven-Mile Canyon has some decent rainbows and browns and easy wading. Anyway, it will be good for Millie to see her sister. I owe my wife a great deal, a great deal."

Doctor Brandon hesitated and said, "We'll take care of your patients and Helen. Not to worry. And you, Doctor, you take care of yourself," his voice wavered, "and you take care of that wife of yours."

As Tim Brandon hung up, a great sadness swept over him. Doctor Walters' wife, Millie, had died two years before.

CHAPTER 14: Laura Menard

W hile restocking the display racks behind Maggie's counter, Laura smiled recalling her fishing trip with Professor Leonard Russell and his two daughters, Megan who was seven and Mandy, five. Laura instantly adored the girls who were inquisitive about seemingly everything—insects, fish, rocks, flowers, the mountains, the river, even the mole on Laura's arm. Both girls asked interesting questions, not just the usual *why*, but questions advanced for their ages and they were well-mannered, polite and courteous. Obviously they admired their father. Laura was willing to bet that their mother looked on and was proud of them.

In Maggie's drift boat, Laura was able to guide the Professor and his girls to a protected pool. The deep water pocket was apparently a nursery for eight to ten-inch rainbows. Megan caught the most fish, but actually seemed happier when her little sister *tied into one.*

Until Laura put Professor Russell onto an eighteen-inch brown trout, both girls had caught larger fish then their father. Finally, he whip-lashed, not cast, a Royal Coachman dry fly ten feet off the side of the craft with twenty feet of excess line piling up near the stern. Part of a good guide's job is to keep the boat in sync with the river's flow which creates a perfect drift for fly line and fly. With one stroke of the oars, Laura quickly maneuvered so that the line straightened out over a long glade of water. The Coachman drifted the shoot into a small eddy created by a barely visible submerged rock shelf. This brought the fly, still atop the water, back upstream. Before it could circle and find the way back downriver, a fish smacked it, nearly tearing the rod from the Professor's hand. Laura had made sure the leader was oversized and the knots secure, just for this moment. Now an eighteen-inch brown trout from the Whoosh River is a very nice fish, but it would not be considered large by any means. It was no *hawg*. The girls whooped and hollered as their father horsed the fish into the boat. Leonard's grin lasted all afternoon. Laura recorded the moment on film and posted a print on the wall at Maggie's. Certainly not the biggest fish pictured there, but the guy holding it has the biggest smile. Another print is framed and prominently displayed on the Professor's desk.

◅●◅

Professor Russell called to book another fishing trip with Laura. When the phone rang, she recognized his voice. She was afraid he needed a decision about the teaching job. He never mentioned it. Instead he said his sister was flying out to take the girls to her home in California for the rest of the summer, returning by Labor Day. Laura wasn't sure why that bothered her. Was this an attempt by his family to coach the Professor back to California?

"Forget it. Don't you dare suggest that. It's just a chance for his family to see the girls," Laura chided herself. "Besides, you don't want to scare off Maggie's newest fishing client."

Laura grinned and went back to stuffing cigarette packages into the display rack. What did Maggie call them? Coffin nails? Cancer sticks?

Laura was born in the Meriter Hospital in Madison, Wisconsin, just blocks from her large, three-story home on Lake Mendota. The youngest of four sisters, she was the straggler.

Her father kept a twenty-three foot *Chris Craft* in their boathouse. The power boat floated alongside a late 1930s Carleton Canoe Company's *Indian Princess.* It was in immaculate condition, with mahogany gunwales, thwarts and seats. The older girls' only interest in their father's *Chris Craft* was to impress their friends, mainly boys. The three had absolutely no interest in the vintage canoe.

One evening in late spring Laura's father came home and found her sitting in the *Princess* just off the front of their dock. She was attempting to cast a popper to several bluegill redds, not with a spinning rod, but with a classic *Granger Victory* split bamboo fly rod, unfortunately with the tip section missing.

A new aspect to their father-daughter relationship was born. It eventually took them trout fishing all over Wisconsin, to the Kinnickinnic River, up to the Brule and Wolf, across Michigan to Hemingway's Two Hearted River (actually the Fox Watershed), down to the Lower Peninsula's Manistee, Muskegon, Au Sable and Pere Marquette Rivers. Most of their fishing, however, was done in the Driftless Area, a large part of SE Minnesota, SW Wisconsin and a small part of NE Iowa. The glaciers of the last ice age surrounded, but spared, this area containing 24,000 square miles of the world's greatest concentration of limestone spring creeks comparable only to England's chalk streams. Geology in the area has remained unchanged for the last 50,000 years.

◀►

Dry fly fishing the Driftless Area requires not only stealth to catch trout, but permission from the land holder, usually a farmer, to make it legal. Laura could not recall her father ever failing to negotiate access. They would park at a midway point on the chosen selection of river and one would fly fish upstream and walk back; the other would walk downstream and fly fish back upstream. That allowed them both to always fish upstream, normally an advantage to a dry fly fisherman. After fishing, Laura and her father would meet at the vehicle, usually about the same time, for cold sandwiches and a ride home.

In comparison, dry fly fishing a freestone Rocky Mountain river, from a drift boat, amounts to floating downstream while casting artificial flies at a three-quarter angle upriver. If the line is properly mended, the fly will settle on a placid spot for a second or two, hopefully where a fish is holding, and then race downriver through a likely chute. The first chance to hook a trout is where the fly dead-drifts over that holding area. The second is where a fish may be finning along the side of the chute in slower water, possibly paralleling the river's bank. From the trout's viewpoint, the ideal location is a hiding place where food is visible as it floats past and where the expenditure of calories to grab the food is less then the calories provided in nourishment. If the fish can't achieve this advantage, they will starve to death. This method is totally different than fishing the Driftless Area where the thinnest of leaders and the smallest of flies usually gives the best chance at extremely selective trout on quiet waters. The universal warning is "don't spook the fish."

The four Menard girls, and presumably their mother, knew little of what their father did for a living. Whenever asked, Laura explained, "He works in his office." The office was upstairs overlooking the lake. He never spent more than four hours a day working and never past noon. Other than an occasional charter flight out of either Dane County Regional or Middleton Municipal airports this allowed them plenty of time for trout fishing. As Laura grew older, she began to wonder about her father's occupation. But, as the years passed, she really didn't care. He was her father, her best friend, and fishing partner.

Laura's mom kept a garden, played bridge and tennis, and was involved in most of the local charities and many national ones. She had more than earned the right. She had paid her dues. In the early years of her marriage, she labored long and hard raising four daughters on a tight budget. Through a series of events, conditions changed financially for the better—extremely so. Now it was her time to pursue the things she enjoyed, none of which involved fishing.

"Fishing? God forbid," was her exact phrase. What made her life even more enjoyable was the realization she could quit her job as a Pampered Chef sales consultant. It was no longer necessary to impose on her friends.

"Oh, just come to my party. You really don't have to buy anything." Yeah, right.

In her junior year of college Laura moved to an apartment only blocks from her parents and just off campus. Schoolwork came easy and there was always enough time to trout fish with her father. When she graduated, Laura loaded her used Dodge pickup, kissed her parents goodbye, and took off for the Whoosh River in hopes of finding work. If that didn't pan out, she planned to return to Wisconsin in the fall for graduate school.

CHAPTER 15: Camp Hosts

M aggie watched as Grace and Barney Westbrook pulled their weather beaten motor home up to the gas pumps. The Westbrooks had been camp hosts at the Whoosh River Dam for ten years and did not plan to return the following spring.

The Westbrooks took the job when they left school teaching, having saved an impossible amount of money while managing to put two kids through college. They wanted to follow their dream of mountain living, filling the days with hiking, fishing, and photographing wildlife and wildflowers.

Cautious people, the camp host position seemed to suit them well enough, so they purchased a modest motor home, hooked their vintage Volkswagen to the back, and headed to Alaska. After six months living in the confines of their home on wheels, they agreed that it was a lot of *closeness,* but they felt, with effort and restraint, they would manage. Returning home, they sold their house, purchased a condo, leased it, and left for New Mexico to serve as hosts at a national park. When spring came Grace and Barney made their way to Towne where they assumed similar duties at the Whoosh River Dam.

There was no pay, but the camping site for their motor home, with electric and water hook-up, came free. Work included keeping campers happy and relatively quiet while maintaining the grounds. On occasion it was necessary to clean up after a foraging black bear. The Westbrooks were, however, on call twenty-four hours a day with only one day a week off. Not much free time, but they made the best of it. When, as it occasionally happened, they got on each other's nerves, they went for long hikes in different directions. Grace enjoyed her photography and Barney became a decent fly fisherman.

As the years passed, the number of campers dwindled at the Whoosh Dam Campground. Those that did show up seemed more interested in partying than enjoying nature. Barney never was one for confrontation, so more and more, Grace had to *talk* to the camp guests and control them the best she could. Rangers and Sheriff's deputies were more than cooperative when a problem arose, but Grace hesitated to call for help. Slowly, it became apparent that the Westbrook's had exchanged one career of baby-sitting school children for another career—baby-sitting adult campers. Their retirement plans were no longer recognizable.

The breaking point came one night when a motorcycle gang trashed the campgrounds. Yeah, yeah, most motorcyclists are respected schoolteachers, lawyers and bankers out for a little weekend relaxation. Not this tattooed bunch of sub-humans. They would be called terrorists, even by the left-wing media.

Barney snapped and confronted the unruly mob with a rake handle. In seconds, the bikers' second-in-command disarmed Barney. The gang leader, a closet coward, allowed his lieutenant to beat Barney nearly to death. The bikers were halfway to Sundance, Wyoming, before Barney even reached the hospital, and they were safely in Sturgis, South Dakota, before the police decided not to pursue them. "Hey, they're out of our jurisdiction by now. What do you expect us to do?" shrugged one deputy.

While recuperating in the Big City County Hospital, Barney revised the retirement plan. He studied maps of New England and drew up a road tour, which would pass through his grandparent's hometown of Stewartstown. He became obsessed with hiking the White Mountains and fly-fishing small streams for native brook trout. It took some work to convince Grace, but Barney offered to stay at bed-and-breakfasts and haunt the antiques shops throughout New Hampshire and Vermont. He knew there would be beautiful wildflowers for Grace to photograph. With rumors of the Whoosh River Dam removal, the timing seemed right and Grace reluctantly accepted the plan.

After Barney was discharged from the hospital, the Westbrooks notified the Forest Service they would not be returning to New Mexico the following fall or to the Whoosh River in the spring. True to their nature, they cleaned the campground before hitching their Volkswagen to the motor home, and heading for Maggie's to fill the gas tanks and say goodbye.

Three months later Maggie received a Christmas card with no return address. Below the greeting, Grace had penned a note that Barney had suffered a massive heart attack and died and that she believed his death was a direct result of the beating he had taken at the campground. She was very matter-of-fact, but Maggie could feel her pain and bitterness. Grace was grateful they had been able to spend Thanksgiving with their kids and grandchildren. She was far from grateful for Barney's death.

Grace lost interest in Barney's New England adventure and began a search for her own identity—her own history. As a child she had been passed from foster home to foster home with no real connection to any of her de facto parents. Her only human bond, other than her children, was with Barney, a bond that had lasted most of her life. Grace had no idea why she suddenly wanted to reconstruct her family's history, but wrote that if the search for her heritage brought her back through the Whoosh River Watershed, she would most certainly stop and see Maggie.

Another year passed. Maggie didn't receive a Christmas card from Grace Westbrook. And she still hasn't.

CHAPTER 16: Oscar Finds Doc

S heriff Oscar Cowdrey sat behind the steering wheel of his Ford Bronco with the big County Sheriff's insignia painted on both front doors. Red and blue rotating lights were mounted on the top of the cruiser with the mandatory cow catcher/brush guard bolted to the front frame. Cowdrey had just stopped to check on the campgrounds at the Whoosh River Dam. The lower grounds, below the impoundment, were now permanently closed to campers. Only the boat ramp and the vaulted toilet were usable. On the upper grounds, the camp host's oversized lot stood empty.

Today only three campsites were occupied along the backwater of the dam. A huge motor home, worth more than Oscar would make legally in a lifetime, sat on one spot. A second held a rusty old red pickup carrying a beat up topper, hand painted a slightly different shade of red. A brand new multi-colored backpacker's tent occupied a third site, with an expensive mountain bike chained securely to a nearby loblolly pine. Nobody was up yet, and besides it wasn't Oscar's job to collect the camping fees. Cowdrey usually enjoyed getting out and talking with the campers, just another way to let them know the Sheriff was on the job. Above all else, he was a politician.

He quietly drove the Bronco out of the grounds, back to Canyon Road and stopped. Should he go north up Canyon Road to the headwater meadows or back to Big City and his office? His office meant paperwork and phone messages. North was the route along some of the most beautiful scenery in the state and probably the least-traveled. The road twisted its way along the canyon's edge until it reached two large meadows containing dozens of beaver dams, numerous Big Horn sheep, a herd of elk, several lynx families, a population of black bear, an abundance of fowl and one lone resident Bull Moose. A horticulturist could spend a lifetime examining the various wildflowers.

If Oscar were honest with himself he would have admitted he planned to head north, even before he left the office. Of course, Oscar wasn't always honest with himself, or anyone else. He liked stopping at a primitive campground and horse corral at the upper end of the canyon. He rarely found anyone there, but at least he could pick up trash and haul it back to the County's *Recycling Plant.* The *Plant* was just a landfill referred to as the County Dump by locals. Any *recycling* was done by nature. While trash hauling wasn't a job for a *prominent elected official,* at least he could justify the mileage.

After creeping up the steep gravel road for three or four miles, sunlight reflected off an object over the canyon's edge and caught Oscar's attention. He didn't have a good feeling. Stopping the Bronco, he set the parking break, turned on the overhead flashers, and got out to take a look. A hundred feet below he saw Doc Walters' *Pink Cadillac,* what was left of it, wedged between two enormous boulders. Oscar walked back to the Bronco, got out his binoculars and sighted in on the rear-bumper license plate. It was Doc Walter's car all right. Nobody else was eccentric enough to own a pink Cadillac in this country, let alone drive it up Canyon Road. Oscar smiled to himself, recalling how the normally gentle-natured doctor always bristled at the description of his automobile.

"Any dang fool knows that's a Lincoln. And it is not, I repeat, not pink. It is Desert Rose...Desert Rose." To emphasis his point Doc's face would change from rose to an off-shade of crimson.

Oscar's smile faded as he focused on the vanity plate of the demolished Lincoln. *Doc W* it read. That hadn't been Doc's doing. It was his wife, Millie's idea. She loved that plate. The paint job was her idea, too.

Oscar shifted the glasses to the driver's seat where he could see Doc Walters slumped over the wheel. He held the binoculars steady for a long moment. It appeared that Doc's head had bounced, shattered the windshield, and now lay at an impossible angle back across his shoulder. He was dead, no doubt.

Years earlier, when Oscar was a junior deputy, he would have called the Emergency Unit and the newspaper in Big City, but not in that order. His cousin Ruth Anne Ledbetter was the managing editor, only full-time reporter, and majority owner of the *Buzz*. Rather than pay a staff of reporters, she used a few stringers, some well-placed sources, and relied heavily on gossip and rumors.

The *Buzz* was the area's only daily newspaper other than the *Capital City Correspondent*, which handled the state news. Reporting of the national and world news was left pretty much to *U.S. Today* and network television.

The sale of Ruth Anne's paper always increased dramatically when there was an accident involving a local. The old adage *IF IT BLEEDS IT LEADS*, general applied to the paper's format. Arrests of prominent citizens for petty infractions sold a lot of papers. Yet, when a well-known resident was involved in any type of corruption there was little, if any, coverage. You never knew where an investigation might lead and to whom. "We'll just let things sort themselves out before we jump in," was Ruth Anne's standard dodge. A cop-out if you will.

A younger Deputy Sheriff Cowdrey could be credited with impeccable timing. At most automobile accidents, he managed to reach the trapped driver, and any passengers, just as Ruth Anne, with her photographer son, Melvin, arrived at the site. Melvin had an eye for finding the maximum carnage in the most minor of accident scenes. As the flash of the camera faded, the ambulance crew would arrive and note Deputy Oscar's bravery and dedication to duty. The next day an editorial would ask: *Wouldn't Oscar Cowdrey make an excellent candidate for County Sheriff?* As the only member of the editorial staff, Ruth Anne could express her views with no obligation to respond to negative comments. She knew how to boost Cousin Oscar's ambitions. It was a cozy setup.

After the former sheriff retired, with more money than possible from his modest salary, Oscar was elected Sheriff. The *Buzz's* continued endorsement brought election after election. Oscar looked forward to a lucrative retirement package, much like that of his predecessor. Golden parachutes aren't always limited to Wall Street and often include more than stock options.

Now, years later, a much older and heavier Oscar Cowdrey reached through the Bronco's window. He grabbed the car radio and called Hazel Mertz, his dispatcher, secretary, jailer, and if you asked Hazel, his keeper. He told her to send an ambulance up but there was no need to hurry. It was far too late to save Doc Walters.

Oscar asked Hazel to call Helen, Doc Walters' nurse. He'd talk to her in person later, but didn't want Helen to hear about Doc's death on the street.

"After you talk to her, call Ruth Anne," he said. "She's gonna love this one, but tell her to cool it a little, no use getting the rumor mill rolling. For the record, Doc was headed up Canyon Road to do a little fishing. He swerved to avoid an elk or a mule deer...who knows? Don't see an animal carcass, so Doc saved another life by just getting out of its way. Maybe, Ruth Anne could play up the humanitarian angle for once. There's no need for an investigation. Keep any other agencies out of it, if you can, and then phone Charlie and get a wrecker up here...the big one. Take care of it for me, Hazel." He hesitated, "Much obliged."

Sheriff Cowdrey and Doc Walters went way back. Years before, Doc had removed the only *bullet* ever fired in anger at the good sheriff. Doc didn't exactly remove the bullet. He patched a minor scattergun wound on the sheriff's forearm, but you know how stories grow.

As Oscar Cowdrey cut the connection with Hazel, he was overwhelmed with sadness, a sensation he rarely experienced and had difficulty handling.

"Damn, maybe I am getting too old for this job...too soft. Good to have known you, Doc." Oscar nodded and tipped his hat toward the wreckage of the rose-colored Lincoln and climbed back into his Bronco.

There was still plenty of time to regain his tough guy image before the ambulance arrived. He had time to ponder if it was even worth the effort. Was the facade he had so carefully constructed beginning to crumble? Was it time to wrap it up? Could he make it financially with what he had stowed away? Maybe one more *opportunity* and he could cash it all in. No more worrying about being tripped up—no more staring at the ceiling nightly trying to remember the lies he had told—trying to remember who he had told them to—no more mental bookkeeping of who owed him and how much—and was payment overdue?

"Snap out of it, boy. Snap out of it now." Sheriff Oscar Crowley heard the sirens moving up Canyon Road.

CHAPTER 17: Melvin Ledbetter - Photographer

◀►

Melvin Ledbetter was Ruth Anne Ledbetter's only child. The whereabouts of his father was unknown, since Ruth Anne announced she was pregnant. Seems some prospective fathers take the news better than others.

As a child, and throughout adulthood, Melvin was vertically challenged for his weight. In spite of his shortcomings he was extremely dexterous and fairly athletic. He would have made a good offensive lineman for Big City High School's football team, the Lassos. Only problem was that Melvin was embarrassingly shy. Nobody thought he would be interested in football. Nobody ever asked. The cheerleading team mistakenly believed he wouldn't be interested in girls either and therefore it was safe to make him their mascot. They dressed him in a rodeo outfit that would have put Buffalo Bill Cody to shame. They gave him a lariat and at half time of the football games he'd run around the field trying to lasso one of the cheerleaders. This was unsuccessful, as intended, until his senior year. During the last game of the season, Melvin managed to loop his rope around the waist of the prettiest cheerleader and wrestle her down in the visiting team's end zone. Before the home football squad, lead by the captain, could separate them, Melvin had gotten his hand inside the girl's uniform and his tongue halfway down her throat. The visiting football squad, already up by three touchdowns, stood by and, naturally enough, cheered. The Big City marching band interrupted their performance to watch—all but the tuba section.

Melvin Ledbetter was suspended from all extracurricular activities until his graduation. The lassoed cheerleader, bless her heart, never complained.

After high school, Melvin took a job at the *Buzz*. Ruth Anne put Melvin on the payroll, gave him a press pass, placed a camera in his hand, and told him to "go photograph something interesting, something I can use in the newspaper."

Melvin's first two-week vacation came only a month after he started his job. He headed for Las Vegas with the *Buzz Van*. He found he could hire a sweet young thing by the week and decided that was how he would spend all future vacation time and money.

Melvin lived rent-free in an apartment attached to his mother's house and whenever possible Ruth Anne cooked his meals. He enjoyed unlimited use of the *Buzz Van* and with a generous expense account to cover miscellaneous items, Melvin could afford two Vegas trips per year.

Between vacations Melvin threw himself into his work and eventually became an excellent professional photographer. He did freelance work for the athletic department at the State University and assisted in the production of their promotional brochures and programs.

While Melvin enjoyed action photography, he developed a real passion for wildlife. He had met Grace Westbrook up in the Whoosh River Meadows taking pictures of, as he remembered, small white Arctic Gentians growing in the boggy areas of the meadows. The two hit it off immediately. Grace, forever the teacher, was a patient instructor. She enjoyed sharing her knowledge of plant life and photography with somebody willing to learn. Her husband, Barney, always showed interest in her pictures, but Grace felt that was more out of a sense of loyalty to her than any real enjoyment of her images.

Unfortunately, Grace and Barney left their camp host jobs at the Whoosh River Dam before Melvin heard the news that they were not returning. He asked his mother why she hadn't run a human-interest article about the Westbrooks, but Ruth Anne said she hadn't heard they were leaving either. Melvin would miss Grace. She was his only real friend.

Melvin hoped to bring home a hooker from Vegas one day and make her his wife—a woman with the proverbial heart of gold. She would have to truly love Melvin to exchange the neon lights of Vegas for nature's sun, moon and stars that illuminated the Whoosh River Watershed. Talk about an adjustment.

Melvin would have to choose this woman very carefully. But, rest assured, he was looking forward to a long and detailed selection process.

CHAPTER 18: Greta Heinzel - Café Owner

Greta Heinzel locked the front door of The Café, turned the red and white plastic open sign to *CLOSED*, dimmed the lights, and eased herself down at the end of the lunch counter. Closing time was seven, but everybody knew she would stay open until every customer was served and gone. Tonight it was well past eight.

As an afterthought, Greta checked behind the counter to be sure the deep-fat fryer was turned off. It was, but the evening cook had only done a half-assed job of cleaning the flat grill. If she didn't finish the chore herself, the morning cook would have a cow. It was her fault the fry cook hadn't cleaned up. She should have made him stay until it was done, but they had already had one confrontation about not ordering enough roast beef. What's a short order joint without hot-beef sandwiches?

Greta had a long history with The Café. She started working there while still in high school. The Big City school bus dropped the Towne kids off at Chester's Mercantile where Greta would cross the street to the restaurant. She would wash dishes until closing, and then walk home. When she graduated, she became a full-time waitress and part-time grill cook. Soon she was preparing the specials, scheduling employees, and keeping the books. Not long after that the owners, an elderly married couple, sold her the business at a very reasonable price.

"Pay us what you can, when you can, Greta," they said. "Don't worry about a down payment. We've finally saved enough money to give it up and go home. We're going back to North Carolina." The overwhelming relief in their voices was plain. Had even a hint of a Carolina accent returned? What brought them to the Whoosh River was a distant memory, forgotten with years of toil and sacrifice. They were finally going *home*.

The Café fit a dining niche in Towne between the Roadhouse Bar & Grill and the two fast food restaurants at the Interstate exit. Although the two taverns in town nuked pre-packaged sandwiches, Greta didn't consider them competition.

She was good to her employees—the good ones that is because she didn't want to lose them to the Roadhouse where the tips were much bigger. Greta told the bad employees to head out to the fast food places to apply for new jobs. She wasn't sure the employees or employers appreciated that.

Greta was able to make a decent living, if you didn't figure her per hour income. She loved her small café and her loyal patrons. What she didn't love was opening at six in the morning and staying until closing. It made for a very long day. After hours she did payroll and paid the bills. The Café was closed on Sundays, but Greta spent her morning in church and was usually involved with some church function in the afternoon. Then the work week began all over again.

Now, Greta was faced with a decision she had put off for almost a year. In ten days her winning lotto ticket would expire. She knew that if she cashed in the seven-figure lottery ticket her life would change drastically. There would be no hiding the news. Did she want to sell the Café and leave Towne? If she did sell, she would have to find something else to keep her busy. If she kept the business and the lotto money, she'd be hounded to death by schemers, charities, and the budget committee from the church, not to mention hoards of newfound relatives. On the other hand, at her age she was downright scared to pack up and move on, money or not. Where would she go? What would she do? She could cash the ticket, pay the taxes, and donate the money to a charity—probably her church. But if news leaked that she had turned her back on a fortune—well, the questions, the razzing, the weird looks—she didn't think she could handle that either.

Maybe she could buy the Roadhouse Bar & Grill, hire somebody to run it and just sit back and count the receipts. Dream on, Greta. Actually, she didn't even know who the owners were. Rumors had it that Mike Tapio and Freda Morrison were operating it for the Mafia. Besides, there was something about Mike Tapio that bothered her. Maybe it was the way he tried to disguise his East Coast accent.

Apparently, Mike's life was as strictly structured as Greta's. Every morning, around ten, he would enter The Café and order black coffee and a bagel. She never served bagels until Mike appeared one day and asked for one. He would sit in the rear booth and read a day old *New Jersey Herald,* front to back. Leaving a big tip, he would head for the Roadhouse to open at noon. Greta figured Mike was in as big a rut as she was, or was it a well-worn groove? Was that a difference without distinction or a distinction without difference?

"Maybe I should have gone to college," she thought, but then decided, semantics aside, she was not going to exchange The Café for the Roadhouse, be it a rut or a groove.

Since winning the lotto, Greta was aware of one thing: she was too young to retire. Unlike everybody else in Towne, she wasn't into trout fishing (bite your tongue) and the Whoosh River had no beaches to sun on and be served tall, cold Mai Tais. Of course, she could always go out to Maggie's, rent a cabin, and count her millions along with the semis on the Interstate. Gawd, she was starting to depress herself.

Greta had resolved one thing for sure. Her on-again-off-again relationship with Stu Letterman, the food service truck driver out of Big City, would end. Actually, she really didn't care, lotto winnings or not. She had an inkling Stuart Letterman was married. Hell, she knew damn well he was married, she just wouldn't allow herself to admit it.

Probably the hardest part of making a decision about the lotto winnings was the fact that she had to make it alone. In her mind, her life as a self-sufficient middle-aged woman excluded her from asking anyone's advice. She never had and probably never would. Who could she confide in anyway, Maggie? She was another business woman who might understand. As much as she respected Maggie she couldn't just pour her heart out—ask her for advice and what—hold her partially responsible if things went wrong? No, this was her choice. She would make it, good or bad, and then live with it.

What Greta really wanted to do was walk over to Charlie's Auto Repair Shop, take Charlie's grease-covered hands and ask him to marry her.

"Let's raise a family, Charlie."

They had been friends since grade school and had fallen into similar situations. Charlie inherited the garage while Greta, in a sense, inherited the Café. Neither of them had ever come close to getting married.

"Too damn busy," as Charlie put it.

"Just waiting for the right man," Greta would say, while gazing at Charlie.

They remained friends through the years and in her heart she knew he was exactly the right man. Well, okay, he was certainly more than adequate. What's wrong with adequate? How many people do you know that are even adequate?

How should she play it? She would have to tell Charlie about the lotto winnings. If she didn't tell him of her newfound riches, she could just hear him:

"There's no way we can get married and have kids. You'd have to sell your cafe and there aren't enough days in the week for me to afford a family. Not on what I make running this garage. Hey there's a couple of beers in my cooler, help yourself," before sticking his head back under the hood of a disabled truck.

On the other hand, if she did tell him about her newly acquired wealth, he'd blow her off because of some misplaced *male pride*. Whatever the hell that was.

"Are you kidding me, Greta? I can't marry a millionaire. I wouldn't know how to act." He'd slowly shake his head at the thought. "I'd have to get all dressed up and wash *all* the grease off my hands…every night. Do you know how tough that is? No, it wouldn't work, but I sure am happy for you, Greta. I sure the hell am happy for you. Hey, there's a couple of beers in my cooler, help yourself. Ah shit, bring me one too," and he'd slam the hood of the disabled truck and join her.

❦

The threat of the dam removal loomed over the entire area, but Greta didn't consider that a problem for her. Even if she closed the café, her winnings would more than carry her through the rest of her life, providing she didn't give it all away.

Maybe she should just chuck everything. Ditch her friends, her church, give up on Charlie, sell her restaurant and modest home, take all the cash and head for Hawaii. Wait, she had heard of people moving to small islands and coming down with Island Fever, a claustrophobic condition caused by the confining spaces of island living. If there was any truth to all that, Greta figured it would be a deadly ailment for a person born and raised in the mountains. Besides, it was an awfully long plane ride. Greta had never even been in an airplane.

Greta reminded herself just how innocently she had gotten into her current situation. She had never bought a lotto ticket in her life, but several ladies from the church had come into The Café selling raffle tickets. They were raising money for some charity or other. Like the owners of all small businesses, she was always getting hit up for donations. If it wasn't for Little League uniforms, or to send someone to camp, it was for a local fundraiser, or a national charity. Then there were the area catastrophes. Some local rancher gets tangled up in a hay bailer and loses. He has ten kids to support and, of course, there is no insurance: PLEASE DONATE!

Because she owned her own business, people assumed she was wealthy. Greta did what she could and more, but was an easy target for the do-gooders of the world. To be honest, the ladies did sit down and order English Muffins and tea. So, Greta bought a handful of church raffle tickets. At the church carnival on Sunday, Greta was walking across the shade-covered lawn inspecting a display of canning jars filled with fruits and vegetables, some with blue, red or yellow placement ribbons. While checking out the pies, she heard her name announced over the loud speaker. She had won third prize in the church's raffle—five state lotto tickets. One of those tickets turned out to be the only winner in the Mega-Bucks Lottery. It hadn't paid out in months. She told no one of her *luck*.

Now, time was running out to cash that ticket. Monday morning she would tell her employees she was going to Big City for provisions and be back before supper. Once in Big City, she would pick up restaurant supplies, tell Stu Letterman their arrangement was over, and go to the state office to claim her winnings. Maybe with the check in hand, she'd have a whole new perspective. Everything would become clear.

"Eureka! I see the light!"

Who was she kidding? Right now all she wanted to do was turn off the *light*, go home, take a long, hot shower and sleep for seven hours. And that wouldn't happen until she finished scrubbing the grill.

CHAPTER 19: Laura and the Rainbow

Laura swung the drift boat out of a whitewater run, pulled hard on the oars and drove the hull well up into a sand bar. Before she could say a word, Professor Leonard Russell jumped over the bow, grabbed the anchor and flung it far up on the bank. He wrapped the slack anchor rope around a dislodged tree trunk, came back and helped Laura over the side. They both knew that wasn't necessary, but Leonard was determined to show that he was thoughtful, if not useful. This was his fourth trip down the Whoosh with Laura. The first three floats included his two daughters and had been a tremendous success. They caught fish, enjoyed picnic lunches, and played games on shore.

Leonard was extremely apprehensive on this day. With the girls in California, this would be a float with just him and Laura. By the time they launched, drifted through the village of Towne and under the Interstate Bridge, Leonard had forgotten his nervousness. To his great relief Laura had stopped calling him Professor Russell. It was now Leonard. What next, Len? One could only hope.

Laughing at the slightest opportunity, he had actually casted a Royal Wulff dry fly over thirty feet, somewhere near the spot

Laura suggested. His technique had vastly improved with practice on his front lawn. One of his neighbors had yelled over and told him he should take up golf. "Or, mow your lawn!"

><

After the oars were secured, Leonard said, "Show me how you catch fish from shore and I'll get the food ready." Laura watched as he spread a plastic tablecloth, made to look like fine linen, and began to unload the picnic basket and cooler.

He had stopped at a classy over-priced restaurant in Big City to have the staff fill a basket with gourmet sandwiches, fancy crackers and cheeses, two bottles of expensive imported wine and other goodies. Caviar was an afterthought. He found it in a specialty shop across from the restaurant. This meal was in sharp contrast to Laura's cold fried chicken, potato salad, cokes and beer she brought along on past trips.

"It certainly looks elegant. Sure I can't help you?"

"Please, I'm catering this party. You catch a fish."

Laura retrieved her fly rod from the boat and tied on a #12 elk-hair caddis. Didn't he realize that catching a fish on demand wasn't all that easy? With one false cast, she sent the dry fly sailing some fifty feet to a calm spot just upstream where a huge boulder protruded mid-river. With a quick upstream mend of the fly line, the artificial caddis held where it landed for one, two, three seconds, before bobbing slowly around the side of the big rock and then shot downstream. Laura retrieved the line with a roll cast and then sailed the fly to the exact same spot. This time she increased the mend and the caddis held for one, two, three, four seconds before it disappeared. Laura set the hook, and a large rainbow skyrocketed out of the rapids, did a mid-air flip trying to shake the hook and dove back into the run, sending spray clear across the river. One more leap and the fish headed back toward the protection of the boulder. Applying just enough line pressure, Laura kept the fish away from the bottom of the rock, without breaking her leader. Now the fish was fighting, not only the rod pressure, but the weight of the current. Within another minute the pink-striped trout was spent. As Laura reeled in near shore, the twenty-one inch fish made one last feeble run and then followed the fly, leader and line onto the stony shore, flopping on its side.

Laura's only concern had been to control the large trout without losing it. For those moments nothing else existed. Time stood still. She was exactly where she wanted to be, doing exactly what she wanted to do, oblivious to all else.

"Fantastic!" Leonard startled her when he came up from behind.

"What a beautiful fish." Leonard ran back to the picnic basket and grabbed his disposable camera. Laura was a little embarrassed, but posed with the fish, holding it just out of the water. An idea occurred to her as she detached the fly.

"Leonard, do you want to have supper with me this evening? Maggie lets me borrow her char-broiler and I've got an excellent recipe for rainbow trout fillets. The ambiance won't match your shore lunch…nothing like this beautiful setting, but we could grab some potatoes and maybe a bag of mixed salad in Towne."

"How could I refuse an invitation like that?" Taken somewhat off guard, Leonard broke into a big smile, "You're on."

"Great. While you finish setting up, I'll clean and fillet this beauty. Just grab a couple of plastic bags out of the cooler for me." Suddenly Laura wondered if she was upstaging him—catching a fish and offering to cook it, all before they had even begun to enjoy Leonard's spread. Had her stomach overcome her common sense? "He'll deal with it," she muttered to the rainbow. "God, I do love baked potatoes."

Laura slipped her favorite knife, a cross between a hunting knife and a fillet blade, out of the well-worn sheath and honed it on a pocket sized shark-tooth sharpener. She rapped the large rainbow hard behind the skull with the handle of the knife. The fish shuddered once and died instantly. Laura hadn't kept a fish this size in all the time she'd been west. She had eaten a few stunted brook trout for breakfast when she camped in the upper meadows, but for the most part she practiced catch-and-release although it wasn't necessary in the Whoosh River—not presently, with enough food, aeration and cold water to keep the biomass of fish in the river at a near constant level. Take a few big trout out and smaller ones soon find those vacant holding spots and quickly grow to the same size as their predecessors.

South, below the Interstate Bridge where they had pulled out for lunch, there was no limit to the number of fish you could keep or how you caught them. Well, short of spearing them that is. The water warmed to an extent where big browns dominated. A few northern pike and small mouth bass occasionally cruised through the reaches. Laura's big rainbow was an unexpected exception.

From the Whoosh Dam south through the lower canyon to the Interstate Bridge, the legal limit was two trout and only one could be over eighteen inches. Catch and release was encouraged with time to take a photo of the prize. If the client knew the official limit and insisted on keeping his fish, the guides did not argue. The size of their tip depended on how tactful they were.

At the City Park, live bait could be used if you were thirteen or under. Amazing how old some of those kids looked. Some even shaved.

From the river inlet to the reservoir and north to the meadows, the upper canyon was impassable with a drift boat. Only a few guides had tried it with an inflatable raft, never with a client. That stretch was the domain of expert kayakers and fools that thought they were. As far as walk-in fishermen were concerned, anyone who could clamber up the steep canyon walls, or hike up from the head of the reservoir, was entitled to all the trout they could haul out. The fish population had little to worry about.

The East Branch of the Whoosh River connected to the Main Branch deep in the upper canyon, upstream of the reservoir. A fifty-foot waterfall stopped any migration of fish. Helicopter drops of hatchery cutthroats above the falls had been attempted, but apparently there wasn't enough nourishment or holding spots for them to survive the harsh winters. Spring surveys showed no carry-over trout.

Below the dam The West Branch merges with the river before meandering languidly through ranch land where herds of cattle, elk, mule deer, and antelope destroyed the banks and in general wrecked havoc on the slow moving stream, making it a very poor habitat for trout. The Department of Wildlife had negotiated a deal with Rufus Jefferson who owned much of the land the river traversed. The plan was to run fencing along both sides of the stream, just above the high water level. This would at least keep the cattle out of the river. The Department would rebuild the banks, construct riprap where trout could hold, and then plant cottonwood trees to provide shade that would cool the river and hold the bank. Fishermen would eventually be allowed access to the stream by climbing stiles built over the fence. A diversion channel, to carry water for Rufus' crops and cattle, was to be dug, allowing his full allotment of water. The channel would hold a series of experimental gates meant to keep the fish in the water instead of fertilizing Rufus' fields. That was the theory. If the theory failed, Rufus' fields would certainly benefit from all the nutrients dead fish could provide.

After reconstructing the riverbed of the West Branch, to follow the historical path of the stream, a whirling-disease-resistant-strain of rainbow trout would be introduced by the Department of Wildlife. Fishing would not be allowed until it was determined if the rainbows could self sustain. If the rainbow thrived, fishing would resume on a catch-and-release basis. Meanwhile, Rufus would receive an annual payment from the Department of Wildlife for use of *his river*—whether the project was a success or not. Rufus had nothing against people fishing on his land and he certainly had nothing against accepting money from the agency. The allotment Rufus received came from the fishermen's license fees.

Above the upper canyon, in the high meadows, there was no limit to the number of fish one could keep. A ten-inch brook trout was large—a twelve incher, a monster. Stories of an occasional fourteen-inch lunker circulated. They were usually caught behind a new beaver dam, one that hadn't as yet filled with silt.

While this discussion of bag limits and river geography went on ad nauseam, Laura filleted the rainbow, slipped them into one of the bags and stuffed the entrails in the other. She knew by keeping the fish guts she was depriving an otter or raccoon family of their supper, but she also knew of persistent sightings of foraging black bears meandering down from the upper meadows. Some of those sightings had come from the summer homeowners who lived a short distance downstream near Pine Bluff. That was a long way from the meadows. Bears were usually attracted by the careless disposal of garbage, but Laura had heard of one elderly lady that bought jars of peanut butter and day-old donuts to spread in her backyard.

"Got some of the dangdest photos of those old bear," she

explained to the ranger. Then the ranger explained a few things to her, but she continued to ignore his warnings. Nuisance bears were becoming a big problem. Plans to tag and helicopter them out of the area were on the drawing board. A plan to tag and helicopter the old lady out of the area was being considered.

Laura slipped the two bags of fish parts into the cooler and placed her fly rod in the boat. She washed her hands with bar soap she kept in her pack. She had yet to adapt to the waterless sanitizers and probably never would. She ran over to Leonard and dropped down next to his impressive lunch.

"Where in the world did you come up with all this? Caviar, come on." Leonard smiled. From his pants pocket he produced a brand new Swiss Army knife with corkscrew. He popped the cork of the first wine bottle with a little more fanfare than necessary. Laura might not have been that impressed, but the Professor certainly was proud of himself. He poured the wine into plastic champagne glasses.

"Madam, what shall we toast…to more fish, to world peace, to this wonderful country?" he asked, gazing around.

"Kind sir, let us drink to this glorious day, and slather some of that caviar all over those crackers—pronto. You have given new meaning to the term shore lunch. There's not a guide this side of the Rockies that could match this. Not the other side either." Laura grinned, lifted her glass to Leonard and then remembered to sip, not gulp, the way she tended to drink beer.

After eating, they packed up the leftovers and sat silently atop a massive pile of rocks. Tossing stones into the river, they watched dippers, *Cinclus mexicanus,* an aquatic songbird, diving in and out of the river's surface searching for their own delicacies—fat snails or stonefly nymphs. They emptied the last of the wine into their glasses and decided to save the second bottle for evening.

Leonard finally broke the silence. "Tell me more about fly fishing."

"What do you want to know? You seem to be getting the hang of it. Your fly casting certainly has improved. I'm really impressed. You, Professor, are one great student."

He couldn't repress a grin. "Tell me about this dry fly fishing thing. You've rigged me up to fish nymphs, some wet flies and a few streamers, but we always seem to come back to dry flies floating on top. I've never seen you cast anything but dries. Does that make sense? I've read that trout feed ninety percent of the time on bugs in the water below the surface. Why dry flies?"

Laura tried to skip a flat stone off the roiling surface of the river. The stone popped straight up and back down, disappearing in a swirl of foam—lost for another 10,000 years?

"Ninety percent…that's true enough. You must be studying. There's tons of information about trout fishing, some of it is even useful. Unfortunately, a lot of it is just rehash…old ideas presented in a different form, old ideas to sell new magazines." She smiled, hoping she wasn't sounding too condescending. Talking down to a professor resulted in her only B in college. Funny, she didn't even remember what the class was.

"If you stick with fishing long enough, you'll learn that there are no absolutes, absolutely *no* absolutes. Fly fishing is not your basic math class. Two plus two isn't always four," she paused. "Maybe it's more like your theoretical math where you make up an equation to fit an imaginary problem." Laura glanced at the Professor for a reaction. He didn't take the bait.

"Anyway," she went on, "for every ten guys who hold with a fishing theory that seems to make sense, someone else comes along with the opposite take and it's just as convincing. You're right though, trout do tend to do most of their feeding below the surface. However, when there's a big hatch of insects they'll also be feeding on top where the bugs have broken through the film, or are laying their eggs, or have fallen back on the water to die. You've seen trout leap out of the water to take a bug just as it emerges from the water? The real showoffs will take the bug on their way back down. With a poor cast I've hung up flies on brush draped over the surface of a river and seen trout take a lunge for them. They're the little naive ones, but they do take a shot. Probably they've seen insects hanging from strands of spider web. Who knows?" She took a deep breath.

"But your question was about dry fly fishing. I guess the real reason for fishing drys is not so much just to catch fish, but to see the action. It's a visual thing. It's watching the dry fly float, bobbing up top and following the river flow downstream. It's the anticipation of the fish striking the fly and seeing the reaction to the hook." Leonard just grinned and shrugged one shoulder. "You don't look convinced." Laura continued. "Well, after awhile, when the number or size of the fish you've caught doesn't matter as much, you'll start appreciating the visual part of it." She drained the last drop of her wine. Leonard was silent, so she took another breath, exhaled and decided, what the hell, and plunged on.

"Let's say you've got a chance to make love to the most beautiful woman in the world, but there's one condition. The only way she'll go along is if it's totally dark...no lamps, no candles, no moon or starlight, just pitch black. It will probably be great and you'll remember it. But just imagine how much better it would be if there was just a little light, and you had your eyes open. Remember, she's drop-dead, world-class gorgeous. You'd probably remember it forever. Like I said, it's a visual thing." Leonard was staring at Laura as she tried to explain—his face turning a deep red.

"Geez, I'm sorry professor. I didn't mean to embarrass you."

Laura jumped up, gave him a peck on the cheek, and ran over to pack up the boat.

Leonard went over to untie the anchor rope. Still red in the face, he mumbled, "Well, I'm not sorry."

They drifted the remaining stretch of the river, catching a few small browns on tiny dry flies. Leonard tied into a *big one* that bent his fly rod double. It had apparently been slurping midges in a tight backwater eddy. They saw the take, but never really saw the trout. As brown trout are wont to do, the fish took a dive, dragged the leader across a submerged log or rock, freed itself and was gone.

After Laura negotiated the final river run, George Otis was waiting at the public access ramp just north of the Pine Bluff Fish Hatchery. He helped load the drift boat onto the trailer and they drove to Towne, stopping at the supermarket on the way. There was a long embarrassing silence between George and Leonard as Laura ran in and picked out two huge Michigan baking potatoes, a package of precut tossed salad, a bottle of dressing (not low-fat), a bag of pine nuts, one fat lemon, parsley, a bottle of canola oil, and a pound of butter. Oh yeah, and a couple ears of corn. The corn didn't look like it was grown in Central Iowa. Well, you do have to give up some things if you want to live in the mountains.

While Laura was in the store, there was only one exchange of words between the two men. "Professor Russell, don't ever hurt Laura." Leonard just stared at George. He was either astounded by what George had said, or scared to death.

"Aaah, no," was his exact response.

The meal at Maggie's was a smash and the fresh grilled rainbow delicious. Laura ate all of her baked potato, plus the skin of the Professor's. The second bottle of wine was even better than the first and helped the less than perfect sweet corn go down. Leonard and Laura sat on two of Rufus Jefferson's hand-built Adirondack lawn chairs in front of Cabin #1. They watched the embers in the char-broiler twinkle and fade out just as the wine bottle emptied. Not exactly a romantic camp fire, but nice. The silver moon, barely evident during the day, was gaining brightness. Stars appeared once the moon set below the mountain range in the west. Sounds from the Interstate were muted by a gentle breeze out of the north. Even the occasional trucker pulling into Maggie's didn't distract from the mood of the evening. What finally changed the atmosphere was Professor Leonard Russell looking at his wristwatch and reluctantly admitting he had to be at State University for an early morning conference. It was about forty-five miles from Maggie's over one impressive mountain range and up the foothills of another. Leonard's room at the hotel was reserved for three nights. Laura watched him over the top of her plastic champagne glass, as she slowly rotated the stem. If this was a dodge or a brush off, it was a good one, but she couldn't believe the Professor was all that practiced at dumping women. Remorsefully, Leonard asked when they could run the river again.

Laura couldn't resist a chuckle. "I'll check with Maggie and see when the boat's free. Call me early tomorrow…after six is too late. I'll be out guiding all day."

"Laura, please ask her tonight and I'll call you first thing in the morning. It's a three-day conference, but anytime after that is great. The kids still have another couple of weeks with my sister, so it would be just the two of us. I *will* call you first thing in the morning, I promise."

◗◖

At 5:00 a.m. Laura's cell phone woke her just ahead of her alarm clock. It was the Professor calling from the State University Hotel.

CHAPTER 20: Reverend Berkshire

Reverend Berkshire sat on a planked bench seat attached to an old carved-up picnic table. He had driven to the unimproved campsite in the Whoosh River Meadows immediately after performing the interment ceremony for his friend, John Schipper.

The Reverend's heart was heavy. He and John had fished this area often. Now he sat alone staring at his legs and a brand new pair of waders and wading boots. He had never been able to afford such luxury. Oh, long ago, he had discarded his rubber-booted waders for a canvas pair with sock feet. He wore oversized tennis shoes as boots. These were Cabela's Dry-Plus®, breathable with attached gravel guards. What next, waders with a zipper fly? The felt-soled boots laced high over his ankles, were imbedded with small tungsten cleats much like the studded snow tires of the 70s. Amazingly, everything fit perfectly. Being, let's face it, short and fat, regular-sized waders never fit. They were either too long or too tight. The label said *Short Stout,* which sounded much better than *Short Fat, Vertically-Challenged, Obese,* or how about *Gawd, You Look Awful*?

The waders and boots were to be a Christmas present from

his fishing friend. John Schipper had purchased them at a huge sporting goods outlet store in Cheyenne. His wife had carefully wrapped them in holiday paper. She gave them to Reverend Berkshire when the two met to make funeral arrangements, explaining there was no reason to wait until Christmas. "You, more than anyone, know how much he dearly loved to fish," a sad smile crossed her lips. "Wear those boots and waders in good health…that's what John would have wanted. That's what John *did* want. Catch a big one for him.

"Enjoy them Reverend, while you can," she smiled. The implication hit him like a large brown trout nailing its first grasshopper of the season. "John planned his retirement for years…six months is all he had. That wasn't nearly enough…for either of us." Berkshire's friend had been a vice president of the largest bank in Capital City. Five years before retirement, John took a demotion with a big cut in salary and moved to Towne. He was named the branch manager of the village's only financial institution. The Whoosh River Watershed and its trout fishing were the main reason he had made the move, along with the chance to get away from all the time-consuming social obligations demanded of a bank's VP. That was precious time away from fishing. The Whoosh River became John Schipper's home water.

About the same time the Reverend was considering his own retirement. Every four years he and his wife were transferred to a new city and its congregation, a move dictated by the board of the mother church. The Reverend never admitted it aloud, but he suspected that the reason he was chosen to relocate was that he may have been the only pastor who graciously packed up and departed for another small congregation, in another small village, out in the boonies. The incentive was always a trout stream nearby.

In reality, it was a good deal for the *"Powers That Be."* While they liked Reverend Berkshire as a person, they had never been impressed with his oratorical skills, though his sermons were carefully and lovingly prepared. Expressed another way—the good Reverend, while being compassionate guardian of his flock, was a lousy speaker.

His wife never complained about the constant relocations. She had always adapted well to each new community. In every church she ever served, the ladies loved her dearly. Maybe Towne should be their last stop. Towne could become their retirement home.

Reverend Berkshire had met John Schipper, the banker, before Schipper and his wife began attending his church, the United Protestant Church of Towne. Late one afternoon, after walking down from a high mountain feeder stream to his brand new Dodge Durango, John spotted Berkshire. The good Reverend had apparently pushed his old Ford station wagon to the limit up the same two-track John had negotiated earlier. A broken shock, along with a shredded tire, had brought a halt to Berkshire's uphill ascent. The two vehicles sat side by side in stark contrast to one another.

"Hello there." The Reverend made no response. He seemed to be deep in meditation or prayer—probably, the most useful thing he could do at that moment.

John cleared his throat and tried again. "Good afternoon."

The Reverend bolted upright, more shocked than afraid. "Sorry, didn't hear you."

"No problem. I hope I didn't alarm you. Looks like you're in somewhat of a fix." John took a moment to observe the crippled vehicle and then stuck out his hand and introduced himself. "I'm John Schipper…manager of the bank in Towne. Don't believe I've had the privilege."

"I'm Berkshire…Reverend Berkshire…the Protestant Church in Towne. I may, however, be forced to reconsider my occupation. The words I have been using aren't…well, I might have taken the Lord's name in vain…"

"No problem, Reverend. If you did, I was too far up the trail to hear you," John grinned. "Mum's the word, I promise."

"If you're done…er, when you're finished fishing, could I impose upon you to drive me to Towne? If you're going the other direction you could just drop me off at Maggie's Corner. I'm sure she has a phone there," he ended lamely.

"I can do much better than that." John reached into one of the many pockets of his fly jacket and pulled out a cell phone. The small instrument seemed completely alien to the Reverend. "I'll give Charlie's Auto Repair Shop a buzz and see what they can do for us."

By the time Charlie's tow truck arrived, Berkshire the minister, and Schipper the money exchanger were fast friends. They even agreed on terms for a new car loan.

Over the years the two men fished the entire watershed, together and separately, exchanging locations of hidden honey holes where enormous browns or rainbows resided and barren stretches only a few shiners or chubs called home.

The two made retirement plans for trout fishing trips outside their home waters. The wives would certainly be invited to go along, but let's not encourage them too much. The two adventurers knew that they were capable of traveling without their spouses with few regrets. Well, maybe the Reverend wasn't completely comfortable with that approach. The banker on the other hand, saw no problem.

"Hey, when was the last time either of them asked to go along fishing?"

Before John died, the Reverend considered it prudent to hold off his retirement until he was sixty-five or older believing the extra Social Security money would be needed. When John was struck down by a massive heart attack six months after his retirement party, in the third row pew of Berkshire's church, the Reverend was no longer sure he was making the right decision delaying his retirement. Maybe he would get out at sixty-two. Maybe he would just get out.

Wasn't that what John's wife was implying when she had presented him with his Christmas presents? John had died quickly, a blessing, long before they could take even one of their extended fishing trips. That was not a blessing. They would never fish together again, not in this world." Reverend Berkshire wondered if he should be feeling more sorrow for Mrs. Schipper. He certainly felt sorry enough for himself.

Well, he was not there to dwell on such matters. He was there to try out his brand new waders and boots.

"By golly, you *Oncorhynchus clarki* just better look out. It ain't da judge a comin'— it's da Preacher!"

CHAPTER 21: Frank & Freda

F rank Zebb had carefully mapped out his cross-country summer bicycle trip. What he failed to do was take the same care in picking his riding companions. They had bragged of their ability to "ride the mountains" with stamina and without whining. Total bullshit. His five *teammates* were weak-kneed, hot air wimps. Besides being first class nerds, they all listened to NPR and probably wet their beds. Calm down Frank, at least none of them had ever been accused of blood doping.

Whether the charges against Frank were true or not, he had lost his sponsorship: *"We're going with a younger rider."*

He lost his job: *"It would be better for everyone if you moved on."*

And, he lost his wife: *"It's not that I don't still love you, Frank, but Maurice just, well, he just swept me off my feet."*

Maurice, for God's sake. Not Morris, or even Morrie, but Maurice. His wife had left him for a Maurice! "God, I hope he isn't a hair dresser." Then again, maybe Frank really did wish that.

It was three years before Frank Zebb got back on a bicycle.

After only four days of the scheduled fourteen-day trip, Frank left his teammates, who were drinking dry Martinis and bragging about their biking accomplishments at a fancy hotel in Capital City. Frank rode alone to Maggie's Corner where he rented a cabin. He had to sleep somewhere. His tent, sleeping bag, and cooking supplies were left behind in the support vehicle, and the team was at least two day's ride behind him. He left a message in voice mail telling them he would wait at Maggie's Corner until they caught up. God only knew how long that would be.

Frank rented Cabin #3 and bought soap, a razor, toothpaste, and a comb. He washed and dried out his riding shorts and shirt, took a shower and went back into Maggie's store looking for something to eat. It was only one o'clock in the afternoon. After considering a pre-wrapped sandwich, he wandered up to the front counter.

"Excuse me. I was the guy who just rented one of your cabins. Could you tell me where I can I get a good sit-down meal?"

Laura smiled. "Yes, I remember you. Gee, it must have been at least an hour ago."

"I'm sorry," Frank laughed. "Guess I was a little preoccupied."

"That's okay. It was Maggie who waited on you. Anyway, in Towne there's the Roadhouse Bar & Grill…if you're up to another six-mile bike ride."

"No problem," Frank said.

"Two more miles south of Towne you'll find a couple of fast food joints and a truck stop…at the Interstate exit. Oh, there's a small café right downtown. It's called The Café. Clever, huh?"

"No problem with another ride, I've got all afternoon. How's the food at the Roadhouse?" Frank asked.

"Well, if you like steak, it's the best. Seafood is excellent. Once in awhile they get rainbow trout in…in from somewhere," she smiled. "Occasionally they have something more exotic to offer, like lobster or Alaskan crab. Who knows where it comes from? If you want simpler food, I'd stick with The Café. It's across the bridge from the Roadhouse, next to the supermarket."

"You know what?" Frank announced. "I'm going to splurge. Roadhouse it is. You wouldn't be able to join me later, after you get off work...for dinner or a drink?" he asked hopefully.

"Oh, thanks, but I'm here until ten tonight and have a big day on the river tomorrow. I'm guiding an elderly couple from North Dakota down the Whoosh River. If I understood them correctly, it's a second honeymoon of sorts. But, if you hang around the Roadhouse long enough some type of band will show up...about eight o'clock or so. You never know what it will be until they start. Chances are it's one of the country and western bands from Big City. If you're really lucky, you might catch a little bluegrass. Some of the local guys get together occasionally. I don't know if jamming applies to bluegrass, but they're good...awfully good for never practicing together."

"Well," Frank said, "if you change your mind, I'll be the one with the biker shorts." Coming close to an apology he added, "...got nothing else with me. I'm sure everybody else will have chaps and boots and cowboy hats."

Laura laughed. "That's about right, although, most of them wouldn't know a horse from a mule."

"Or their dancing partner?" Frank asked.

"Now that *is* cruel but probably true," Laura grinned. "Hey, if you'll be around here a few days, check with Maggie in the morning. Maybe she could schedule you for a float trip or even a fishing trip. She's got all the equipment and I'm a good guide... damn good."

The ride into Towne was an easy six miles west on County Road 64. The road was flat, paved, and had little traffic as it paralleled the Interstate.

Frank locked his Trek Equinox TTX 9.9 to a modern day hitching post in front of the Roadhouse and pocketed his odometer. Okay, so his bike wasn't new, but reconditioning was part of the ridiculous price he had paid.

He looked into the bar and decided he'd do better in the restaurant at least for now. The sign at the cashier's stand said *Seat Yourself*, so he did. He found a table by the far wall where he could watch who came in to eat and who turned into the bar.

A menu lay on the table. The *Daily Specials* were printed on a white index card attached with a paper clip to the inside page.

24oz. T-bone, hash browns.
Green beans, and tossed salad.
Apple pie 99 cents extra.

That was a lot of food. How about *Sea Bass*? Wasn't that illegal to sell? What had Laura said? "…seafood in from somewhere."

Frank checked out the breakfast offerings: *Served until 11 a.m.* Maybe he'd come back in the morning—he had a whole day to kill.

Deloris Jankowski walked over to his table holding an order pad in one hand and a pencil in the other. Frank beat her to the greeting.

"Hi, sweetheart. On the advice of the little gal at Maggie's Corner I just rode six miles on a bicycle to eat at the finest restaurant in the city and here I am."

"Well, I guess that explains your colorful shirt and shorts… you're a bicyclist, but Greta at The Café might argue who has the best food. What do you want to drink?"

"How about you tell me about your specialties…er, specials," Frank smirked.

"How about you tell me what you want to drink." Deloris smirked back.

He finally settled for the pasta which, as usual, was twice as much as he could eat, and a piece of *homemade* huckleberry pie. The pie was good. His attempt at conversation with Deloris was not.

"Not my day," he spoke to his reflection in the window. "Hell, this hasn't been my decade."

Frank paid the bill, left a huge tip (that'd show her), checked on his bike, and went into the bar where stools formed an L-shape. They were empty except for the far corner where a woman sat talking quietly to the bartender. Frank sat near the two and ordered a diet coke. Mike Tapio, the bartender, poured his drink and left to refill a beer pitcher for some locals sitting in a rear booth.

"Hi, I'm Frank Zebb. I'm new in town."

"Well, I might not have guessed your name, but I sure figured you weren't from around here." They both smiled. "Today they call me Freda Morrison. You can call me Freda."

"Hi, Freda, it's nice to meet you. What will they call you tomorrow?" Freda stared at him, without answering

"What's happening in Towne tonight?" Frank went on feebly.

Freda chuckled, "Well, there's a group of college kids due in here about eight for a jam session. We don't pay them, so it will probably be more like nine before they get here and set up. I have no idea how good they are, but I'm sure they'll have fun.

We turn the ventilating system way up. Some of them have weird smelling cigarettes. Just kidding," Freda amended, "in case you're working undercover." Mike grimaced as he returned with the empty pitcher.

"Of course, there's always an easy mark at the What Are You Lookin' At Saloon—it's a tavern down the street, but then you don't look like a pool shark."

"No, I'm not a pool shark. I'm not even a very good swimmer."

Freda choked on her beer, trying to suppress a laugh, but managed an unladylike snort instead. "Well, other than that..." she trailed off. "Oh, there are always a few garage sales on Saturday. I think its Towne's biggest industry." She thought a second, "And, there's a meeting of SOD this afternoon at the Catholic Church. Don't see why you'd be interested in that."

"What is SOD?" Frank asked.

"Sorry, that's the Save Our Dam committee. They're some locals that want to save our dam from a bunch of do-gooders who think the world would be a better place without dams...even better, without people. They want the government to rip out the Whoosh Dam and drain the reservoir. I'm sure the local chapter of PETA will be protesting the meeting—all four members."

Frank shrugged. She was right. That was nothing he wanted to hear about.

Mike pointed to a poster on the wall advertising a slo-pitch softball tournament that very afternoon.

"That's an idea. Softball games in the City Park this afternoon. Just a bunch of beer guzzlers trying to regain their youth. The first thing they do is tap a keg and set it on second base. Actually, the first thing they do is have their wives notify Doc Walters...just in case. Usually one of the teams will try to sneak in a couple of ringers from the University, which makes somebody mad, which makes somebody else madder, which means they end up calling Doc Walters…but, they claim it's all in fun," she grinned.

"Freda, it's early, how would you like to take a walk with me, show me your town and then we can watch some beer guzzlers play softball?" Freda studied him for the longest time. Frank was about to withdraw the invitation, drink his Coke, and then excuse himself.

"Mike, I'm going to take Mr. Frank Zebb on a walking tour of Towne. We'll be back before you get busy." Taken completely off guard, Mike said nothing. Just nodded and watched the two walk off.

◂━◂

By the time Frank and Freda had circled the village, checked out a softball game (one was more than enough) and returned to the Roadhouse, they were friends. When the music ended that night, they loaded Frank's bike into the back of Freda's pickup and told Mike they were heading for Jackson, Wyoming, in the morning—for just a couple of days. They had come up with the idea while the band played a version of Johnny Cash and June Carter's *Jackson*. I know, I know—it's Jackson, Mississippi, but give them a break.

By the time the sun had risen over Maggie's Corner the next morning, Laura had her honeymooners out on the Whoosh and Frank and Freda were more than friends. Frank left a phone message for his cyclist partners telling them to finish without him. He would pick up his camping gear when they all got back home.

While Frank paid Maggie for Cabin #5, Freda made a call to a restricted number in San Francisco, and left a message:

"I'm out of here. Mike is on his own now. Freda."

Freda stood on the cabin porch and watched Frank walk back from Maggie's store. A great wave of relief swept through her. The San Francisco office would not be happy, but they would assign someone else to baby sit Mr. Tapio or they would consider him out of danger. Whatever, she was a private contractor working month-to-month and she had had enough of Mike Tapio and, more to the point, the village of Towne. After a few days traveling with Frank, she would drop him off at his home, kiss him goodbye, and call the office. She would be reamed out, threatened, and then offered a new assignment. Whatever it involved, she would no longer be labeled "Freda Morrison from Towne."

"God, I hate that name," she hissed under her breath, as Frank ran up the cabin steps and gave her a big hug.

CHAPTER 22: Short History of the Village of Towne

◅►

U ntil the automobile became popular, Towne was known as Ratzigg's Ford. It was named after Chester Ratzigg the area's first white settler. This evolved, some would say regressed, into Rat's Ford and finally Ratsford.

Chester's house, where his wife raised their ten children, slowly grew into a huge general store, now known as Chester's Mercantile. His other dwelling, a log cabin, is still up in the high meadows beyond the dam. The cabin has been rebuilt and modified several times over the years and now serves as a makeshift ranger station and shelter for hikers and cross country skiers—hardly a posh mountain retreat.

Before his home became a general store, Chester eked out a living running trap lines near the cabin and by panning for placer gold on his homestead. For most of the year the Whoosh River ran wide and shallow right past Chester's side porch. During the snow runoff in late spring, Chester's house sat far enough above the average high water level to be safe from flooding. Most years that is. Once or twice every twenty years the river spilled over its banks and inundated the area. On one of those rare occasions,

Chester came up with the name Whoosh. As he told it: "One day that darned old river just upped and whooshed right through my front parlor." When the Whoosh River Dam was built in the 30s, some ten miles upstream, the flooding problem was solved.

As wagons forged west, they forded the river on Chester's land. Soon Chester's adult children were repairing wagon wheels and replacing horseshoes for the *Great Migration West*. Mrs. Ratzigg cooked meals for the weary travelers and sold them homemade remedies for every ailment imaginable. In Council Bluffs, Chester traded furs for merchandise and then hauled the goods home to sell or trade with travelers that crossed the river. Many transplanted sojourners realized a few more pots and pans, another couple of blankets, or warmer coats were more valuable than Grandma's Spinet Piano or any other weighty heirloom they had dragged along. Consequently, Chester amassed a fine assortment of vintage furniture that he gladly resold for a fine profit.

It wasn't long before other businesses opened up in the area, usually owned by the travelers that had gone as far as they could stomach.

"*This may **not** be the Promised Land, but it dang sure is close enough,*" they proclaimed, to the relief of their families. Anyone who ever transplanted a clan and household via wooden wagon would certainly understand.

Years later, townspeople built a one-lane bridge across the Whoosh. It remained a single lane until the daughter of a state senator, driving one of the area's first sports cars, challenged the area's first International Harvester Farmall tractor. When they met somewhere in the middle, the senator's daughter, not surprisingly, lost and within a month construction began on a new two lane bridge.

For years, the village of Ratsford remained basically unchanged. Locals had two taverns to chose from, the I Dare Ya

Bar and the What Are You Lookin' At Saloon. Chester's General Store continued to expand. His descendents added hardware, lumber, and bottled liquor. And his ice cream window was the first west of Kansas City, or so they claimed. Scattered on four principal streets were an assortment of buildings including the post office, a doctor's office, a bank branch, and two churches. Later, a full service gas station and used car lot took up a main corner of the village.

Around Ratsford, if you weren't a rancher, your choice of occupations included logging, saw blade sharpening, poaching, and meat processing which, naturally enough depended largely upon the poaching. Then there was, dare we mention it, cattle rustling?

If you've ever been to any of several small river towns in northern Michigan, and survived, you'll have a pretty good idea of what Ratsford was like until the Whoosh River Dam became a reality in the late 30s. The real difference was that Ratsford encouraged tourists, while some of the Michigan towns looked upon the tourists as intruders—probably still do.

"Don't be a fishin' in *my* trout stream, ya dumb sum-a-bitch," could well be the village motto.

After the Whoosh River Dam was completed, and the promised prosperity and building boom never materialized, the town barely changed until the Interstate Highway was built in the early 80s. No one seems to know what possessed the engineers, or influenced the Feds to put an exit at Ratsford. Actually the exit was six miles east of Ratsford at Maggie's Corner, which made some sense as it was the shortest route to the dam. Eventually another exit was built that led directly north to Ratsford and south to the community of Pine Bluff, which should not be confused with Pine Bluffs, Wyoming. This village, overlooking the Whoosh River, sadly has but one bluff.

With two freeway exits, the State decided to construct a few office buildings at Ratsford—a welfare and unemployment center, a Secretary of State branch, and a health clinic. All subsidized by the taxpayers, of course. Along with the state's building program, came the not so subtle suggesting that the Ratsford's village fathers:

"Change that God-awful name of your God-awful town."

Rather than taking insult, the mayor called the village fathers to an emergency session at one of the local taverns. Didn't matter which one, as they usually alternated meeting sites between the two. The only topic that evening was the renaming of the town.

Actually, nobody but strangers referred to Chester's homestead site as Ratsford anymore. All the locals called it *town*, as in; "Are you going to town?" or, "Have you been to town lately?"

After several rounds of liquid refreshment, someone said, "Hell's sake, let's just call it Town?" Everyone, except for old Zeke Astor, agreed happily and the group of men and one woman ordered another round to toast the new moniker. It was a simple, practical solution.

"Excuse me gentlemen...er, and lady," Zeke interrupted as his barstool did a one-eighty to face the council table. The lady he was referring to was Phyllis Grimsley, the village secretary.

"Don't you think Town is a little plain, a bit mundane?" Zeke questioned. Rumors had it that Zeke was a direct descendent of the fur trading Astor family, which Zeke had never denied.

After a snicker or two, one of the council members asked: "Okay, Zeke. Just what would you call our Town?" Notice they were already using the new name.

"Call it Towne." Everyone gawked at Zeke. "That's T-O-W-

N-E, you damn fools...Towne with an '*e*' ... *a silent 'e' on the end*. You idiots wouldn't know class if it bit you in your...," he spluttered.

While they didn't especially appreciate Zeke's approach, they did accept his idea. Ratsford was renamed a third time. The mayor had Phyllis order new stationary and asked her to inform the State of their decision. She also called Big City Billboard Company to order new Village Limit signs—three of them—one for each end of their community—east, west, and south. Only locals came in from the north and they knew damn well what they were getting into without any sign to warn them.

The meeting adjourned after several more rounds and the council left the tavern, congratulating themselves on their originality and creativity. Old Zeke just stared into his wine glass filled with Napa Valley Red.

"Talk about class," he carefully enunciated with a mordant smile. "It don't get no classier than Napa Valley Red - 1976."

The bartender smiled and poured Zeke another glass of "class."

CHAPTER 23: Clunkers, Junkers and Casey Romanak

><

The simple plywood sign bolted securely to two pine poles across the road from Maggie's Corner read: *AVAILABLE*. This was the former site of the old restaurant and motel that the Barnes boys torched. After the County razed the charred remains and passed the title to Maggie they occasionally sent someone to mow the weeds and clear the litter.

One Saturday morning, near the end of a hot summer, old Casey Romanak pulled his flatbed truck, loaded with a huge yellow Caterpillar, onto the lot and slapped a *For Sale* sign on the inside window. Climbing out, he stared at the rig for a few moments, seemingly undecided. Finally, he reached inside the cab and pulled out a worn leather travel bag. Disgustedly, he shot a stream of tobacco juice against the front tire. Slamming the door, Casey turned and walked across the road, past the gas pumps and through Maggie's front door dropping his bag by the cashier's counter. Pulling titles and registration slips from his back pant's pocket, he laid them on the counter, along with two sets of keys. Maggie didn't know it then, but she was about to go into the used-vehicle business.

Maggie had been stocking coolers when Casey walked in. She turned to watch the wiry old man. Well, truthfully, she didn't know exactly how old he really was. Working outside his entire life had weathered Casey's skin, bleached his thinning hair, and hardened his muscles. The expression "tough as wet leather" seemed to describe him best.

Casey came to the Whoosh River Watershed on a circus train. People say it was the last time the old NNW & WNW Railroad tracks were ever used.

After the final performance, Casey broke his arm helping pack the main circus tent into a boxcar. While a young Doc Walters was setting the bone, the train moved on without Casey. He threatened to chase after it if he was forced to return to his home in Oklahoma. Instead, Doc Walters and his wife accepted Casey as a boarder until his arm healed. Then they reluctantly gave the teenager their blessing along with fifty dollars and sent him on his way. Within two years, he returned to repay their kindness. Casey had caught on with an earth moving company in Pine Bluff, but after several years of hard work and miserly living, had bought their equipment for ten-cents-on-the-dollar, a deal the bankruptcy court was happy to accept. His employer had gone belly-up owing Casey several months back pay and so he figured that his low-ball offer made them about even.

Casey ran his business as a one-man operation. Oh, he would hire an occasional temp, but always said, "I'd rather do it myself than havin' to tell somebody else what to do. They never listen and I end up doing it, anyway…makes no sense."

Casey's business thrived, at least enough to support a wife and put their only child through Cal Tech. His wife, Alice, had lived to see their son graduate with honors, take a job with a start-up computer company, and become wealthy at a very young age.

Their son never made it home before his mother succumbed to cancer.

❦

Maggie watched Casey. His was a face showing grim strength and the seasoning of many years of high altitude, sun, and wind—a face with a set of lips that could change a grin into a sneer by merely lowering his eyebrows. What was missing was the usual twinkle in his eye and his mischievous smile, both rarely seen since he buried his wife.

Casey's Adam's apple bobbed in his scrawny neck as if he were talking to himself. Perhaps rehearsing what he was going to say.

"What's up, Casey?" Maggie obviously startled him, but he recovered quickly.

"What's up?" he repeated. "Up to my scrawny neck, that's what's up." Maggie sputtered and broke out laughing. "What's so dang funny?" Casey demanded.

"Casey, that's funny because I was just admiring your scrawny neck."

"My luck…how about my scrawny butt?"

"No. No, thank you. Please."

"Yeah, well, you just might be missin' something. Anyways, there's titles, registrations, and keys for my rig across the road. Sell them for whatever you can get and I'll split it with you. Or, split it anyway you want, just see if you can dump 'um for me. This'll finally get me out of the dirt pushin' business. That's the last of the equipment. Now none of my so-called friends will be lookin' for no favors."

After a moment of thought, Maggie agreed. "I guess I can do that. If they don't sell in a month or two, I'm sure Charlie can get rid…er, dispose of that rig somewhere for you."

Casey nearly choked on his tobacco chew. "You ain't a gonna hurt my feelings whattin' you do with them," Casey said with more bravado than necessary. It was apparent to Maggie that it was mostly an act. He was hurting big time. "Well, I'm out of here." He reached down to pick up his bag."

"Hold on, Casey. Where are you going? And, how are you getting there?" Maggie demanded.

"Headed to San Diego, California…just for awhile, mind 'ya. My boy wants me to move out there. Move in with him and his wife and kids. He says he's got a guesthouse next to an outdoor swimming pool with all the…what's the word…amenities? Says he's a willin' to throw some trout in the pool for me to catch. Dang fool probably thinks they'd live. Anyway, I told him I'd try it for a few days…would like to see my grandkids. I truly would. Then, I don't know, probably come back here and hang out with you." A shy grin crossed his face. Was that a hint of the twinkle he had lost? "If them fools haven't ripped the dam out by then, I'll be back to catch up on my trout fishin' and do a little reading. Bet you didn't even know I could read, did ya?"

"Casey, I'm sure there are a lot of things I don't know about you or want to know for that matter." Maggie did know that the man was struggling with his decision and she loved the old coot. She had adored his wife Alice who had often wondered if she'd given birth to a daughter, instead of a son, might they have had a much closer relationship. Oh, Alice loved her boy and was so proud of him, but once he left Towne, he never returned. Would a daughter have done that?

After Alice died, Casey lived alone and worked from dawn to dusk. Maggie was able to keep tabs on him, as he would go out of his way to pull in and fill up his rig. From his home in Pine Bluff it was only seven miles to the truck stop south of Towne and fifteen miles to Maggie's, but Casey never bought fuel from anyone but Maggie—out of his way or not.

Every year Maggie would wrap a ribbon around two cases of Miller High Life beer for his Christmas present. On his birthday, she gave him a fifth of Johnnie Walker Gold Label Scotch Whiskey, the really good stuff. It was the only two things she was sure he enjoyed—other than his chewing tobacco and she wasn't about to give him any of that. Although she still sold it over the counter, she claimed to be the first "Spit Free" business in the state. The spittoons had disappeared long ago.

"Well, I'm going to hoof it into Towne and catch a bus to California. Bye, Maggie, I'll be seein' ya."

"Nonsense, you slow down a second. George will drive you to Big City. You know there aren't any buses out of Towne...not anymore. George, come here please," she yelled toward the back room. "You know darn well nobody is going to pick you up if you hitchhike. Poor people would be scared to death of you. Probably try to run you over. You'd be road kill."

❦

So that's how Maggie got into the used vehicle business. Before she even sold Casey's rig, word got around. Soon she had two pickups, a van, four sedans, and a septic tank cleaning truck all sitting on the old motel lot. The deal was the same. If you could drive it in, just leave your title and keys and a forwarding address. When Maggie sold your rig, she would send you, not half, but two-thirds of the selling price. If it didn't sell, Charlie would haul it away and vandalize it for parts, then mail you a check for what he thought it was worth. As long as he knew Maggie was watching, he was fair.

ᐁ

But that's not the end of this story. A young hotshot attorney, Samuel Cowdrey, opened a new law practice in Big City just days out of law school. It's rumored that his grandfather, Sheriff Cowdrey, and County Commissioner Fred Barnes had promised him enormous retainers for his services, not that they would ever need a lawyer—certainly not, don't be silly.

Soon after the lot opened, young Cowdrey paid Maggie a visit. Just a social call, you understand. After stilted pleasantries, he informed Maggie that his specialty was tax law and he would be willing to make his talents available to her for a small monthly fee. If not, he would accept a single large retainer. Maggie could save herself a ton of money that way.

Hardly able to restrain her laughter, Maggie thanked the Sherriff's grandson and said if she ever needed any legal advice she would certainly consider his offer. A smirk crossed young Cowdrey's face, changing his features from acceptable to unpleasant, a definite sign that the grandfather's genes ran through this young man. The acorn doesn't fall far from the oak tree.

Attorney Cowdrey handed Maggie an expensive looking embossed business card and before leaving reminded her that tax problems could be the most expensive kind.

Taking a final shot he said, "Don't let the I.R.S. get involved. You don't want them snooping around."

"What in the world was that all about?" Maggie wondered as she watched Cowdrey drive away in his shiny new Mercedes-Benz. Her eyes came to rest on the "Maggie's Clunker" sign across the road. "Bet that's it. Well, it's about time I took care of that little matter," she mumbled to a disinterested little boy buying a chocolate fudge bar.

Maggie picked up the phone and called Stella, the County

Clerk and told her that she had just received an inquiry about the property across the street, hinting that it sounded like an out-of-state development firm, possibly mall oriented. Problem was that she had no idea what the appraised value of the land was, or how much the property taxes would be. After only two or three minutes on hold, an over-excited Stella quoted Maggie some figures and wished her luck, lots of luck, in selling the lot.

Maggie hung up, multiplied the tax amount by the number of years she had owned the land and wrote a single check to the County Clerk, noting the description of the parcel next to her signature. She scribbled a note stating that, because of an apparent oversight by the county, she had never received a tax bill for that piece of property.

"As ridiculously high as my taxes are on the store, I naturally assumed they included the lot across the road," she wrote. "As I am bringing the mistake to the County's attention, I feel no obligation for any accrued interest or penalty." She made no mention of the earlier verbal agreement with the County.

Maggie signed and dated the paper, not knowing how legal it really was. "Maybe I should have Cowdrey's grandson prepare it. Ha." Grinning, she called for George. "George, come witness something for me, please." He appeared from the back room, carefully signed his name and then disappeared again. Why in the world did he spend so much time in that back room?

Maggie plugged a nickel into her copy machine (thinking she should have raised the price to fifteen cents long ago) and waited for the clunk, bang, and shudder of the old contraption before grabbing a copy of her note and check. Maybe ten cents was enough.

Maggie addressed an envelope, sealed it, stuck a stamp on it, and walked outside to the blue U.S. Postbox. Hearing the envelope hit the bottom of the nearly empty container, she smiled. Surprised how relieved she was, she went back inside, grabbed a fudge bar for herself and climbed on her stool behind the counter.

Maggie couldn't believe that County Commissioner Fred Barnes had anything to do with the not-so-subtle threat of legal problems over a delinquent tax payment. She had seen Barnes' sons torch the motel and restaurant. He certainly wouldn't want that made public. Maybe it was just petty harassment from Sheriff Cowdrey, but that didn't make much sense either. Sheriff Cowdrey and Commissioner Barnes had a lock on all the shady deals in Whoosh County and they certainly would not risk that cozy setup for a childish chance to pester her, or to collect a few more tax dollars for the Whoosh County coffers. The only thing that made sense was that young Samuel Cowdrey had come across some information that he thought would parlay into a retainer fee from Maggie.

"You know what, Margaret Elizabeth? You're just being paranoid—not cut out to be a crook." She laughed out loud. "You're just afraid you might be embarrassed by those clowns. Talk about paranoia.

"Then again, just because you're paranoid, doesn't mean they aren't out to get ya."

Whatever. Maggie knew one thing for sure: after her conversation with Stella Hemlock, it would not be long before rumors swept through the Whoosh River Watershed that a megamall was being planned for the land across from Maggie's corner. Maybe even a Cabela's outlet store. How about a Bass Pro Shop? She wasn't sure the area was ready for an Ikea.

Aaah, a neo-renewal of the Whoosh River Watershed appears on the horizon. Or would this be considered a neo-neo-renewal? One could only fantasize.

And, all this got started because Casey Romanak merely wanted out of the dirt pushin' business.

CHAPTER 24: Sandy Rhodes & Sweetwater Drilling

><

Ronald "Dusty" Rhodes left his Kentucky home when he was fifteen, passing through the Whoosh River Watershed. There were rumors that he was in the area long enough to be romantically involved with Ruth Anne Ledbetter of the *Buzz,* but those were only rumors. After his abbreviated stay, Dusty left for South America. Nobody in Whoosh River ever heard from him again, least of all, Ruth Anne.

Dusty's younger brother, Raymond "Sandy" Rhodes left home at sixteen and trailed his brother to the same Whoosh River area. The Rhodes family never tried to contact either of the boys. Well, they were a family of twelve.

Maggie gave Sandy a home in Cabin #4 and a job pumping gasoline, until an exploration company hired him on during the *oil boom* in the area. This particular oil boom quickly turned into the *oil bust*, taking Sandy's employer with it.

Like Casey Romanak, Sandy, with the bankruptcy court's blessing, scavenged equipment, hired a crew and went into the exploration business for himself. Because of his personality, he was usually able to raise enough capital for a chance at the next *gusher*. His track record for locating oil wasn't all that good, but it was good enough to keep him financially afloat, pay his crew, and occasionally return a small profit to his backers. This was an unprecedented accomplishment in comparison to the transient wildcatters passing through the region.

Sandy Rhodes was a man most folks took to right off. He was a big man, built like George Otis, only some eight inches taller. Where George had thinning brown hair, Sandy had a full head. When he forgot to shave for a few days, a beard appeared that was—well, sandy colored.

Where George Otis had seen violence all his adult life, Sandy Rhodes rarely encountered any type of physical confrontation. His size alone discouraged problems, for himself as well as anyone associated with him. George Otis, if not trained in all the Martial Arts, was at least familiar with them and, of necessity, had put most to use. In contrast, Sandy had never struck anyone out of anger, fear, or duty. His shy smile, warm humor, and physical presence took the fire out of nearly every ugly situation. In looks and stature, Sandy resembled the former Los Angeles Rams defensive lineman, Merlin Olsen, who played the part of Jonathan Garvey on the TV series "Little House on the Prairie."

Don't be a fool. His mild, almost shy, mannerism belied an instinctive intelligence that gave him an edge over most of his competitors in whatever the situation. Anyone thinking he was naive or gullible was wrong.

❦

Thomas "Winter Wolf" Bennett, a full-blooded Indian and lifelong resident of the Whoosh River Watershed, had known Sandy since he came to Towne. They had met at Maggie's Corner and at Maggie's urging, Thomas had taken him hunting and fishing, even after Sandy began working in the oil business.

At first, Sandy saw Thomas as a surrogate big brother. He missed his real brother, Dusty who promised he would come back to Oklahoma and together they would vagabond around the world. Through some connections in the oil business, Sandy eventually found the name, Ronald Rhodes, on payroll records of an exploration company operating in Central America. Before he could make contact, the government nationalized the oil industry, the name disappeared, and access to the records ended.

Sandy's relationship with Thomas Bennett gradually changed from big brother to best friend, though an older and wiser one. He never quite understood why Thomas had taken to him and eventually didn't care. The friendship grew to a point where Sandy finally felt comfortable enough to ask Thomas about his given Indian name.

"What's with the *Winter Wolf?*"

"Who knows?" Thomas answered. "Something about being born during a howling winter storm. Some claim it was a pack of wolves making the racket, not the wind. My father says it wasn't the wind or the wolves. It was my mother. I was a very big baby."

Sandy met the love of his life while negotiating with a local tribal Council. That fateful day he sought permission to drill two wells on their reservation north of Big City and east of Capital City. This tribe respected Sandy as much as they could any outsider.

Rarely late for anything, Sandy arrived at the Council Hall promptly. He realized that the Council did not necessarily operate on White Man's time (by the clock). They could call him in at once or leave him sitting in the small alcove indefinitely. He wasn't sure if this was a test of his patience or the Council just showing him who was in charge. Today Sandy would receive a *go* or a *no go.* His final offer would be accepted or rejected. Chances of oil on the reservation were two—slim or none. Both sides knew it. Sandy had not proposed much upfront money, but had generously back-loaded the deal just in case they hit big. It was the most favorable offer the Council was liable to receive—possibly the only.

Sandy had a feeling that the decision had already been made, but this was the Council's final chance to make him sweat it out. Maybe more accurately, make him run a modern day gauntlet.

After only ten minutes, the double doors swung open. Thomas "Winter Wolf" Bennett came out and escorted Sandy into the main hall. Eight elders sat behind two long folding tables. The windowless room was illuminated by several fluorescent light fixtures hung from a stark-white drop ceiling. Long-bladed fans stirred the air softly with their sibilant circular motion. A small stage in the far corner held a piano, a drum set, and huge amplifying equipment.

Thomas walked behind the Council and remained standing. How much authority or influence he had, Sandy wasn't sure, but he did serve as their spokesman-interpreter. Thomas' input probably carried a great deal of weight.

Sandy hated speeches. He was known for direct and concise talk—one-on-one. Anyone who knew him for any length of time never questioned his honesty, but the Council was known for long drawn-out negotiations.

After greeting the elders, using the long respected term *Grandfathers*, Sandy began his final appeal, then stopped short.

He hadn't noticed *her* when he entered the room. At the end of the table, dressed in a business suit, blouse and high heels, sat the most beautiful creature Sandy had ever seen.

Sandy stared open-mouthed at the woman. She returned his dazed look. Her mouth closed tightly. After a moment Thomas cleared his throat to break the silence.

"Mr. Rhodes, the young lady is here as an advisor to the Council. Hell, Sandy, she's here to check you out. The Council relies big time on her judgment."

Sandy was suddenly at a loss for words. If you had asked him what he was even doing there in the Council Hall, he might not have come up with an answer.

"Sandy, this is Lizabeth Dupree. Ms. Dupree, meet Raymond Rhodes. Everybody calls him Sandy."

"Ms. Dupree," Thomas addressed the young woman, "Sandy wants to drill for oil on our sovereign and sacred lands. Being a White Man he is probably a crook. We'd like you to tell us how big a crook." While Sandy's face flushed, Thomas broke out with the biggest grin you'll ever see on an American Indian's face. Only one of the elders winced. The others retained their impassive expressions, sitting silently. Maybe they just didn't understand English, the language, or the people that spoke it.

With difficulty, Sandy finally averted his eyes from the woman and found himself staring at Thomas.

"Lizabeth is not of our tribe," Thomas went on. "She is a full-blooded Nez Perce, a direct descendent of Chief Joseph. Her Indian name is Sweet-Running-Water. I'll let her pronounce it for you."

Lizabeth Dupree said nothing. She shifted her position slightly, cleared her throat and glared at Thomas, his signal to "sit down and shut up."

Thomas quickly added, "Apparently she prefers to be called Ms. Dupree." With that he found his chair behind the elders and did indeed sit down and shut up.

Ms. Lizabeth "Sweet-Running-Water" Dupree was obviously of Indian descent, but in truth, she was closer to a Hollywood stereotype of an Indian Princess than any Indian woman Sandy had ever met. She was tall, although he couldn't tell how tall, as she sat observing him. Yes, tall and thin, but she gave the impression of a strong woman. Not overtly muscular, but a woman with inner strength. Her skin was dark. Her eyes picked up various colors at different moments from dark blue to green to gray. And though Sandy didn't hear her speak that day, he soon learned that she was a determined, self-reliant woman fighting battles that Sandy did not fully understand—the biggest, perhaps the battle she fought within herself.

Flustered, Sandy took out his notes and began reading the lines he had highlighted in yellow. Mid-paragraph he stopped, stuffed the notes into his shirt pocket, scanned the elder's faces, inhaled deeply, and said: "Gentlemen, if I hit oil, I could become wealthy…," he paused, "but that wealth will be shared with your people. We all know the terms. Let's do it."

He thanked the elders, thanked Thomas, nodded toward Lizabeth, and left the room. Before Sandy could close the doors behind him and wipe the sweat from his forehead, Thomas followed him outdoors into a brilliantly blue Rocky Mountain day.

They looked toward the eastern mountain range, still partially shrouded in an unusually late morning mist. Thomas smoked one Camel, field stripped what was left of it into the wind and lit another. Finally, the silence became too much even for Thomas.

"It's a done deal," he said, without looking at Sandy. "The

elders will haggle all day and then give you their approval. I'll call you first thing in the morning and you can get started."

"What about the woman? Did she approve?"

"She approved."

Sandy stared at his friend. "She approved? I didn't get that feeling. I didn't get any feeling at all."

"Trust me."

Thomas kicked a loose stone and watched it bounce down the dirt-hardened driveway. It separated two Yellowbellied Marmots, who scurried to rocky dens on opposite sides of the road, interrupting their discussion. Or was it Sheriff Cowdrey's Bronco pulling up to the tribal building that disturbed them?

"Maybe that's why the Council was more-or-less on time this morning. They may have bigger fish to fry with the good Sheriff Cowdrey than they do with you," Thomas said.

"Cowdrey's a little out of his jurisdiction, isn't he?"

"Not if he was invited. Something must be going on that I'm not in on. Who knows?" They watched Sheriff Cowdrey get out of his vehicle, look around and disappear into the building.

"Anyway," Thomas continued, "Ms. Dupree will recommend they approve your deal. Good or bad, it's a *go*."

◄━►

Whatever love life Sandy had, past or present, was instantly forgotten the moment he saw Ms. Lizabeth Dupree.

Sandy was thrilled when the Council okayed the wells with the one condition—their oversight be conducted by Ms. Dupree. Every Saturday afternoon thereafter, he shut down the drilling operation early, sent his crew off to the nearest bar, and went home to his trailer where he showered, ate a huge meal, and went to bed.

Every Sunday morning he picked up Lizabeth from her home in Capital City. First they would check out the drilling sites, then go over reports, and take endless rides throughout the Whoosh River Watershed in Sandy's four-wheel drive Jeep.

◄━►

Lizabeth loved this country she so steadfastly tried to reject. She was born and raised in Lapwai, Idaho, the seat of government for the Nez Perce Indian Reservation. She spoke English, Spanish, French, and numerous Indian languages and dialects.

While still in high school she received a full ride scholarship to Arizona State University. At ASU, Lizabeth completed a four-year degree in the American Indian Studies Program in two-and-a-half years. She earned a master's degree at UCLA and collected enough education credits to teach at either the high school or college level. Her only detour was two semesters at the Yale Law School where she learned she did not want to be a lawyer and that she most definitely did not want to be in New Haven, Connecticut. She missed the land she left behind—the mountains, the high plains, the towers of billowing clouds, and the tall pines reaching skyward in an endless sea of blue.

So she returned to the Rockies and took a teaching job at State University in Capital City where she taught Indian Culture Appreciation classes four days a week. On Thursday evenings she taught the same course to an adult education group. And on weekends, she worked on her doctorate degree through UCLA.

Lizabeth experienced pressures, both covert and overt, to return to the reservation, any reservation, and teach. She chose instead the public school system on the theory that it would be more productive to explain the Indian culture to the White Man's children than to attempt to merge the Indians with the White Man's world. She was never quite at ease with that reasoning. It occurred to her that it might just be a convenient rationalization. But the bottom line was she did not want to be back on the reservation, any reservation. Besides, who was she kidding—the pay was far better at the University.

━●━

Sandy Rhodes also loved this country he so persistently exploited. With a ninth-grade education, he came west to fulfill his capitalist dream. Well, okay, he wouldn't have expressed it that way or even thought along those lines. He would say he followed his brother to the Whoosh River hoping to catch up with him. Here he found, not his brother, but enormous challenges and, in his own way, he measured himself against those challenges. He also found Maggie and Thomas. Without their guidance and compassion, he wouldn't have become the man he was.

━●━

It was early fall and drilling on Sandy's first well had gone deeper than the geologist's *best-chance* depth. No oil in another week and the pipe would be pulled and drilling would begin on the *second-best* site. This particular Sunday he didn't want to think about the possibility of another failure.

Sandy and Lizabeth were a half-mile northeast of the soon-to-be-dry hole. The derrick, now in sight, had been erected on a small, treeless tract of land. It rested on a cement pad measuring a hundred feet on each side. Piles of pipe, in various sizes, were stacked lengthwise around the tired outbuildings. One was a large corrugated aluminum shed, the other, a beat-up house trailer that served as an office and a place to flop for a nap or an overnighter. A flatbed, tanker, and concrete mixer were parked between the structures.

Lizabeth stood some fifty yards away amidst acres of fragrant wildflowers. Spineless Horse Brush with its creamy yellow flowers contrasted with the plump red-orange berries of the Skunk Bush. The field was blanketed with Pasqueflower loaded with purple, cup-shaped flowers, Cliff Brush sporting waxy-white blossoms, and Deerhorn Clarkia boasting brilliant pink lobes.

Her raven-black hair blew with the slight breeze from the foothills. Her oversized blue plaid shirt hung loosely over a tight-fitting pair of designer jeans tucked neatly into custom-made roper-style cowboy boots. No, Lizabeth did not own any Indian moccasins. She stretched her arms upward to the cloudless sky, closed her eyes for several seconds, opened them, and gave Sandy a rarely seen smile.

"Raymond, there's no oil here." She was the only person to ever call him Raymond. Even his mother abandoned his chosen Christian name when he was born with a gigantic mop of blond hair that screamed Sandy.

"There's no oil here," he silently repeated to himself. He believed Liz. Snake eyes it was. First thing in the morning he would start pulling the pipe, notify his investors, apologize to the Council, arrange other jobs for his crew and head for Alaska, the Gulf of Mexico, or the Near East. Finding a job in the petroleum business was not the problem. The problem was leaving Lizabeth.

"There's no oil here," he said aloud and turned to leave. He didn't want to believe it.

"No, wait. Wait. Raymond, please wait." It was as close to a plea as Sandy had ever heard from Liz. "What is more precious than oil out here?" she called after him. He turned with a blank stare. She stood in a patch of thick, ankle-high Sulfur Buckwheat, golden and beautiful in the morning sun. All Sandy could think of was an old prospector's saying: *"Look where the buckwheat grows—it has an affinity for silver."*

"Silver," Sandy cried.

"Silver, what in the world are you talking about? Raymond, look around you. We're miles from any river. There are no creeks, no springs, no marshy areas. Other than fields of flowers this land appears desolate, but it's alive. Come stand with me." She took his hands and closed her eyes again. Next to her, his size seemed to shrink.

"Feel it? It's here."

He stood there dumbfounded. To this day Sandy won't admit that the only thing he felt was Liz's trembling hands.

"It's water!" She opened her eyes and jumped up and hugged him. "It's water," she cried.

Occasional travelers to the Rocky Mountains can be easily deceived by the amount of cascading water that flows from high snow-capped peaks into lush meadows and man-made reservoirs. In the mountains, naturally enough, most roads follow the river's path, usually the easiest route up or down—a route the river has forged after centuries of eroding gravitational forces. What is not seen from ground level is the expansive stretch of barren land between those river beds, with mile upon mile of gigantic ranges that often hold nearly vertical rock formations—areas with little if any ability to retain moisture.

Where Lizabeth stood was an abnormality of huge proportions. It was an enormous aquifer where unseen seams, cracks and splits directed millions of gallons of high mountain water to a reservoir deeply hidden for thousands of years. This desolate land had been undiscovered because this was indeed sacred land to Thomas Bennett's people, mostly ignored by them and totally off limits to all others. Sandy's first oil well had missed the aquifer by only feet.

The rest was predictable. Sandy drilled for water and hit big time. The Indian Council held a ceremony removing the land from sacred status and they immediately went into the real estate racket, selling hundred-year leases on four-acre ranchettes, to the White Man. Of course they did. The bleak landscape was turned into a large green subdivision of Big City. With easy access to Capital City, it became a bedroom community for many of the State workers. Where sage brush once grew; lush lawns took its place. Where dusty two-track roads ran; paved cul-de-sacs protected expensive homes. Where Colombian ground squirrel colonies once thrived; children played on plush, manicured soccer fields and baseball diamonds. The land was transformed. Some would argue that it was *not* a transformation for the better, but it *was* a transformation. The Council took the longer, more practical view. In 100 years, after the leases ran out, the land would revert to the tribe for anything their children's children desired. It could even be reinstated as holy ground and allowed to grow free.

Sandy settled with his oil investors and came to an agreement with the Council. Now he was in the water business. He named it after Lizabeth; you guessed it—*The Sweet-Running-Water Drilling Company.*

Sandy Rhodes parked his Jeep in Maggie's Over-Da-Hill Clunker Lot. Lizabeth stood by the gas pumps across the street. Picture, if you will, a Penske rental trailer full of personal belongings hitched to a brand new midnight blue BMW.

Maggie watched Sandy climb out of his Jeep. The company logo on the door, though spray painted over, still showed a faint outline of a waterfall. Sandy rapped his knuckles on the hood several times. People in the West develop a strange and personal relationship with their vehicles, almost like their attachment to horses in a bygone era.

Taking a long, deep breath Sandy straightened his shoulders and walked across the road toward Liz. She stepped up and ran her hand gently along the side of Sandy's face, stood on tiptoes, and kissed his cheek. Sandy smiled and they both turned and walked into Maggie's Corner.

"Why is that old trailer hooked to such a beautiful car?" Maggie greeted them from behind the cashier's counter. "By the looks, it's loaded."

"Hi, Maggie," Sandy replied. "Yeah, we're all packed up and headed for Vegas...then on to Tucson. You heard I sold the drilling business?"

"Yes. News travels pretty fast around here...rumors even faster. You know that."

"Sold to an outfit from the East. Made a few bucks."

Maggie chuckled. "I heard that Eastern outfit you're talking about was from East Kansas. I also heard you soaked them good. Didn't they want your Jeep?" she asked, as she nodded toward the lot.

"Well, I thought Laura could use it...costs her a dollar. Got the title all signed...if she wants it," his voice trailed off.

"Laura's on the river with a couple from Wisconsin...kind of old home week for her. They know her parents. Anyway, I'll see if she wants your Jeep, but you know how fond she is of that old Dodge of hers?"

"Sure, but please ask her...if she passes, no hard feelings... turn it over to the Lodge. They can sell raffle tickets and maybe make a few bucks. It has a lot of miles on it, lots of them, but your cousin Charlie has taken real good care of it...ever since I bought it new."

"That's mighty nice of you, Sandy. I'm sure Laura will appreciate the gesture." Maggie turned to Liz and, as if noticing her for the first time, said, "You're sure lookin' pretty Ms. Dupree, dressed up and all."

Before Liz could respond, Sandy blurted, "We were married in front of the Council...up on the reservation this morning... Thomas was my best man... we slipped out before the party really got rolling. It's kind of weird, what with neither of us being from their tribe. Made us honorary members and then married us. It's all legal, but we're headed for Las Vegas to do it again... in English." The pride in his voice and the huge smile on his face said as much as his words.

"Well, bless your hearts. It's about time you two were hitched. Sure will end all the gossip around here." Maggie came around the counter and took both of Liz's hands in hers. "You're getting a fine man."

"I know, that's what he says." A hint of a smile crossed Liz's face.

"No, I'm the lucky one." With that, Sandy lifted Maggie up off the floor and gave her a hug. Bear hug hardly describes it. By the time he set her down she was gasping for breath. That's probably why there were tears in her eyes—then again, maybe not.

"God bless you both. I know He will," Maggie stammered.

"Did you say you're headed for Tucson after Vegas? What's that all about?"

"I've taken a position at the University of Arizona," Liz said.

"Position? Maggie, she's going to be head of a whole dang department, now that she's a doctor." Sandy's face glowed.

"UCLA approved my paper and they granted me a Ph.D. in American Indian Culture. Not exactly a medicine woman." Liz attempted to downplay Sandy's enthusiasm, to no avail.

"I always figured her to be some sort of shaman...the way she finds water and all. Now it's official and she's got a piece of paper to prove it," Sandy beamed.

"Shut up, Raymond." Then Liz added, "Please. And I'm *not* the head of the whole department." Sandy's face turned redder than normal.

"What in the world will you do in Southern Arizona, Sandy," Maggie asked?

"I hate to admit it, but it's sort of a sweetheart deal. Liz's job offer included work for me. Seems they need a new sprinkling system for the college golf course. Can you imagine a college golf course in Southern Arizona? Anyway, it sounds interesting. All I have to do is figure out the system, hire the contractors, and supervise the job. They didn't need any of my equipment. Maybe, if I do a good job, I'll write a paper and they'll make me a doctor like Liz," Sandy beamed. "Can you imagine if I created a trout stream for them in the desert? Maybe the Chamber of Commerce would nominate me for mayor...might not even have to write a paper."

"Gracious, sounds like you've got it all figured out."

"Well, Maggie, we're out of here. George is done filling the tank. Haven't you explained self-serve to him? Give the man a break." Sandy dumped a wad of bills on the counter.

"Oh, George is just trying to do something nice for you two. He thinks the world of you. Now you both come back here on vacation sometime soon. Sandy, you can have your old cabin. Got new hot water heaters for all the units…not like when you first came out here, Mr. Rhodes. Mr. and Mrs. Rhodes, that sounds nice…real nice."

Sandy couldn't speak, or didn't dare. He gave Maggie another embrace and walked towards the door. Lizabeth mouthed the words, "Thank you, Maggie," and followed him out.

Oh, and Maggie did explain self-serve to a grinning George Otis for the umpteenth time, while she devoured another chocolate fudge bar.

CHAPTER 25: Veterans Day Massacre

Darwin Caxton Worde, Whoosh County's Acting District Attorney, watched Sheriff Oscar Cowdrey's fat ass, as his secretary Hazel Mertz had so eloquently dubbed it, sway down the corridor and out the bulletproof glass doors into a gloriously sunny Tuesday. The Sheriff had, however, just ruined Darwin's *gloriously sunny* Tuesday. Out of character, the Sheriff had not strutted into his office unannounced, wearing those silver-coated, redneck sunglasses, making demands on Darwin and his staff. Actually, Sheriff Cowdrey seemed contrite, downright meek.

Cowdrey came to the office and presented a one-page report recommending the District Attorney bring charges against George Otis for an incident that occurred the previous day. Commissioner Fred Barnes had scribbled his name across the top with a red felt pen. It made the request appear more like a demand than a recommendation. Cowdrey had signed lightly on the bottom in pencil. In Whoosh County, the District Attorney and Prosecuting Attorney are synonymous, possibly a money-saving measure. With unspoken reluctance, Darwin agreed to seek an arrest warrant for George Otis. The charge was felonious assault. He needed a judge's signature before authorities could take George into custody. After having the document signed, Darwin would consider the ramifications of what he had done. Remember, this is George Otis of Maggie's Corner.

◗◀

How did this all get started?

Twice a year the Lodge in Towne invites patients from the Veterans Administration Hospital in Big City to a fish fry and afternoon of bingo. Volunteers aid the mentally and physically disabled war veterans on and off a specially equipped bus. Vets get assistance marking their bingo cards and collecting donated prizes. After bingo, they eat as much fish and chips as they can possibly hold—usually rainbow trout from the Whoosh River, not from some fish farm, or frozen food locker. On occasion this has put the Lodge at odds with the Department of Wildlife. The Grand Pooh-Bah of the Lodge would remind the Head of Wildlife that the river had plenty of fish and…"for God's sake, these are our disabled war veterans, you idiot! They are heroes." A war veteran himself, he did not often mince words.

Maggie and George Otis were always ready to help, even though that meant Maggie's Corner was left in the hands of the students she employed. Not a problem this year, now that Laura Menard was working for her.

The summer fish fry took place on a Monday. After the "Bingo and Rainbows," the veterans were given gift certificates from Big City and Towne merchants, to use in their stores, and free packs of outdated cigarettes. Then they were herded back on the bus and sent back to the hospital—some would say, out of sight, out of mind.

While the loading process took place, Fred Barnes' sons, Worthless and Moreso (as they were locally known), along with

three or four other freaks, came out of the What Are You Lookin'
At Saloon. They started directing comments about *gimps, misfits,*
and *baby killers* at the veterans. When the last vet was safely
aboard and secured, George gave the okay sign to the driver and
the bus headed toward Big City in a cloud of diesel fumes and
street dust. As it disappeared around the corner, Maggie climbed
behind the steering wheel of her Blazer. George remained on the
sidewalk. While the Barnes boys turned their verbal abuse on
George, their friends wisely vanished back into the bar or down
the alley.

Maggie's only comment to her steering wheel was, "Oh, my."
She grabbed a pen and pad and quickly wrote the names of the
disappearing hecklers and the volunteers that still stood on the
sidewalk. At this point, Maggie was in no hurry to help George.
He would need help later.

As George approached them, the Barnes boys froze. Was it
fear or inane stupidity? No one could imagine them standing up
to George. Even though he was four inches shorter than either of
the brothers, George picked one up in each hand, banged their
heads together and gently laid them on the sidewalk. A cheer rose
from the remaining spectators.

George walked into the saloon and returning with the bartender,
pointed to the unconscious bodies. The bartender nodded, patted
him on the shoulder, and disappeared to make some phone calls.
George got in Maggie's Blazer, hooked his seat belt, and listened
with no comment as Maggie quietly said: "George, you probably
shouldn't have done that." That was the basis of what is now
known as Towne's "Veterans Day Massacre."

Tuesday morning Fred Barnes, long-time County
Commissioner, went to the Big City County Hospital where his
sons had been transported, not by ambulance, but by an unmarked

sheriff's car. The boys waited for him in the lobby, heads hanging practically to their knees. Fred ignored them, marched into the hospital's administration office and demanded to see the medical reports. He left with revised copies. The notations indicating high blood alcohol levels had been removed.

Barnes went straight to the Sheriff's office, located in the county jail building and handed Oscar the medical reports. Then Hazel typed a request addressed to the District Attorney's Office asking the Prosecutor to issue an arrest warrant for George Otis.

Before the ink could dry, Sheriff Cowdrey made his way across the street, entered the County Court House building. He huffed up one flight of wide, marble stairs to Acting District Attorney Darwin Worde's office. Handing the paperwork to Darwin, Cowdrey decided to take the rest of the day to go check out the old bridge across the East Branch of the Whoosh. If the county didn't do something to shore it up, the shaky span would be condemned soon. He would take a long look and fill out an inspection report. It wouldn't change anything, but it would justify an eighty-mile round trip voucher and, more importantly, get him out of town.

While the Sheriff was heading north, Darwin drove south with the arrest warrant to Pine Bluff where a judge signed the document. Well, he wasn't really a full-blown judge. He was a justice of the peace. Darwin knew that Judge Elliott (whose office was downstairs from his) would never sign the warrant.

While all this took place, two anonymous phone calls went out from the County Hospital, one to the *Buzz,* and the other to Maggie's Corner.

Nothing more official happened that Tuesday, but the calm betrayed undercurrents set in motion. It was like watching a hushed, high-mountain lake during the fall— completely quiet and still, while just beneath the surface gathering brook trout scurry about readying for their annual spawning ritual.

Rumors flew, like startled pigeons, from Maggie's Corner on the east, to Capital City on the west. The basic question: Had Commissioner Barnes and his attached-at-the-hip cohort, Sheriff Cowdrey, finally stepped over the line?

At exactly seven Wednesday morning, George's day off from Maggie's, four, that's right, four sheriff's patrol cars pulled up in front of his apartment complex. Six deputy sheriffs cautiously approached the apartment and quietly arrested a nonresistant George Otis. The Sheriff, notably absent, had taken the only other available county car to Capital City. He was hauling a three-time drug offender to the state penitentiary. For the second day in a row, the good Sheriff went missing.

Charlie, Maggie's cousin, observed George's arrest. He had been hitching an abandoned station wagon to his wrecker. The vehicle had been left at the apartment complex in lieu of unpaid rent. Charlie gave the manager a hundred dollars in exchange for the title and registration. After the transaction, he flipped open his cell phone and called Maggie.

Maggie listened quietly, thanked Charlie and turned to Laura, "It's all yours. I'll be in Judge Elliott's office in Big City. If the Blazer holds up, I'll be there in an hour."

Having heard the rumors, Laura didn't ask why Maggie was leaving. "Be careful," was all she said.

Maggie despised cities, especially Big City. Towne was plenty large enough for her. She made it to the courthouse in sixty minutes exactly as predicted. It took another twenty to find a parking place.

She had a handicapped card to hang from her mirror, but adamantly refused to use it. It had been issued to her when George was released from the VA Hospital. She had never shown it to him, but held on to it just in case he ever had a relapse. She did not consider it a relapse that he was now sitting in a county jail cell.

Maggie walked into the County Courthouse and went straight to Judge Elliott's outer office. She nodded to Ester, his secretary and legal clerk. Ester pointed toward the Judge's door. Before Maggie could sit down the Judge asked, "What took you so long?"

"Big City's parking. There isn't any," she sputtered. "I hate cities. Why don't they take some of my tax money and build a parking garage, for heaven's sake?"

"Maggie, Big City is less than twenty thousand people. That's not large at all." Maggie repressed a snarl—the Judge repressed a grin.

"I guess this is about George?"

"Elliott, you know it's about George." Because they were friends, the Judge, Elliott T. Elliott, always assumed she was calling him by his first name, not his last. At least that's what he hoped.

"Did you see what happened?" he asked.

"Yes."

"Did anybody else see what happened?"

"Yes." Maggie handed him a two-column list of names with addresses and some phone numbers—one column for witnesses and another for participants.

"Aaah, you do come prepared. Tell me what happened."

Maggie repeated, as distinctly as possible, what took place. By the time she finished, she was even more disgusted with the whole turn of events.

"Hmm, have you seen today's *Buzz?*"

"No, I left before our delivery." Elliott handed her the Wednesday morning edition.

"They must have gone to press before they knew George had been arrested. I can't wait to see tomorrow's paper," the Judge grinned.

FALSIFIED REPORT PUTS MAGGIE'S CORNER EMPLOYEE IN BIG TROUBLE

*Reliable sources say an arrest warrant,
based on a falsified hospital report,
may put George Otis behind bars.*

The article detailed Monday's events in front of the Lodge, and the Barnes boys' involvement, stressing verbal abuse the *victims* had directed at the disabled veterans— Our American War Heroes. The paper's version was nearly identical to Maggie's.

Three pictures followed. One, of George Otis, showed him lifting the back end of a Suburban off a puppy.

The second picture was of Worthless and Moreso Barnes at the county fair hog-calling contest. Dressed in bib overalls and dirty Chicago Cub's baseball hats, they had just finished 2nd and 3rd in the annual competition. Nobody beats Harold Hofstadter at calling hogs. He could be the state champion, but believes his Amish faith prevents him from traveling to Capital City to compete. That is really a shame if you're a fan of pig calling.

The third picture, with no caption, showed Commissioner Fred Barnes handing Sheriff Oscar Cowdrey a check. It was taken at a campaign rally in front of the County Courthouse. Barnes was presenting Cowdrey a check for his re-election campaign, presumably all legal and aboveboard. Faithful readers of the *Buzz* may have noticed the original background showing the courthouse had been replaced by the interior of the I Dare Ya Bar. The *New York Times* or *Reuters News Agency* do not have sole license for creative photojournalism. Coincidently, the I Dare Ya Bar is where Cowdrey's recent prisoner, the three-time-pot-smoking loser, was busted.

With the slightest smile, Maggie carefully refolded the newspaper and handed it to Judge Elliott.

"You and George must have very good friends at the *Buzz*," the judge commented.

"We buy a lot of advertising space," Maggie deadpanned.

With a more authoritative demeanor, the judge continued. "As of this moment, I have not heard anything about George's arrest…officially. Here's the scenario." Notice the good judge didn't use the word *deal*.

"When the paper work arrives, a personal recognizant bond will be set at fifty dollars. It will be immediately waived. No reason George should spend another minute in jail. We'll just wait and see how the acting district attorney wants to proceed. It's his decision…regardless of who's pressuring him.

"Ester," Judge Elliott hollered. "Call across to the jail and tell them to have George Otis in the lobby in ten minutes ready to go home with Maggie. And have the paperwork in my office in five."

"Not a problem," Ester called back.

"What day is the county employees' golf league?" he asked.

"Tomorrow…every Thursday…till fall." Ester was standing in the doorway between offices grinning at Maggie and the Judge. "It's a shotgun start. Everybody's tee-off time is at five."

"Perfect," the judge responded. "Get hold of Sheriff Cowdrey…

on his radio if necessary. I understand he's making another out-of-town trip. Tell him to be in my office at four tomorrow afternoon…four o'clock exactly…no sooner, no later. Then call District Attorney Worde and tell him to be here at four-thirty. If that golf game doesn't expedite this meeting, nothing will." He winked at Maggie. "Grab George and go home."

Maggie dropped George off at his apartment. They had driven the twenty miles from Big City to Towne without exchanging a word. "I shouldn't have roughed up Mr. Barnes' sons," George finally offered before unhooking his seat belt.

"Nonsense, I'm the one who should have dropped the hammer on those punks…long ago," Maggie retorted, with as hateful inflection as George had ever heard in her voice.

"Hey, you still have time to get your groceries and go have a drink at the Roadhouse. Come in a little early and help Laurie load up the drift boat. I'll get one of the kids to spot her truck. She's got a rich couple in from Dallas tomorrow and then her professor friend again on Friday. Don't think his daughters are back from California yet, but he certainly has become a regular. If that keeps up we'll have to invest in another boat…got a brochure in the mail from the Hog Island Boat Works. They're out of Boulder, Colorado…claiming their boats are stronger and lighter and the price isn't too bad, either." Suddenly Maggie realized she was babbling. Taking a deep breath, she slowed her voice and continued. "You get on out of here, George. Everything will work out just fine. Think of Laurie."

George shut the door gently, and gave Maggie a halfhearted wave as she pulled away. No, he would not forget Laurie. He liked her and was beginning to like the professor. He downright adored his little girls. Thinking of them, he smiled, probably for the first time all week.

He picked up enough TV dinners and frozen pizzas for the week, dropped them at his apartment and pedaled over to the Roadhouse. He walked into the dimly lit bar. As his eyes adjusted to the light, he noticed, not surprisingly, that the Barnes boys were missing. He spotted Rufus Jefferson sitting at the far end of the bar. George went over and sat down next to him. Mike set him up with a draft beer and poured Rufus a fresh one.

"Tough," was all Rufus said. George nodded and drained his glass. Mike immediately filled the glass.

"I couldn't have spent another minute in that cell," George said softly, enunciating each word slowly and carefully.

Rufus nodded and drained his beer glass. "I know," he said.

George had spent two and a half hours in custody and less than sixty minutes in a jail cell. Who knows, to George it might well have seemed like an eternity—or an eternity revisited?

◄━

Early Thursday morning, Acting District Attorney Darwin Worde made the drive from Big City to Towne and was waiting patiently on the sidewalk as Greta Heinzel unlocked the front door to The Café. Greta gave no indication that she recognized him.

"Good morning," he greeted pleasantly.

"Morning, yourself. Pick up that bundle of newspapers and come on in. I'll get the coffee going. The cook will be here in a few minutes. If not, I'll cook you breakfast myself." Greta flipped on the overhead lights. The place was immaculate. Her little chat with the staff had done wonders.

Darwin set the papers on the corner of the counter, slid the top copy out from under the binding cord and sat down on the nearest stool. Thursday's edition of the *Buzz* was extra thick. There was a colored insert all about Maggie's Corner. It explained how Maggie had taken a rundown bait shop and dilapidated tourist cabins and turned them into a thriving business.

"Maggie's Corner remains a show place—an enterprise that does enormous credit to the entire region. Her thriving business is a reminder of all the possibilities available in Whoosh County."

The article included pictures of the Maggie's Corner Little League teams, of the bicycle ride Maggie sponsored for MS victims, and of her and George Otis helping rebuild the softball field and refurbish the town park. In one picture, George and Maggie wore American flag pins and stood in the old railroad station they had helped renovate. The building now served as an open-once-a-week township museum. In every picture, conspicuously placed, were the red, white and blue of Old Glory. Talk about overkill.

"Do you know this Maggie the paper is talking about?" Darwin asked.

"Haven't read it yet, but if it's Maggie from Maggie's Corner, then I know her. What's it about?" Greta asked.

"It talks about all the wonderful things she's done for your community."

"Well, there's not much she isn't involved in…don't know where she gets the time. Everybody loves her, sure enough."

"Hmmm," was his only response. He went back to reading the paper.

The sole mention of Monday's Veteran's Day Massacre, noted

on page two of the front section stated that felony charges against George Otis were pending.

> *A rumored meeting in Judge Elliott T. Elliott's*
> *office has been scheduled for this afternoon."*

Later that morning, Ruth Ann Ledbetter picked up her phone at the *Buzz* and heard Sheriff Oscar Cowdrey plead, "What in God's name are you doing to me? I'm your blood relative for God's sake. I'm your cousin. You're destroying me!"

"Cousin Oscar, it's nothing personal, but times they are a changing."

><

Darwin Worde grew up in North St. Louis, receiving his education in the public school system. Later, he graduated from an obscure law school. His grades didn't allow him admission into a more prestigious institution of learning. His parents, Burt and Ida Wordeczeski, owned a plumbing parts supply store located on Broadway Avenue. Their business wasn't profitable enough to buy their son's way into a better school and they had no connections or influence to help him. Besides they had hoped he would take over their company someday and then they could move to Branson, Missouri, in the heart of the Ozarks. The American Dream, right?

After Darwin graduated from law school, his poor grades and lack of an influential backer dogged him as he searched across the country for employment. Eventually he found himself in Big City, working in the Whoosh County District Attorney's Office.

Edward "Teddy" Moore, Darwin's boss, was the DA at the

time. It was an elected position just as Sheriff Cowdrey's and Commissioner Fred Barnes' positions were. They pretty much controlled the county. It was Barnes' money that kept them in office year after year. Someone foolish enough to run against any of the three would be snowed under with an avalanche of campaign money. Funds were raised by committees set up by FOFB, Friends of Fred Barnes. The reward for opposing the triumvirate would be less than thirty percent of the vote. Vote early, vote often. These guys were reason enough to impose term limits.

No one doubted where Barnes came up with his campaign money. Initially, it had been his wife's family fortune, but as he repeatedly won re-election he developed his own means of generating money. Sometimes they were innovative, sometimes even legal.

When young Darwin Worde took the job, he had no idea he would soon be appointed *Top Dog*. The appointment as acting DA was effective until the next regular election. At that time, it was implied that Commissioner Barnes and Sheriff Cowdrey would support Darwin for a full six-year term. Naturally, his complete and unconditional cooperation was expected.

"A new face just might be a good thing in the prosecutor's office," Barnes told Cowdrey, his smirk sickening, even to Cowdrey. "Times, they are a changing," he stated. Seems he had heard that recently.

∈◀

How did Darwin Worde move up the food chain so quickly?

As it happened, Edward "Teddy" Moore, who claimed he was connected to the Kennedy clan, had died in a single car accident out on the Interstate. The sheriff's report stated that, while executing official business for the county, Moore lost control of his automobile. The report asserted that he hit an icy spot that spun him into a bridge abutment. Speed of the car was estimated at between sixty-five and seventy mph. The person in the passenger seat, an unidentified female, was also on official business. That summarizes the official report. Actually, that was the report.

The unofficial version going around the Roadhouse where Teddy hung out, said he had been doing between ninety and one hundred mph on the Interstate in his vintage, flaming-red Corvette. Teddy had rarely been seen on the open road driving slower than the legal limit of seventy-five. No doubt he lost control of his sports car, but as for the freezing temperature that night—it was fifty degrees under a star-filled sky. How was again, an icy spot?

True, Teddy had hit the bridge abutment, sending a huge hunk of the cement pillar flying. It is still obvious to all westbound Interstate travelers. The motor block from his car was discovered some two hundred feet down the road in a dry riverbed. By the deep gouges in the freeway surface, it appeared the block had bounced twice before burying itself in the arroyo. County deputies on the scene found no piece of the Corvette's fiberglass body bigger than three by five inches.

The unidentified female was Missy Reynolds, an employee of a gentlemen's club located in downtown Capital City, right across the street from the governor's mansion. Initial identification was only speculative. Missy's body was as mutilated as the Corvette. Police discovered her wallet at the crash site and her husband recognized the tattoo on a small piece of her *back upper-thigh*.

Mr. Reynolds had his wife's body parts cremated—those that were found. Hungry wildlife discovered the rest. No further official inquiry or follow-up ever occurred.

A closed casket funeral, with great pomp and ceremony, honored District Attorney Moore. Mrs. Moore, the bereaved widow, was pictured in the *Buzz* clutching a folded United States flag, apparently holding back her tears. According to wags at the Roadhouse, what she was holding back were whoops of joy. Teddy, her cheating husband, had died on *official* business. Can you imagine the insurance settlement?

After the funeral, Commissioner Barnes and Sheriff Cowdrey met with Darwin Worde, the youngest, least experienced attorney on the District Attorney's staff. Even grade school students in Whoosh River understand that the shares of something divided by two are greater than divided by three. Former D.A. Moore's share of "something" would not automatically be passed to his successor. They'd have to see how things worked out.

Darwin knew why the county commission, with prompting from Barnes and Cowdrey, chose him over the much more experienced attorneys in the office. The Commission hoped that he didn't know where the county's skeletons were buried if he were so inclined to dig for them.

"Who am I to buck the system? Who am I to fight this inbred tradition of, can I whisper, corruption?" Darwin questioned himself with a derisive smile.

It was oh, so damn, tempting. For a small county D.A., the risk was seemingly low and the benefits endless. Darwin Worde accepted the temporary promotion graciously.

So, here sat Darwin reading the *Buzz* in Greta's Café in Towne. He knew you could gage the mood of a small town's populace by just listening in the cafes and barbershops. After breakfast he would walk across the street, get his hair trimmed, and then wander over to the Roadhouse for another cup of coffee, just to listen—maybe decaf this time. He wasn't due in Judge Elliott's office until four-thirty so he would have time for a few more coffee shops back in Big City. Then Darwin would have to decide how to proceed. He really did want to be elected as the new DA and drop the *acting* from his title. Since being hired, his thinking had evolved. He was not on any one-man-crusade, but if he could clean up the county's image by putting a few bigwigs in jail, who knows, maybe he could parlay that into a state office or, eventually, a judgeship. The *rewards* would then far exceed the payoffs for petty corruption at the county level. Then again, perhaps Darwin held the naïve concept that a District Attorney was elected to protect the people, not rip them off.

Darwin knew that Judge Elliott would discourage further action against George Otis. If Darwin's office insisted, it could be the quickest dismissal of charges in the history of the Whoosh River Judicial System. Darwin's problem was convincing Commissioner Barnes that he had really tried to bring action against George. But, with Barnes' flagging popularity, Darwin did not want to be associated with the trashing of George Otis—not Maggie's George Otis. It came down to Barnes' money versus the vast respect people held for Maggie.

Of course, it wasn't beyond Judge Elliott T. Elliott's code of ethics to take credit for defending George. Judge Elliott, while an elected official himself, was one of the few that owed absolutely nothing to Fred Barnes and Company—absolutely nothing. Being independently wealthy insured that.

If Darwin could get Judge Elliott and Commissioner Barnes to cross swords, he might well slip out of the middle and be elected to a full six-year term as Whoosh County's DA. What's the worst that could happen to a boy from North St. Louis? If he lost the election, he could always return home and learn the plumbing business. Actually, he rather missed what was left of the aging brick neighborhoods and the historic water towers of his boyhood home. Darwin would never forget Piekutowski's European Sausage Factory on North Florissant or Crown Candy Kitchen's soda shack on the corner of St. Louis Avenue and North 14th Street. Talk about *good stuff.*

Darwin would have to play the "Veteran's Day Massacre" very close to the vest. He now had until four-thirty to decide the best approach to turn this mess to his greatest advantage. After the meeting with Judge Elliott, he would go and beat some golf balls around that cow pasture Big City called a Municipal Golf Course. He had heard rumors that some big money guys were planning to build a private golf course up on the reservoir. A membership would certainly be offered to the District Attorney, but for now the city course would have to suffice.

Fore!

CHAPTER 26: The Skier

❦

If you appreciate the wholesome, healthy outdoor woman, then you would consider Sydney Babcock pretty—the proverbial *girl next door*. All her life she was a snow skier. That's all she ever wanted to be. If you were insensitive, you'd say that's all she ever was.

At the age of six, Sidney was out-skiing adults on the slopes of Colorado's highest and steepest mountains. When she turned sixteen she was ranked the United States' number one Olympic hopeful in downhill and slalom, and third on the giant slalom list. Three days after being featured on the cover of *Sports Illustrated*, she caught an edge and smashed into an unprotected pylon. As the mystic of the *Sports Illustrated* cover jinx grew, the pylon was padded, and Sydney was finished.

It was a near-fatal accident. After months of rehab, Sydney could stand. Several months later, she was getting around with a walker, then a cane. Four years later, she was recreational skiing. She hated it. She had lost her strength, her coordination, and her grace to ever compete at world-class level again. Her new body was a stranger to her, a husk that no longer responded to the demands of either the slopes or her mind. And she was getting *old*.

Skiing had been Sydney's lifelong dream, her obsession, her only ambition. Her one goal was to be a world champion. Maybe because of her notoriety, teachers had been too easy on her. She had done just well enough in school to slip by. Now her body convinced her that any skiing dream was over. By accepting that reality, Sydney was left with another. She had no reason to live. Now she sat on a large, river-worn boulder deep in the Whoosh River Canyon.

Laura had swapped her usual day off with Maggie for a chance to do a little moonlighting for Richard Whendelstat and his Flies & Lies Shop. Richard had purchased three new drift boats on the condition they could be tested on the Whoosh River. The chance to guide the latest design through the Whoosh Canyon was too big a temptation for Laura to turn down. That and all those twenty-dollar bills Richard had stuffed into her hand. And there was the opportunity to report back to Maggie, just in case Maggie wanted to expand her own guide business.

Laura asked Richard why his top guide, Brad Hawkins, wasn't in charge of the test run. Richard simply replied, "I trust your opinion."

Brad hooked the trailer loaded with the first drift boat to Laura's pickup. They rode together to the launch ramp below the Whoosh River Dam and unloaded the boat into the river. While Laura headed downstream Brad would drive back to Towne and spot her truck and trailer at the landing site just below the Roadhouse Bar & Grill. On the ride out to the river, Brad never asked Laura why she got the job of testing the boats and he didn't. Laura was grateful.

She had started out late in the afternoon on purpose, not wanting to risk the possibility that other fishing guides or rafters would plug up the river. She wanted a clear shot to see how the craft handled through every run, every whitewater rapid, every pool, eddy, channel, slough, or hole. Being the last boat on the river meant she would have to explain herself to no one. This should be a fun ride.

After putting the new boat through every extreme situation she could think of, Laura lined up the final rapids into the only major hole on the river—*Devil's Gulp*. In whitewater terms, the *Gulp* was rated as a class three, on a scale of one to five. Five, the most difficult class, was an open-ended rating. As this was only the second river Laura had ever run in a drift boat, she had little frame of reference to judge whether or not *Devil's Gulp* was overrated. Listening to the more experienced guides, she thought three might be high.

Maneuvering downstream Laura recalled a family vacation one summer in West Virginia. Her father made reservations to whitewater raft on the upper Gauley River. Her mother and three older sisters backed out after seeing a television promotional at the hotel. Laura and her dad went ahead and ran the rapids, while her mother and sisters went shopping. She never forgot the exhilaration of that trip.

Laura begged her father to stay two more days and take on the New River's Lower Gorge. Outvoted four to two, her father decided to head for Sandusky, Ohio, and the Cedar Point Amusement Park. After the Gauley River, the roller coasters held no thrill for Laura. Her father promised they would return to the Lower Gorge one day, but they never did. Years later, he mentioned the possibility of meeting somewhere in the Allegheny Mountains, but like many fathers who promise their children something, he never was able to follow through. He often felt the guilt and regret of something lost, something precious gone forever.

◄◄◄

The last boat down the river picks up any straggler—someone dumped out of a boat or raft where it is impossible for the guide to get back to them—a point-of-no-return. Night in the canyon awaits anyone falling out of the last craft down the river. In the morning, the first boat through picks up the bedraggled adventurer. At least that's the theory. Riding the rapids directly at the *Gulp* Laura noticed a lone woman perched on a huge rock overhanging the rapids. Just in time she applied opposing pressure to the oars, did a forty-five degree turn and slid the drift boat up on the gravel bar next to boulder.

"Hi," Laura greeted the young woman.

"Hi, yourself," was the cheerful return. The woman wore faded Levi's, Nike running shoes with no socks, and a T-shirt with a picture of Innsbruck silkscreened on the front. There was no indication of a sports bra or any bra for that matter. Her bottom rested on a faded blue sweatshirt, obscuring any logo. Her hair, a dull brown, was cut to the top of her shoulders, just long enough to show below a ski helmet.

"I'm Laura. Laura Menard,"

"Hi, Laura Menard," the woman responded.

Laura swung the oars into the boat. "You want a water?" Before the woman could respond, Laura flipped her a plastic bottle, grabbed one for herself, and scrambled out of the high-sided boat. Giving two tugs on the bow to secure the landing she climbed on the rock.

"That was beautiful…the way you handled that boat. It was almost like you were above the water…suspended, almost flying. It was absolutely amazing." There was a quiet awe in the woman's voice, or was it envy?

"You're right. This one is sweet. It only draws about five inches of water and responds like a dream. It reacts with very little effort."

"I was ready to watch you take those rapids," the woman nodded toward the hole. "I can see why you chickened out," she said, smiling at Laura with a half wink.

"With this rig, I don't think there's a problem. That's why I'm on the river…to find out. Certainly can't lug it out of this canyon on my back, not from here…unless you want to help?" After a questioning look from the woman, Laura grinned. "Just kidding. The last boat stops and picks up anybody that's stranded. Through this stretch the guides can't turn around and paddle back to retrieve you. They just have to wait until tomorrow. Whose raft were you in?" Laura questioned.

"Oh. I wasn't rafting. I was just…just hiking," the woman answered.

"You're alone?" Laura sounded almost incredulous.

"Yeah, alone…all alone."

Laura took a long drag from her water bottle, looked up the cliffs that formed the steepest part of the canyon and asked, "How did you get down here?"

The woman looked where Laura was staring. "Mostly straight down…it was a trip," she laughed. "I almost wore through the bottom of my pants. Glad there weren't any cameramen around."

"Do cameramen normally follow you around?" Laura asked.

The young woman smiled, shook her head once and said softly, "Not anymore, they don't."

"You must be camped around here?" When the woman didn't respond, Laura continued. "There's only about an hour of daylight left. When the sun hits the rim of the canyon, it gets dark awfully fast down here."

The woman hesitated. "Yeah, I know. I've got a backpacker's tent and sleeping bag, and some sandwiches." She looked up and down the river, as if searching. "My tent is upriver, ahead of those rapids you just came through. I'll stay the night and climb out in the morning." With a slight shrug of her shoulders, she flipped a stone into the rapids.

"Hope that's a great sleeping bag. Not only does it get dark down here, but it gets pretty cold. Not much driftwood or deadfall for a fire."

"I can scrounge up enough. Besides, I've got a couple cans of Sterno. I'll be just fine…kinda looking forward to it."

"Say, look," Laura said, still skeptical, "Why don't you pack up your stuff and float out of here with me? I'll give you the ride of a lifetime…promise. You can camp at the takeout spot. There's a bar and grill nearby. I'll even buy you a drink, maybe two."

"No, really, but thanks. I've got my car parked on the rim. It would be a long hike back to retrieve it. I'll be fine tonight."

"That must have been some road trip to get to the rim. Don't know of any two tracks this side of the river. You must have a four-wheel drive."

Again, the woman hesitated, took another sip of water and nodded. "I'll be fine."

"Well, obviously I'm being too nosy. And I don't like running this river at night, not in somebody else's brand new drift boat. Everything seems to change after dark…dimension, depth, size… even time, if you can believe that." Laura slid off the rock, shoved the boat back into the river, climbed in, stowed her water bottle and, in her best imitation of a public service message announced, "Be sure to pack out what you pack in," and pointed to the plastic bottle the woman held. "Minimal impact camping, you know." They both laughed and Laura swung out into the rapids, negotiated the hole and was gone.

Sidney Babcock stood on the boulder, waved and mouthed, "Thank you. Thank you, Laura Menard."

One week later, early in the morning before anyone else was on the river, Brad and Laura were towing the second of the three drift boats.

"Did you hear about the body that washed up below the Roadhouse landing?" Brad asked.

"A body?" Laura questioned.

"Yeah, a woman. Guess it was Thursday. Nobody knows her, no ID, nothing. That old fart, Zeke Astor, found her. They took her to County Hospital to do an autopsy. Friday the BLM had a fly over and found a rental car, all beat up, on the rim...above *Devil's Gulp*. Sheriff claims it was an accidental drowning. Hiker falls in, drowns, washes down the river. Cut and dry...according to him."

To be historically correct, it was the local tomcat, Bucky, who discovered the woman first, but being of no obvious concern of his, Bucky allowed Zeke to take full credit.

Brad launched Laura from below the dam. She literally flew down the river, taking the fastest route possible. Laura had, over the last three summers, learned more about this waterway than any river map would ever show.

She pulled out of the current and slid up beside the same boulder where she had met the young woman. After securing the boat, she climbed the boulder and tried to spot where the woman could have pitched a tent—nothing. Carefully picking her way upriver to the head of the run, Laura saw no evidence of a campsite.

Why did she say she was camping? Just to get rid of me? If she had a backpack loaded with a sleeping bag and tent, wouldn't she have told me how difficult it was to get down here?

Back at the drift boat, Laura took out a bottle of water and pulled herself back up on the boulder. Crossing her legs yoga-style she closed her eyes, under no illusion that she might have any psychic ability. Nothing of the paranormal had ever happened to her. She never had a premonition that panned out. Never saw an apparition. No Zen-like understanding ever percolated her consciousness. Yet, she sat there concentrating on the image of the woman as she remembered her. Not surprisingly to Laura, nothing happened; no revelation, no sense of another's presence. No Perry Mason courtroom *aha* moment—nothing.

Laura opened her eyes, lay back, and gazed at the steep incline above. Downstream sheer rock squeezed the river into a narrow whitewater run before it plunged into the *Gulp*. You would need rock climbing gear to edge yourself along the cliff, maybe two hundred yards before you would find enough room to scrabble out. While the woman looked fit enough, she was wearing Levi's, and Nike running shoes with no socks, not exactly climbing clothes.

Upstream it was possible for her to edge along the river, but it would be at least two miles before there was a way to reach the rim and her car. If the woman started her climb where Laura had beached, she certainly could have slipped and fallen to her death, but would not have landed in the river. This time of year it was running low and the distance between the water's edge and the base of the climb was some thirty to forty feet. If she fell, she would be a bloody mass of crushed bones and flesh, laying somewhere in the rubble of rock at the foot of the cliff. How badly she was beaten up would depend on how often her body bounced, but that would never be far enough to deposit her in the river.

Attempting to get out of this part of the canyon, by going either upstream or downstream, could certainly result in slipping and drowning. It didn't matter how good a swimmer she was. But again, she said her car was directly above. The only logical way out was right here where she claimed she had come down.

Finally, Laura stood up and stretched. Then she saw it. A plastic water bottle, exactly like the one she had tossed to the woman, was wedged between two large rocks just beyond the boulder. Laura made her way carefully to the bottle. Inside was a note. Written in pencil, it simply said:

Thank you, Laura Menard.

Laura made record time through the hole and down to the takeout. She loaded the drift boat on the trailer Brad had spotted and drove up the hill to the Flies & Lies Shop. She walked into the shop and told Richard to buy the drift boats.

"If the third boat is anything like the first two, there's no reason to even test it," although thought Laura, another handful of twenty-dollar bills would be nice. In her opinion, the boats showed excellent craftsmanship and were worth more than the asking price.

Avoiding the Interstate, Laura drove along County Road 64 northwest to Big City. The road was well maintained, but even on a good day the twisting twenty miles of blacktop took forty minutes or more to cover. And, for those winding twenty miles, Laura mentally beat herself up.

Why didn't I insist she come out of the there with me? Laura knew she wasn't camped. Well, she guessed she wasn't camped.

What was I supposed to do? Throw the woman in the boat kicking and screaming and float her down the river? The woman looked like she could match her muscle for muscle.

The woman didn't seem suicidal. Seem suicidal? What do I know about suicide...other than what I learned in that dumb freshman psychology class? Suicide is stupid! Truth was, she had never known anyone that had taken their own life. Oh, she had heard of a few students on campus that did. Usually it turned out to be some freshman that just couldn't cope. Probably wasn't well adjusted enough for college life in the first place. And then she had heard of others dying while under the influence of drugs. Is that a form of suicide?

Why was I in such a big hurry to leave that woman? I could have stayed and talked with her longer. It wouldn't have mattered if it did turn dark. After the hole, the river's a piece of cake...all the way downstream to the takeout, night or day.

Reaching the downtown section of Big City, Laura parallel parked in front of the county jail as easily as she handled one of Whendelstat's drift boats. Putting two quarters into the meter, she climbed the huge flight of cement steps, looked across the street at the even more ponderous courthouse and then pushed her way through the bulletproof doors. The outer door to the sheriff's office was open. Hazel Mertz was at her desk working a crossword puzzle.

"Is Sheriff Cowdrey in?" Hazel looked up briefly, pumped her pencil toward the inner office, and went back to her puzzle.

Laura entered the Sheriff's office. Cowdrey had his feet, cowboy boots and all, propped against the windowsill balancing his mammoth body in a swivel chair. The over-taxed chair was dangerously close to the tipping point. His eyes were half closed against the last of the day's sunlight pouring through windows that extended beyond the dropped acoustical ceiling. Recent renovations were an obvious slam at the public buildings of the 1920s with their high ceilings and pompous architectural design. Labor was cheap in those days, but still, what a waste of time and effort.

Aviator sunglasses and a wide-brimmed Stetson hat lay on the Sheriff's desk hiding his name plaque. His flat-brimmed Smokey Bear hat, with the department's silver badge, hung in the corner. Several 10 x 12 glossy prints rested on Cowdrey's massive chest.

"Excuse me, Sheriff Cowdrey." Cowdrey, unaware of Laura's entry, jerked straight up.

"Damn it, Hazel!" he bellowed. "You're supposed to announce people."

Hazel stuck her head into the room and said, "This young lady asked if you were in. You're in." Suppressing a grin, she closed the door.

"God, I wish I didn't need that woman," Cowdrey mumbled to himself. Recognizing Laura, his demeanor changed immediately. Realizing he may have lost charge of the situation, his boots hit the floor as he swiveled his creaking chair to face Laura. He gave her a lopsided smirk. "I know you. You're Maggie's grocery clerk." Laura bristled. The derision in his voice was either for Laura or for

Maggie. If it were directed toward her, Laura didn't understand. It was most likely aimed at Maggie. It was generally known that Maggie and Sheriff Cowdrey had a *history* of mild confrontation going way back, not that Maggie had ever confided any of it to her. Okay, thought Laura, maybe as a child Sheriff Cowdrey had a bad experience with a grocery clerk. Give the man a break.

"What can I do for you, Missy?"

"The name's Menard. Laura Menard."

"Mmmmm," was his only response.

"I understand somebody found a woman's body at the landing in Towne last week." When Cowdrey didn't respond she went on. "I may have some information for...," she hesitated over the word *you*. "I may have some information that is relevant to the investigation and the department."

"You knew the woman," Cowdrey asked?

"No, but last Tuesday I was running the river with one of Richard Whendelstat's new drift boats. Just above the rapids, before *Devil's Gulp*, I saw a woman sitting on a rock. I figured I was the last boat through the canyon that day, so I stopped to see if she needed a ride out. I pulled over and talked to her for awhile. Claimed she was camping at the base of the canyon overnight and would climb out in the morning...said she had a car at the rim." She caught her breath. "The bottom line is that I left her there. Today, before I ran the river with a different boat, I heard about a woman's body washing up. I stopped at the same spot on the river...took a walk upstream. There's no room to walk downstream. I couldn't find any signs of a campsite, anywhere."

"So you think that was the same woman?"

"I haven't heard of any locals missing or any rafters reporting a lost customer...have you?" Sarcasm laced the rhetorical question.

"Do you recognize her?" Cowdrey handed her one of the

pictures he was holding. It was a headshot of a deceased woman. Laura took a noticeable gulp and handed the picture back to him.

"That's her."

"No doubt?"

"No doubt," she repeated.

"We took the body over to County Hospital. Somebody recognized her as some hotshot skier from Colorado Springs. We checked the missing person report and identified her within three hours. Excellent police work."

"Sometimes we get lucky, huh, Sheriff?" Laura smirked.

The sheriff glared at her. "We contacted her parents. They're flying in Thursday to make identification…take the body to Colorado Springs. Then again maybe they will have her cremated here. Not sure if they've decided what to do yet," he hesitantly amended.

"In this state, if we find an unidentified body we're required to perform an autopsy. The autopsy," Cowdrey continued, "showed her lungs were full of water. She drowned. The bruises on her body were consistent with being washed down the river for five or six miles. If this was the same woman you saw, that would be about the right distance from the *Gulp*. The county medical examiner said she had no alcohol in her blood. As far as other drugs…it will be a few more days before the toxicology report is complete, but they're pretty certain that will come back negative. On Sunday a plane from the BLM spotted her car on the rim. You do know what the BLM is, don't you, Missy?"

"I'm familiar with the United States Bureau of Land Management," Laura enunciated very slowly. "It's an agency of the United States Interior. I may even know the pilot. I understood the flyover was Friday, not Sunday," disgust tinged her voice.

"Be that as it may, the car was rented to this woman," he

nodded at the photos, "and it was full of camping equipment. That Missy, er…Menard, is it. She fell in the river by accident and drowned. She overdosed on river water, nothing else. End of story. End of investigation." Cowdrey stacked the pictures neatly, stuffed them into a manila envelope, and slid it into the top drawer of his desk, ceremoniously locking it. He glanced impatiently at his Rolex watch. What county sheriff can afford a Rolex?

"Have you considered that she may have committed suicide, officer?"

"Hold on there." Now it was Cowdrey's turn to bristle. The term *officer* didn't fit his self image. He was an *elected representative of the people,* in his mind, the most important. He was sheriff, after all. He was *The Sheriff.*

Composing himself, Cowdrey rose and reached for his sunglasses and hat. "Like I said, her parents are due into the Big City Airport on Thursday to claim the body. I'll be meeting the plane. And, unless they suggest a possible suicide, the case is closed. If they want any further investigation, and I doubt they will, I'll decide whether or not to take your statement. Until then, the case is, as I said, closed. End of discussion.

"Now, if you will excuse me, I have rounds to make. Give my regards to your boss." He carefully placed his sunglasses on his nose and pulled on his Stetson. Glancing at his reflection in the window, he adjusted the hat, grunted his approval, and turned his back on Laura. With his best John Wayne imitation, he high heeled it out to Stella's office leaving Laura staring out the window.

"Stella, I'm headed for the reservation to have a powwow with the elders. Get it, powwow? If you need me, call me. Don't need me, okay?" Stella nodded without looking up. The Sheriff moved out into the hall and out of the building.

Laura was steamed, or in today's vernacular, she was pissed. She unclenched her fist and carefully smoothed out the note she had taken from the water bottle. "No reason to show that jerk," she muttered, placing the note in her jacket pocket.

Finally, she stood up, took a deep breath, walked out of the inner office and crossed to where Hazel Mertz was pretending to study reports that covered her crossword puzzle.

"What is that man's problem?" Laura demanded. "Why wouldn't he even consider the woman might have committed suicide?"

Hazel smiled at Laura. In small bureaucracies, secretary-dispatchers, are privy to all information in one form or another; letters, faxes, phone calls, e-mails, and, naturally, gossip. Everything, at some point in time, comes across the secretary's desk. No exception for Hazel.

"Look," she said, not too unkindly, "Sheriff Cowdrey has a lot of things to deal with in his life. Call it a life, if you will. He thinks everything is crucial to his re-election. Everything is about getting re-elected. This gives him power. There are rumors that his next re-election may not be a slam-dunk. That incident with your boss and George Otis didn't help…what did the *Buzz* call it, "The Veterans Day Massacre?" That didn't help at all. It was a total embarrassment for the sheriff and the department.

"Anyway, an accidental drowning," she went on, "is no big deal. It happens occasionally. A couple phone calls, a few reports, a small article in the newspaper and it's over. A suicide involves a serious investigation. Maybe other agencies get involved and step on toes, which could mean piles of reports and headlines in the newspaper, especially if it is someone important. Apparently this woman was big in the ski world. Besides, if you suggest suicide, somebody will suggest homicide."

Laura was stunned. She suddenly realized that she was probably the last person to see the woman alive. Would she be a *person of interest?*

"Who said anything about murder?"

"Hopefully, no one has or will." Hazel went back to shuffling the papers on her desk. Laura walked toward the door and turned.

"If you need a seven letter word for sheriff, in that puzzle of yours, try asshole. Or is that two words?" Hazel Mertz snorted, choked, and finally exploded with laughter.

Laura stormed out into the fresh air and fading light. The sun had dropped below the mountain ridge. Streaks of red caroming off the bottoms of a few puffy cotton ball clouds rising over the western range didn't even help her mood. Laura pulled herself up on the huge cement staircase outside the county building, got out her cell phone, punched *Menu* and then *Contacts.* She had to talk to someone. Her father's number was first on the list. She knew that his influence, or at least his connections, reached this far west, but what was she going to ask him to do? Order a hit on a county sheriff? For the first time all day she smiled. She almost got the giggles.

The next number was Professor Leonard Russell's, but he had enough to deal with; keeping the college afloat, his kids and, with any luck, his love life.

Ranger Ted Miller was number three. Even if he answered his cell phone he'd be up on the Meadows with his beloved beaver. If indeed, a signal could reach that far into the mountains. And what in the world would she say to him?

The fourth number was Brad Hawkins' and Laura was sure she could find Bradley at the Roadhouse. He would be glad to listen until he had too much to drink. Then it would be payback time and Laura would be forced to hear about his pathetic life history for the zillionth time. Pathetic wasn't fair, because she did care for him, but it was getting— what, boring?

Maggie's Corner was the last number. She knew Maggie would be working. "Hi, Maggie. Laura."

"Hi, Laurie. What's up?"

"I know you work until ten, but could you meet me at the Roadhouse after you get off?"

"Hold on." After a pause Maggie was back on the phone. "George will cover for me tonight. With the regular crew working we should be fine. Where are you?"

"I'm in Big City…just talked to *your* distinguished County Sheriff. I'm headed back to Towne on 64."

"Be careful…a lot of critters on that road…especially in the evening. Should take you about forty minutes. Don't know what this is all about, but I would guess that, if our sheriff is involved, he just might have upset you a touch. Don't worry about it, he does that to everybody. I'll see you at the Roadhouse."

"Thanks, Maggie. Thanks much." Laura closed her cell phone and made her way to her pickup. "Bet there'll be a parking ticket on the window. No doubt in my mind," she said to herself.

><

By the time Laura negotiated CR64 she had calmed down. She had gone to see Sheriff Cowdrey with good intentions and had left feeling humiliated. The only other time she had felt that degraded was in the ninth grade when she had finally gotten up enough courage to ask a boy to the high school Sadie Hawkins dance and he laughed at her. It was two years before she ever went out on a date.

What exactly had she wanted to accomplish by going to the Sheriff? Nothing would change for the woman—she was dead. If she fell in—she was dead. If she jumped in— she was dead. If somebody threw her in—she was still dead. How dead can you be? Still, Laura was plagued with meaningless *what ifs*. Suicides torment the living, whether intended or not. Still there was an empty sensation in Laura's gut. Maybe it was guilt. Or, maybe it was the helpless feeling, that you were fighting the inevitable and, that no matter what you had done nothing would have made a difference. The end of the story was written before the story line played out.

No, that was not what Laura believed at all. Predestination was bunk, but she also knew that railing against past actions was a waste of time. Suddenly she could hear her father talking to her around a campfire or in a canoe: *"Laura, there are no alternative life paths…no parallel universes like the science fiction writers would have you believe. Do what you can. Do what you think best at the moment. If it doesn't work out, try to do it better next time. Learn, and then get on with your life. Sadly, it's probably the only one you'll ever have. How about another sandwich?"*

◆◀

Laura slid her truck into a parking place behind the Roadhouse and checked her front brush guard for critters. Finding none, she walked to the split-rail fence and looked down at the boat landing some twenty feet below. A large slab of cement extended below the surface of the water where trailers could be backed up to load or unload.

Based on the water currents Laura decided that there were two places where a body could wash up on shore. Rapids from across the river made an s-curve as they swung back by the landing. Most oarsmen used that approach to the takeout. A body could be deposited there in the same manner.

And just upstream, on the landing side of the river, was a cluster of ten to twelve large cottonwood trees that protruded out and over the current causing a sweeper on the upside and a gently eddy below their bent trunks. After the long, torturous run down the whitewater, a body could float peacefully, circling gently until discovered.

Laura pictured the young woman's dead body face up, first floating over the cement-slab landing and then into the lee of the cottonwoods. Suddenly, Laura saw the body in both spots simultaneously. With a snap of her neck and a violent shake of her head, the bloated corpses disappeared. She looked again for the woman, saw nothing, and made her way slowly around to the front doors of the Roadhouse. God, did she need a drink. Maybe food was a better idea, as she hadn't eaten all day. But Laura chose the cocktail lounge, a.k.a. bar with dance floor. She could always order something to eat since the kitchen served both sides of the establishment. Brad Hawkins sat at the bar staring at his reflection in the back mirror. Laura walked up behind him, draped her arms around his neck and ordered a Myers's and Coke.

"Sit down Laura. I'll buy," Brad offered. Mike gave Laura a questioning look.

"No, no. Set up a tab and send my drink over to that back booth," Laura pointed with a turn of her head. "I'll buy Mr. Hawkins a beer."

"Aw, damn, Laura. You never sit and drink with me anymore. You don't realize, I could be the love of your life."

"Bradley, unfortunately you *are* the love of my life, my only love, but I'm meeting somebody."

"Hey, he's obviously not here yet. You've got time for one drink. We'll talk about your run in Richard's new boat today. How about giant cutthroats, dead bodies, or double hauling a line? How about the pending doom of the world as we know it?" He gasped for breath, almost whining. Not a pretty sound from an ex-Big Ten linebacker. Not a pretty sound from anyone. "I'll even say something nice about your damn Republicans."

"Bradley, why don't you go back to Ohio to your wife and kids?" Laura asked as she moved toward the back booth.

"Where have I heard that before?" Brad mumbled, draining his beer. He nodded toward Mike and pointed to the empty mug.

Laura and the waitress arrived at the U-shaped booth at the same time. Laura slid across the worn vinyl and nudged up against Buckheart Beastly who stretched and half opened his eyes. She rubbed his jaw line with her index finger. Bucky stretched again and began to purr. Suddenly, he was fully awake and aware of his undignified behavior. He immediately stopped purring and jumped down, "harrumph." He slowly scanned the room, decided no one was watching, and rubbed up against Laura's leg before leisurely making his way across the dance floor toward the front door, leaving Laura smiling. Bucky stood by the entrance as Maggie walked in. He slipped out between her legs to begin his nightly tour of Towne.

Maggie noticed Laura in the corner, gave her a half wave, and sat down next to Brad. She nodded toward Mike, "I'll try a Belgium Witbier. Bradley, dear, how are you?"

"Oh, hi. Guess you're the person Laura's looking for. She's in the back corner ignoring me." Suddenly, Brad brightened. "Why don't I buy you both a drink and join you?" he asked hopefully. Maggie thanked Mike and picked up the beer schooner—a thin orange slice floated near the top. She took a sip and got down from the bar stool.

"Bradley, why don't you go back to Ohio to your wife and kids?"

"Déjà vu," Brad said to Mike who only shrugged.

Maggie eased herself into the booth across from Laura while brushing black cat hair from the seat.

"You made it," Laura offered. Maggie nodded.

"What's up?"

After several false starts, and a second drink, Laura related her story from the moment Richard Whendelstat asked her to test his drift boats to Sheriff Cowdrey telling her what she should do with her story, drift boats and all. She didn't include the floating body scene.

Maggie was an excellent listener. She was not only interested in Laura's story, but she truly cared about her. Maggie made everyone, small children to aging seniors, want to share their experiences with her. They felt she was genuinely interested and, in most cases, she was.

Maggie wasn't much of a "what-if person" but ever since Laura had barreled up to the store in her dying pickup, Maggie often wondered if her own daughter, dead at two, would have resembled Laura in looks and personality? Maggie cherished the memories of her child and couldn't help but wonder whether Laura wasn't her reincarnated daughter. Or, God making amends for taking her baby?

"Nonsense…total and complete nonsense," Maggie reproached herself silently. "That's repulsive. What's the matter with me? Laura is Laura and I love her for that, not for any of my stupid, screwed-up fantasies."

Not noticing the disgusted look on Maggie's face, Laura

continued. "I went to the sheriff's office thinking I was doing the right thing. My first mistake. I felt I should do something for the woman…at least for her family. Somehow it got all turned around. Made me mad as hell the way your condescending Sheriff Cowdrey treated me. I took it personal. I admit it. Maybe I was just trying to ease my conscience for not dragging that woman's ass out of the canyon before she killed herself…saying something that would convince her to come along." Laura's voice faded with another sip of her drink.

Putting her thoughts aside, Maggie smiled. "Laura, you had no idea she wanted to kill herself." Trying to lighten the mood, she said, "It's true, my mother was a true cynic for such a nice woman, but she always said, 'No good deed ever goes unpunished.' A warning not to expect too much from being a good person."

Changing the subject, Laura asked, "What is it between you and the Sheriff?"

Maggie suppressed a mild obscenity. "Well, we go back a long way…I don't ever remember him not being around. We started together in grade school and neither of us ever left the area. I wouldn't say he holds any real animosity towards me, but he knows that I'm aware of things, things that he wouldn't appreciate coming to light."

"Does he know things that *you* wouldn't like coming to light?" Laura smiled and raised her eyebrows.

"Good question. I'm sure he does, but I'm not the one trying to hold public office. Maybe he could embarrass me because of some, as I like to put it, youthful indiscretions," Maggie laughed, "certainly nothing that could do me any harm…not anymore. I'd like to think I've cleared up all my messes."

"I can't believe you were ever in *too* many messes."

"No matter, but Sheriff Cowdrey might not be above making

life difficult for my friends. He'd get even in a minute if I screwed up his precious political career.

"His reaction really has nothing to do with you," Maggie thought a second. "Well, maybe it does. As Mertz said, you could be creating more legwork or paperwork for Cowdrey if he were forced into a full-blown investigation. God knows, he could use a little legwork." They both laughed loud enough to catch Brad's attention. He dropped off the bar stool and headed directly toward them. Laura put up both hands in mock horror while Maggie gently shook her head. Brad did a military left turn towards the men's room.

At the exact same moment the two women said, "Why doesn't he go back to Ohio to his wife and kids?" and they both cracked up.

❦

"What makes you so sure it was suicide and not an accident?" Maggie asked. The conversation turned serious again, but Laura's tone was not as dire as before.

"First, she went out of her way to convince me that she was camping in the canyon. I checked. No signs of a campsite anywhere near there. And, the Sheriff said they found a tent and sleeping bag in her rental car up on the rim.

"And talking to her, she sounded almost euphoric. I read somewhere, probably in *Screen Star* for God's sake, that people who attempt suicide are crying out for help. It's help they want, not death. But people who actually commit suicide have come to grips with their situation. They are happy, maybe relieved, with their decision to end it all. I think they call it a *leap to health*."

"A leap to health?" Maggie looked doubtful.

"Yeah, instead of a leap off a cliff, I suppose. A buffalo jump... lemmings flying off into space? Anyway," Laura went on, "they've convinced themselves that death is the best alternative. They've made up their minds. They're comfortable with that decision. It's all very logical to them." Laura searched Maggie's eyes for confirmation. People can be understanding, but not understand. Maggie usually got it.

"Well, it makes sense to me," Maggie responded, "but you say she was euphoric? Wouldn't someone that had just scaled down that cliff without the right gear and lived, be euphoric? I've seen it. That cliff is a beast. I've heard it compared to the Black Canyon of the Gunnison...maybe worse."

"You're right. Euphoric is too strong of a word. Obviously I'm trying to prove my case," Laura smiled. "At peace, maybe that describes it better. She was at peace. And there's one thing I didn't tell you. This morning, when I pulled off above the *Gulp*, I found the water bottle I gave her, with a note inside. I know...I know most people who commit suicide don't leave notes. Guess they don't believe their life is worth enough to explain why they're ending it."

"Goodness, you got a lot out of that magazine...about suicide, I mean. I didn't realize you read *Screen Star*."

"Ah, probably it was a *Field and Stream* or maybe it was info from my freshmen course in psychology at Wisconsin," Laura said with a smirk. "Aren't you impressed with my credentials?" Laura reached into her pocket, took out the wrinkled slip of paper and tried to smooth it flat. She pushed it over to Maggie, who read it, paused for a long moment before saying, "Really, her note doesn't explain anything.

"I was a stranger, the last person she talked to, and if she was thinking about suicide, she knew I was the last person she would..." Laura's voice faded off.

After a long silence, Maggie refolded the note and handed it to Laura. "I'll phone the Sheriff first thing in the morning and ask to talk to her parents. Will you trust me on this one, Laura?" Laura shrugged.

"I'll feel them out and, if I think any good will come of it, I'll tell them what you suspect. If they're just looking for closure, I won't say a thing. No use causing any more pain. If they believe their daughter took her own life and want some sort of confirmation, I'll have them get in touch with you. Agreed?"

Laura looked visibly relieved. "Agreed. Maybe that's what Cowdrey had in mind all along." Laura paused, "No, I really doubt it. Think he'll let you talk to the parents?"

"Sure. I'll offer to go with him. He's not too comfortable consoling folks, especially if they're not voters...no upside for him. That's probably a bit harsh. He's not all bad. Sort of a mixed bag, full of contradictory emotions. Rather like all of us. How's that for psycho-babble?" Maggie grinned. "Don't you ever tell him what I said," she winked. "I do *not* want to lose my edge with the man. I don't want him to think I'm going soft."

"Maybe you're not going soft...maybe it's that funny looking beer you're drinking," Laura smiled.

"Right. Anyway, he'll know I've heard your side of the story and the way he treated you. I'll make him sweat a little...or a lot. Then he'll agree." Maggie said.

Looking around, they noticed Brad had left and Bucky had returned to sit by the jukebox to patiently wait for his booth and a fallen pretzel or two.

◀●▶

On Thursday morning, before Maggie met the parents of the late ski champ and long before Bradley Hawkins hit the Whoosh with his fishing clients from Tennessee, three newspapers landed on Sheriff Cowdrey's desk each with an article on the "Former American Olympic Ski Hopeful." A four-sentence obituary in *USA Today* said she tragically drowned in a canoe accident. The *Capital City Correspondent,* had her falling off a houseboat. And holding to tradition, the *Buzz* had plastered howling headlines above her picture, suggesting foul play in the mysterious case of a former world champion snow skier who...

...died right here in our own Whoosh River. Speaking on condition of anonymity, a high ranking County official indicated that further investigation into the baffling incident might be justified.

A Charlie Brown *aaaugh* went up, not from a two-dimensional cartoon character, but from a two-hundred-and-sixty pound piece of humanity known as Sheriff Oscar Cowdrey. At the time he was wearing his Smokey Bear hat, and did in fact resemble a comic strip character.

Legend has it that the sheriff's distress was heard throughout the Watershed; arousing the attention of a gray wolf passing through; ending the playful yipping of a pack of coyotes, who stared at each other in absolute amazement; and scaring the bee-Jeezus out of a young lynx family foraging for breakfast. A lone bull moose, wallowing peacefully in a beaver pond, was hit with a sudden case of indigestion. And before the vibrations faded, another roar exploded:

MERTZ GET IN HERE!

CHAPTER 27: The Meadows

Laura pulled up against the far bank, away from the sheer drop off to the Whoosh River below. Setting the hand brake on her truck, she shifted into park with little room for another vehicle to pass, but on Canyon Road there were few vehicles.

On her way to the meadows she had carefully negotiated the narrow mountain road above the dam. The plan was to fly fish for some gullible little brook trout, maybe cutthroat. Heavy weather showed signs of the coming change of seasons. Patches of fog chased each another through the canyon leaving an occasional spray of moisture on Laura's windshield. Conditions were perfect. No scaring the spooky little trout today.

Laura asked Maggie's cousin, Charlie where Doc Walters had gone over the cliff on Canyon Road. Charlie had been the one to pull Doc Walters' pink Lincoln out of the rock crevasse shortly after medics brought the doctor's body up and whisked it away to Big City County Hospital.

Charlie's directions weren't needed. Someone had carefully wedged a wooden cross between two boulders just over the road's edge. The piece which looked like Rufus Jefferson's craftsmanship, had been routed *Doctor Walters*. Wild raspberry canes, unmolested by the local bear population, intertwined the cross. The canes were nurtured by mountain runoff, diverted through a culvert built under the road and passing by the monument.

Leaving the engine running, Laura got out of her pickup. Gazing over the steep embankment, she could see that Charlie had done a good job cleaning up the wreckage. Laura was no tracker, but she did see a few scraped rocks that indicated something unnatural had occurred. Pressing her lips together hard, Laura nodded and slowly walked away, leaving the ripe raspberries untouched.

Even though Doctor Walters was well known in the area, Laura had only met him once when she had brought a fishing client to his office. The man, obviously a weight lifter, wouldn't even let her extract a small imbedded fish hook from his muscular forearm that was a tanning booth shade of orange. Laura wondered whether his entire body was colored orange. The client insisted the fishing trip be cut short and that Laura rush him down the river to the nearest hospital. In truth, he screamed instructions at her and calmed down only after she threatened to hit him broadside with an oar. Laura convinced Mr. Weightlifter that Doc Walters was probably more qualified than anyone at the hospital and a lot closer and then proceeded to row down the river at a leisurely pace, taking the scenic route, whenever possible.

After Doc was through with the injured patient, a total of ten minutes including paperwork, the heroic fisherman laid an enormous tip on Laura, presumably to keep her mouth shut about his medical emergency, or at least, how he had handled it. Naturally, after composing himself, he reverted to character and offered to buy her a drink at the Roadhouse.

><

Laura was deathly afraid of the medical profession herself. On the theorem that *if it doesn't hurt, don't mess with it,* she religiously avoided doctors. Dentists, that was a different story. Her parents had spent big bucks straightening her teeth. As some sort of repayment, she felt obliged to keep them in decent shape. She wasn't at all vain, but she did know that her 'dentally enhanced' smile was one of her best assets, and she wasn't afraid to use it. Not that she enjoyed sitting in a dentist chair. Her grip marks were imprinted on the armrests of every dentist's chair she ever sat in, displaying her fear over even the simplest of oral procedures, including cleaning.

><

Laura had heard about the good-looking young doctor, Tim Brandon, who took over Doc Walters' practice. She envisioned a married intern with two children, and a wife who had put him through college, then medical school, by working at a laundromat. Now haggard, after raising the children by herself, she would soon be dumped for a trophy wife. No idea if this was true of Doctor Brandon, but it was just one more reason for the somewhat cynical Laura to stay clear of doctors, young or old.

><

After an ungodly number of narrow switchbacks, Laura's pickup finally emerged from the canyon into the serenity of the upper meadow, leaving behind the constant roar of the river raging through the gorge far below. Asked which she enjoyed more, river or meadow, she knew that she would never abandon her beloved river, but she also understood why Ranger Ted Miller was so captivated by these headwaters.

There were in fact two meadows with just a short climb between them, at 7,500 and 7,600 feet. These grasslands resembled a huge marshy soup bowl, a catchment of sorts. The entire area was fed by melting snow from the surrounding mountains; water that ran in hundreds of rivulets to gather behind beaver dams. Only a few of these mountain streams were big enough to sustain trout, and those only up to the timberline. To catch fish between the meadows and the timberline one must be willing, and able, to boulder hop, climb and scramble to find holding spots big enough for small fish. There is no fly casting as such. Using the old English method of dapping, a long pole is extended over a likely hold where a dry fly is bounced up and down on the surface. Small brook trout and cutthroats are deemed naive because they will make a mad dash at most any artificial fly before grabbing it and darting off. Understand that at these altitudes small fish have very little food to seize upon and no time to enjoy it, at best four months in an unusually warm summer. If you realize it only takes two or three years to reach maturity, reproduce and then die, you'll know why they seem eager to attack a piece of fabric tied around a metal hook that suddenly appears before them—regardless how unrealistic it appears. Given the theory that any animal is only as smart as is necessary to propagate the species; then these fish, like most other creatures, are not stupid, they're survivalists. They have spent centuries evolving to do just that. Survive.

Most topographical maps show Canyon Road paralleling the Whoosh River on its east side and ending at a campground, a very primitive area at the foot of the meadows. At the far end of the flat-grassy tent area, there are parking spots for horse trailers. Here, a usually empty, makeshift corral waits the next windstorm that could easily level it. A wooden trail-head sign marks the beginning of a path for hikers and horses, a trail that leads to old trapper Ratzigg's cabin and on up the mountains that surround the meadow. This range claims two 13,000 foot peaks, but most hold in the 11,000 foot reach, topping out just above the timberline.

With a monster truck or Jeep, and plenty of clearance, you could follow the hiking trail to the cabin for a majestic view. This day, rolling clouds tumbling through the canyon had replaced the panoramic view with a ponderous all-encompassing grey, reducing visibility to less than two hundred feet. Laura wasn't about to risk her truck just to prove she could make it to the top of the range. She could stare into the haze right where she was. If it cleared later in the day, the cabin and the view were only a short hike away.

By the time Laura had finished rigging her fishing rod, the mist had turned to a light rain, making even the outline of the mountains invisible. She admired a beaver pond, new since last year, and probably loaded with fish. Trout dimpled the surface, making bigger circles than the small raindrops.

As the light rain diminished, breaks appeared in the clouds to the west, showing pale blue patches of sky. A brisk breeze from the northwest, probably a sign of an approaching high-pressure cell, began shoving the cloud cover out of the meadows. Long rays of sunlight appeared, bathing the marshy land and the surrounding mountains in a muted glow. Laura often watched people fumble with their cameras attempting to capture such a moment. She wondered if these amateur photographers wouldn't appreciate the scene more if they just put down the camera and looked around. Laura knew she was guilty of the same sin and wondered what she had missed while tying on a #22 midge pattern to a #7x tippet. She continually had to remind herself to slow down and appreciate the beauty around her. In the Whoosh River Watershed the *around* was mostly spectacular.

On her first trip with Professor Russell to the meadows, he had thrown out the line: *Piscator non solum piscatur.* "There is more to fishing than catching fish," she translated silently. The man, schooled in Latin, apparently was attempting to impress her. She didn't have the heart to tell him that she knew what it meant.

Anyway, it's probably a little corny for somebody as young as Laura Menard, but wasn't it Mac Davis who sang about taking time to stop and smell the roses? Come to think about it, it's far too corny for anybody, of any age. But, more and more, Laura had come to appreciate and cherish the countryside she had called home for the last three years.

Because the meadows were so difficult to reach by the casual traveler, the animal life was afforded more protection from humans than in most other regions. The meadows were alive with wildlife, not just beaver and trout. In the fall, Elk, known as wapiti (white rump) to the Shawnee, held their annual mating ritual, bugling and all. At times the noises from the oversexed males sounded more like the slaughtering of pigs than sounds from a musical instrument, but please don't be saying that to someone who has just traveled nine hundred miles to experience this autumn ritual.

No antelope herds lived above the reservoir. Black bear were plentiful, but grizzlies had not been seen in the area since the early 1930s. There is no record of buffalo ever living in the meadows—it was simply too high for the prairie loving creatures. In the 1980s, several moose were transplanted from Minnesota, Ontario, and British Columbia. When the batteries gave out on their radio collars, the moose, all but one male, were widely scattered, presumably headed back home—a very long trip. Why the one bull stayed is pure speculation, but it's a known fact the meadows seem to attract isolationists.

While the experiment with moose failed, the transplanting of Canadian lynx was a success and the cats thrived.

Ranger Miller had found wolf prints from a huge male and a much smaller female the previous fall. No sign of them since. Maybe it was a pair out of Yellowstone National Park looking for space to start a new pack.

Zeke Astor claimed that his grandfather and Jim Bridger, while hunting elk, came across a herd of unicorn in the marshes. Since there is no record of Bridger ever being in the Whoosh River Watershed, we probably shouldn't believe old Zeke about the unicorn. He does have a propensity to exaggerate.

The meadows have had their share of natural disasters, mostly due to lightening strikes and straight-line winds reaching over one-hundred-and-twenty miles per hour. That's equal to a category three hurricane. One such storm, a blow-down in local terminology, leveled a thousand acres of pine trees like a set of dominos toppling. As this was an opportunity for an ongoing experiment and an open-air laboratory, the BLM left the trees where they had fallen, clearing trails through the area only when necessary.

The entire watershed is positioned on a minor geologic fault zone adjacent to Yellowstone National Park's major fault. With only a few strike-slip lines, not much damage would be done to the meadows—not until the *Big One,* earthquake or volcano, strikes under Yellowstone. It might be interesting to see the Whoosh River run north instead of south. That's assuming it would run at all.

Probably the most visible damage to the Whoosh Meadows was a *controlled* fire set by the U.S. Forest Service to burn out underbrush. It quickly gained momentum to qualify for *uncontrolled* status. The *Buzz* had a field day with that one. The story didn't have legs, as no lives were lost or homes destroyed, and plant life began regenerating within days. Years later, burned trees still tower over the new growth. Wood decays slowly at these altitudes.

If the proposed removal of the Whoosh River Dam proceeded, the meadows would not be altered. What influences the meadows the most is the differing amounts of winter snow accumulation and runoff the following summer.

><

Laura threaded her two-weight rod with an old beat-up fly line, pulling it through the guides before tying on a leader and a small imitation of a grasshopper. While there are no fields of grain to attract locusts, it wasn't that unusual for weather updrafts to lift terrestrials to the high meadows from the rangeland far below. Those that landed on the beaver ponds made a feast for finned inhabitants that watched and waited.

Preoccupied with thoughts of fish, the meadows and Doc Walters, Laura screamed when Horse gave her a nudge from behind sending her staggering three or four steps before doing a half turn and flopping down on the soft grass.

"You crow bait, don't ever sneak up on me like that again." Some animals sound like they can laugh. Horse really could laugh and did. Laura checked to make sure her fly rod wasn't splintered, and then laughed at herself.

"You dang near scared me to death. What are you doing up here all saddled up and rarin' to go?" She looked around for Ranger Ted Miller, current guardian of Horse, but saw no sign of him. Nobody owned Horse, as Horse will tell you once he masters English. And there was no sign of Ted.

Laura dusted herself off and turning to Horse said, "Well, come on you old retard, I might have an apple or two in the truck." As she rummaged through her cooler, Horse ran up the trail a few yards and stood and watched Laura.

"You don't want an apple? Unbelievable." Horse snorted, stepped backwards, and shook his head from side to side.

"What is this, your Lassie follow me act?" With a hint of concern, Laura stored her rod in the back, under the truck topper, and followed Horse.

"I'm not out for a stroll. Come here, you bag of bones." Horse hesitated and then came back. Laura had never seen anyone but Ted ride him, but she swung up in the saddle just as Horse bolted for the cabin. With her feet hanging short of the stirrups, she never had any sense of control. As they crested the last knoll before the cabin, Laura spotted Ted's Jeep. Then she noticed that the porch had collapsed at one end. Ted, half sitting, half lying against the rubble, appeared dazed. Laura slid out of the saddle and knelt beside him. With nothing more he could do, Horse wandered off.

"You okay, Ted?" the obligatory dumb question to stall for time while she tried to assess the problem. Ted glanced at Laura and then seemed to lose consciousness. He had obviously vomited, at least once. Worried, Laura tried to remember her first aid instruction, a class required by all river guides before they could be licensed. It consisted of a brief two-hour seminar with no test at the end—only a certificate of attendance. She had a current CPR card from the Red Cross, but breathing didn't seem to be Ted's problem.

"Where is the indomitable Ranger Anna Pigeon when you need her?" she asked an unconscious Ted, referring to Nevada Barr's fictional law enforcement ranger, trained in emergency medical care. Laura checked Ted's heartbeat while monitoring his breathing. Both were normal. A large bump on his head seemed to swell as she watched, but she saw no bleeding. Without returning to her truck, she had no ice to apply to the contusion.

"Wake up, Ted. You probably have a concussion." To her surprise, Ted came to.

"What? Who are you?" a dazed Ted mumbled. "Oh, you're Laura...er, Laurie."

"Yeah, yeah, I'm Laura and you need help." She slipped a radio from his belt holster. "Did you get this dumb thing fixed yet?" Apparently he had, as it connected to Headquarters and Sid Rosenburg who sent help immediately.

"Ted, wake up. Ted, what happened to you?"

"Tripped on the corner post...whole roof came down...top of me," Ted stuttered. Changing direction he asked, "...will you marry me?"

Ted drifted in and out of consciousness several times while they waited for the BLM helicopter that would air-lift him to Capital City and the University Hospital. Besides the proposal of marriage, Ted offered to let her work on his research paper. No, she didn't have to type. He even suggested they go skinny-dipping in his favorite beaver pond and then they could honeymoon at his folk's new Amish home in Nebraska. Laura knew his parents were dead. His father had died a few weeks before, and his parents had lived in a ritzy Detroit suburb, not some Amish community in Nebraska.

"Ted, that is the most romantic marriage proposal I've ever gotten," Laura laughed.

"Shoot, I guess it's my first…and it comes from a man who just had his head caved in."

While the helicopter lifted off toward Capital City, Laura stripped Horse of saddle, blanket, bags, and reins. Dumping the gear into Ted's Jeep, she headed back down the trail. Horse followed her and occasionally ran ahead as she headed back down the trail in her truck. District Ranger Rosenburg was sending two backcountry rangers from Big City with a horse trailer. One to haul Horse to Ranger Headquarters and the other to bring Ted's Jeep back. Tomorrow Rosenburg would round up a couple of summer volunteers, probably with college degrees and no jobs, and send them up to rebuild the porch roof.

It wasn't fair to take a person too seriously after a porch had fallen on his head, but some of the things Ted babbled, while holding her hand, were kind of cute—especially the idea of skinny-dipping. Semiconscious, he actually turned red with embarrassment. Why did the men in her life become so *flustrated* (a word she had concocted, combining fluster and frustrated) around her? Well, not all men were shy about their intentions. What about Richard Whendelstat, ex-stockbroker-turned-fishing-entrepreneur? What about Brad Hawkins, ex-school-teacher-turned-river-guide and ski-bum? What about that funny-dressed-guy on a bike? Men, go figure!

The sky had cleared with all but a few delicate, wispy-white cirrus clouds. Stands of Aspen with slender gray-white trunks and bark fissured with rough black scar tissue stood in stark contrast to the mountain pines now being decimated by pine bark beetles. The Aspen's oval-shaped golden leaves meant fall was on its way.

"Yes, it's beautiful," Laura thought, "all the ingredients of a fifty-cent post card or a fifty-dollar coffee table book."

Still, she missed the blazing brilliance of the Midwest hardwoods; the oaks, the elms and maples. The blending of colors, appearing anywhere from late August through October, with shades of orange, fire engine red, maroon, and purple intermixed with the yellows of poplar and birch, cousins of the western aspen. On a sunny day, with a white-capped lake, the scene is outrageously beautiful. A little home sick for Wisconsin, Laura imagined black and white Holsteins grazing in pastures near a traditional farmhouse and red barn with attached silo.

When they reached the beaver pond, Horse foraged for lunch while Laura took her fly rod from the truck, chipped off the artificial hopper and tied on a #18 Adams parachute dry fly. She carefully worked her way down the face of the beaver dam. Unlike older dams in the meadow, this one was not weathered and ignored. Fresh beaver cuttings indicated recent work. One rivulet seeped through the upper structure—a minor repair job. A steady flow of water discharged from the base of the sturdy construction, water that would meander until joining the main branch of the Whoosh.

Laura flipped the Adams up on the backwater. It landed with barely a ripple. The water was crystal clear, but because of the muddy bottom it actually appeared black. The artificial fly floated for a second before disappearing in a swirl. Laura lifted the tip of her rod, felt the weight of a fish, and then heard the scream of the reel. For more than a minute, the fish raced back and forth behind the dam before diving deep into the mud. With the lightest of bamboo poles and the thinnest of fluorocarbon tippets, Laura didn't dare apply too much pressure to the line. After a minute of holding, she was afraid the fish had buried her fly into a sunken tree branch and made an escape. Laura patiently increased the stress on the line until the brook trout, still connected, broke water. In midair it twisted around the leader and plunged back through the surface and the supposed safety of the mud. But the fight was over. The fish had exhausted itself with that last burst of energy and came slowly to the edge of the dam. Laura scrambled to the top, retrieving line as she climbed. She carefully unhooked the twelve-inch speckled colored trout. Holding it gently, she worked the fish back and forth under the surface, forcing water and oxygen through the gills. Before deciding whether to keep him for breakfast, the trout was revived enough to struggle in Laura's hand. She released her grip and the brookie disappeared into the black depths.

No one has ever been able to describe a brook trout without making it sound like a five year old had just painted its picture. Only nature has the ability to combine the extreme tones, wavy lines and spots on this fish, without creating a laughable cartoon character, or a creature from an alien planet. Fantasize, if you can, a brown to olive green fish with dark gray or black squiggly lines covering the back and top part of the tail. Apply random spots of red and yellow, occasionally circled by blue or purple halos, to its sides. Then add a belly changing from yellow to orange to a reddish color depending on the season. Got it? No? Go find a picture.

As Laura was about to cast again, a large ball-shaped object bobbed up in the middle of the pool. A beaver, with fur flattened back over its head, making it look like a Wildroot Cream Oil Hair Tonic advertisement from the fifties, stared at Horse, who ignored the wet intruder.

"You one of Ranger Ted's buddies?" Laura asked softly. In one continuous motion, the beaver jerked his neck around to see who was talking, arched his back and dove, slapping the flat of his tail on the water surface as he disappeared. The amazingly loud sound startled a bald eagle perched high in a ponderosa pine. The massive bird had been watching to see if Laura's released fish would survive the ordeal or float to the top for an effortless supper. The eagle flapped his wings several times struggling to lift off and away from the noise. Regaining his composure and he hoped his dignity, he circled twice and disappeared toward the mountains in search of a different meal. There has to be an easier way to make a living.

Laura smiled and broke down her fly rod. She heard the rattle and squeak of the Forest Service truck and horse trailer as it neared the end of Canyon Road. Enough of nature, she needed a beer, and stopped to uncap a Bud Lite from her cooler. Without her help, and Horse's consent, there was no way the two rangers were going to get Horse into that trailer—although, it might be fun to watch them try. She gulped two quick mouthfuls and putting her beer back in the cooler, picked out a loose length of rope for a tether, grabbed a couple more apples and went to help.

CHAPTER 28: Margaret Elizabeth

Things had certainly changed around Maggie's Corner since that day three years ago when Laura Menard flew into the parking lot in a cloud of loose gravel and dirt. The dirt washed away, but the dents are still visible on the side of the building.

Before Laura appeared in the Whoosh River Watershed, Maggie had renovated and enlarged her main building for the first time since she bought it. Even her upstairs living quarters got an update. It was no longer vintage 1950s. Six tourist cabins were modernized. They were no longer sporting a 1930s look. Maggie replaced the old fuel tanks and pumps with self-service environmentally friendly models and was the first in the area to offer Ethanol. But inevitably, when events are put in motion they seem to build momentum until nothing stands in the way. It was Nevada Barr that said, *"You can get either angry or morose but it won't stop or even slow the change."*

When Laura showed up, Maggie was in possession of an old McKenzie wooden drift boat that George Otis was caulking and refinishing to sell. Laura convinced them to put it in the water and before long she was guiding fishermen down the Whoosh River for, what Maggie thought, exorbitant fees.

"Geesh, you're just taking them out fishing," was Maggie's standard remark. Soon she had to decide whether to order new drift boats and hire more guides to expand her business. Come to think of it, exorbitant fees weren't all bad.

Laura had been at Maggie's nearly two years when Jolene Ouimet and her husband Warren appeared in a huge motor home—a titanic example of motorized locomotion.

"Maggie, I'm Jolene," she introduced herself. "You probably don't remember me, but my mom said you used to baby-sit for me years ago." Maggie stared blankly. "Seems that my mom's brother's cousin was married to your mom's brother's cousin... does that make us cousins of some sort? Mom always said it did. We moved out of the area when I was young...very young. Guess everybody kinda lost contact."

"Jolene, I have so many cousins that you're certainly welcome to be one...related or not," was Maggie's less than enthusiastic reply, but Jolene seem relieved and introduced her to Warren.

As it turned out, they were in the midst of an extended vacation after losing their jobs with a lumber company in Washington State. Environmentalists, or *tree huggers* as the laid-off workers called them, had systematically destroyed the company. Fortunately, it was only a small part of a worldwide conglomerate which had protected the key employee's pensions and given them each the option of a transfer or a large severance check. Jolene and Warren spent their entire married life in the 'Rain Forest' area of Washington and had amassed a small fortune. Extremely frugal and childless, they had few places or reasons to spend their money in the Northwest wilderness. With savings and a protected pension, they accepted the buyout and decided to explore the United States.

Jolene had been the office manager of the company and

Warren was the top maintenance mechanic for the monster-sized logging equipment. Both felt too young to retire so after several Heineken Special Darks with Maggie at the Roadhouse, they drew up plans. Maggie would lease them land across the road adjacent to the *Maggie's Clunker* lot, for a buck-a-year. Jolene and Warren would erect a maintenance garage for diesel repair, and add sleeping quarters and showers for cross-country truckers. They wanted to attach their operation to Maggie's building, but that would have necessitated the razing of the six tourist cabins, and as long as Maggie was around that was not going to happen. Only when pigs flew over Pine Bluff.

Jolene agreed to be the accountant for both enterprises. Warren would run the semi-repair business and purchase two huge wreckers to prowl the Interstate looking for truckers in trouble or travelers in distress. Maggie would still manage her store, fuel pumps, cabins, and any administrative *problems* involving the local politicos.

The next morning, after the Heineken had worn off, the plans still seemed sound. Maggie had warned her 'cousins' that there was a possibility that the dam could be removed and the reservoir drained. The Oiumets agreed that if that happened their projections would have to be changed, but the majority of the business would still come from the Interstate with its ever-increasing traffic, not the reservoir and tourist trade. If the dam remained and the proposed resort projects were built, estimated profits might be even higher.

Maggie filled Laura in on the details of her new business plan while they had drinks at the Roadhouse. "What do you think of my expansion idea," Maggie asked.

"I know very little about business Maggie, but my dad always said it was simple; take in more than you put out," Laura shrugged.

Maggie burst out laughing. "You went to college to learn that?"

"Hey, I studied fish, not marketing. Besides," she grinned, taking no offense, "that's what my dad said, not some professor. I'll take his word for it before some ivory tower recluse."

"Your father was obviously a very wise man, but how do you do that...making sure you take in more than you put out?"

"Dad never went into details or I wasn't interested enough to listen," Laura gave a mock gasp. "Did you listen to everything your father told you, Maggie?" she grinned.

"I would like to think I remember his words of wisdom, but there just weren't that many. He died on my fourteenth birthday."

"Oh, Maggie, I'm so sorry. I wish I hadn't brought it up."

"Nonsense, that was a long time ago. But with expanding the Corners..." she trailed off. "Money aside," she tried again, "I feel like I'm being swept along...swept along into something I have little control over."

"Look," Laura said, "run a check on Warren and Jolene. Find out if they are who they say they are. Find out what their money situation really is. If they're on the level...if they come in with the financing...if your lawyer writes up the papers all nice and legal and *your* financial situation is safe...maybe then you should go for it. That's about all you can do." Laura reached out and covered the older woman's hand. "But Maggie, the question is whether or not you really want to *go for it*. Take your time and don't be afraid to just say no...just say no thank you. You're doing okay as things are. You're doing great. Up until a few weeks ago none of

this was even imaginable. Make sure it's what you really want…
want for yourself, nobody else."

They were silent for the longest time. Laura stared at Maggie
as Maggie stared into her beer glass. It suddenly occurred to Laura
how all alone Maggie really was. All these years she had made
her own decisions with nobody to really confide in—not even a
father. It seemed to Laura that it had all worked out pretty well,
but now there was a huge decision to make. Maggie could well
be risking everything she ever accomplished with people she had
just met and for what? Would it all be worth it, even if it did pay
off? Laura thought of facing decisions on her own, but she had
options, and she was young, she had time to readjust her life if she
screwed up. Did Maggie have those same options?

For the first time Laura realized that Maggie might have
vulnerabilities like everyone else. Maybe she wasn't the super-
strong woman, the totally independent person she seemed. Laura
had come to love her like a mother. Was it time to love her like a
friend, like a sister? Was it time to help share her burden?

"Is it time to grow up, Menard?" Laura reproached herself. "Is
it time to finally grow up?"

Mike Tapio came over with two fresh beers. "They're on
the house. You guys look far too serious. You're depressing the
place."

Maggie looked up, her trance broken. "Mike, what would
you do?"

"Ladies, I have no idea what you're talking about, but CYA…
cover your ass. Whatever it is, cover your ass. Trust me, I know."
That was probably the only personal advice he had ever given since
his arrival in the watershed.

◀●◀

Maggie, Jolene and Warren took several days to check each other out before taking the plunge. The Transportation Department approved Maggie's Corner as an official weigh station and later a man who introduced himself as Willie Nelson came by to discuss putting a bio-diesel fuel plant on the property.

Through all this activity, one of Maggie's biggest concerns was cutting into Charlie's Auto Repair business. When she told Charlie of the tentative plans, Charlie's only response was, "Thank God, I'm getting too old to work on those big-ass rigs." Jolene, Warren and Charlie became fast friends.

When the night manager at the Interstate truck stop at the Towne exit heard news of the expansion, she approached Maggie for a job. The only way Maggie could hire her, and make sense financially, was to stay open around the clock—24/7. With reservations, Maggie finally agreed.

Turns out, the new manager, Marcia Lynn Stonebreaker, was a shirttail cousin of Maggie's. Is Maggie related to everybody?

Marcia Lynn had good business intuition. Three months after she came to work, the Interstate Truck Stop folded. If you didn't include government or school workers, Maggie's Corner was now the area's largest employer. Business was booming.

While construction was finishing up and without Maggie's knowledge, George and Charlie used Casey Romanak's old front loader to transplant a row of conifers between the tourist cabins and the fueling area, alternating fifteen-foot subalpine fir with Colorado blue spruce. They hoped to save some of the fading rustic charm and to shield the cabins from the lights and fumes of Maggie's growing enterprise. The cabins were filled nearly every night, but the whole atmosphere just didn't feel right to George. He didn't think Maggie was all that happy with the changes either.

Fearing the new trees had come from federal land, Maggie confronted George, "I hope you've got a bill of sale." He grinned at her for the longest time and finally reached into his coverall pocket for a piece of notebook paper that he and Rufus Jefferson had both signed. In exchange for the trees from Rufus' ranch, George agreed to take a week of his vacation time to help Rufus round up steers and bring them down from the high country to wait out the winter.

"Guess that's as legal a document as any. I'll just hang on to it," Maggie said. "The BLM might wonder where we got those trees." Switching gears, she asked, "George, you've never taken any of your vacation time before. What in the world is going on?"

George grinned again. "Been out here all these years…time to learn how to ride a horse."

"You're going to learn to ride a horse?" Maggie stared at him for a second. "Okay, fine. That takes care of Rufus, but look at Charlie out there working his bottom off. How are you going to pay him?"

"I promised him I'd never ask him for another favor." George winked and went back to planting pine trees.

When the VA Hospital called to check on George Otis, Maggie made a mental note to let them know that he was finally regaining his sense of humor. Maggie smiled faintly and quickly turned away as tears began to run down her cheeks.

Possibly the one change Maggie regretted the most was that she had agreed to cover the store's tin ceiling and worn wood-planked floor. Jolene and Marcia Lynn had convinced her it would make the place easier to maintain and would appear much brighter and cleaner. They were right, of course, but Maggie missed the feel of the old country store. "Just plain sentimental," Maggie chided herself. "No, just getting old," she corrected. An antiques shop in

Capital City had even made her an offer for the old neon *FUEL* sign atop the roof. Enough was enough. The unlit sign stayed.

Vultures gathered as the money rolled in, with three major oil companies offering to purchase Maggie's Corner. Bidding against each other, they ran the amount to staggering proportions, without Maggie showing any interest in selling. Well, maybe she did show a *little* interest. She even heard that a national motel-restaurant chain had taken an option to buy forty acres of land on the northwest corner of CR64 and Canyon Road, across the street from her. They paid more for the option than the whole parcel would have cost two or three years earlier. Was it Fred Barnes, or Ruth Ann Ledbetter of the *Buzz*, who said, "Times they are a changing?"

CHAPTER 29: American Chop Suey

><

Maggie asked the old guy from Cabin #6 up to her apartment for a farewell dinner. Each year before he left for the winter, they would celebrate at the Roadhouse. This year Maggie feared she had made a gigantic mistake. Asked about his favorite meal, he had said, "American-style chop suey." What the hell was American-style chop suey?

Maggie drove to Towne early Saturday morning to talk to George "Tony" DiMaggio, the butcher at the Towne Supermarket. For a small village, they had one fantastic meat and fish counter. His Italian sausage was *to die for.* If she ever went into the restaurant business, she would surely hire him away from the market, no matter what the cost.

After listening to Maggie, Tony handed her a pound and a half of chop suey meat. "That is it? I fry this and feed it to him?"

"Gawd, Margaret Elizabeth, you've been in that gas station business too long…the fumes, maybe." Tony wiped his hands on his bloodstained white apron, untied it and draped it on a wall hook. Walking around from behind the meat counter, he took Maggie by the elbow and guided her up and down the food aisles until her cart was full of canned chow mien noodles, fresh celery, bean sprouts, water chestnuts, soy sauce, two boxes of Minute Rice (in case she *burned* one batch), a small onion, a bag of flour and a package of Sister Schubert's yeast rolls. Tony grabbed an apple pie and a quart of spumoni ice cream. Apple pie topped with spumoni ice cream certainly isn't Chinese, but it was *his* favorite just in case her friend didn't show, and Maggie needed company—his company. Shoving her toward the checkout counter, he explained what to do with her bounty.

"Let me know how it turns out." Tony walked slowly back to his meat counter. Shaking his head, he stopped to look over his shoulder. "You do have table salt, don't you?" He didn't even consider asking if she had sea salt.

As Maggie unloaded the groceries and started hauling them upstairs, her thoughts turned from what she was going to cook for the old guy to the old guy himself.

"Maybe he's not all that old," she mused. Halfway up the stairs she stopped. "Do you suppose I'm older than he is? Now that's a depressing thought. Hmmm, I probably should stop calling him *old guy*—just in case." A stellar jay, watching from the signpost, ignored her question.

Every year, like clockwork, the old guy would show up a day or two after the winter snow runoff had subsided. Uncanny, as the date could vary as much as six weeks from year to year. It was as if he hovered in the mountains above Maggie's Corner waiting to appear at exactly the right moment. Maybe he did.

He'd walk up to the counter, greet Maggie, ask if the rent had gone up and then write a check for the full season. She would give him the keys to Cabin #6 and after getting settled, he would spend the rest of the summer fishing the Whoosh River Watershed. When he wasn't fishing, he could be seen walking around the area talking to people and writing in an ordinary spiral-bound notebook. Before leaving, usually sometime well after Labor Day, he would hand Maggie his journal and she would lock it in the drawer under the cash register. She didn't remember exactly when that tradition started, but he always said, "In case I don't make it back next year…" So far, he had always returned and every year Maggie seemed happier to see him.

After the summer was over, his usual plan was to head east and fly fish where the weather and local laws allowed. Over the winter holidays he would visit his kids in Pennsylvania. January would find him in South Carolina fishing for Red Drum on the shallow flats of Cape Romain Wildlife Refuge. He then headed toward Key West angling for permit and bonefish. During the early spring months, he worked his way around the Gulf of Mexico through Alabama, Mississippi, and Louisiana, catching the local fish on dry flies—much to the good-old-boys' amazement.

"Dry flies? Are you crazy, Yankee?" was the usual question.

The month of May would find him on the Arkansas River in Colorado, following the famous Mother's Day caddis hatch upstream. During the snow runoff period, he would fish the tail waters of major river dams, where the flow was controlled and stored in the reservoirs, making it possible to fish below most dams in the harshest of winters. By the time the rivers receded to normal summer levels he would be back in the Whoosh area.

For the past five or six years he had asked Maggie to come with him in the fall, travel the country, meet his family and just "…take a vacation. Maggie, you work way too much."

She remembered his first proposal started as a joke over pitchers of Coors Beer at the Roadhouse. In a moment of good humor and the glow of several glasses, Maggie may have even suggested it herself. Each year he would bring up the subject. She would thank him, but decline, claiming she couldn't afford to leave her business. Actually, that was no longer true.

For a gal that had never been east of the Badlands of South Dakota, it was sounding more and more tempting. If Laura stuck around, Maggie might surprise him and say yes. Say yes just to see what his reaction would be.

"Probably he'd run *like the wind,*" she smiled.

Of course, that was the kicker. What was Laura going to do? If she returned to Wisconsin (and Maggie didn't want to consider that possibility) she would seriously think about selling out. With the offers she had in hand, she would have plenty of time and money to travel with whomever she chose. Hell, admit it, the old guy would probably be a great traveling companion. Besides, she always wanted to see Laura's Wisconsin. She and the old guy could swing through the Midwest on the way back East.

Since the loss of her child, Maggie didn't often "talk to God," let alone pray, but when she did, she only asked for strength enough to handle whatever He threw at her. This time she was tempted, oh so tempted, to ask that Laura stay. No, that wasn't fair. That wasn't fair to Laura or to God. "Just give me strength to accept whatever Laura decides," she mumbled as she spread out the chop suey ingredients on the kitchen counter.

Shoot, if Laura did stay at the Corner, Maggie might fly to Key West for a few days and do some fishing with the old guy. That way any possible romance would not start with a road trip. Whatever happened, she was *not* ready to meet his family.

"Now then, what am I supposed to do with these water chestnuts? What in the world are water chestnuts, anyway?"

CHAPTER 30: Old Guy in Cabin #6

S o, that's it for another year. Before his evening with Maggie, the old guy grabbed his journal and started to scribble.

My last day here amounts to buying a case of Fat Tire Beer to take to the kids and then packing my truck camper. I like to get an early start on Sunday morning. Going east I cross two time zones before getting to the coast. That's less daylight for travel. Jet lag... you think?

Every year it gets tougher to leave, but I'm dying to see my kids and grandkids in Pennsylvania. God only knows why they live out there. To be honest, I hear the winters can get pretty harsh around these parts of the Whoosh. And the older I get, the harder it is to take the cold. I can't believe I once ice fished with no shanty.

On the last Saturday night each fall, Maggie and I go to the Roadhouse for dinner. This time it's different. She's going to make me chop suey at her place. First time I've ever been invited to her apartment. I'm bringing the wine. What kind of wine do you drink with chop suey? Maybe I'll check with Zeke Astor. He prides himself as a connoisseur of fine wine. Actually, Zeke prides himself on being a lot of things.

What I've put to paper in this journal is my way of explaining events around the Whoosh River. I've written about what I've heard and seen...what other people told me. As long as no one else writes an account, you'll just have to take my word for it and accept my version.

I have one disclaimer: I have no idea how women think. My favorite author, Louis L'Amour, may describe it best through his character Texas Ranger Chick Bowdrie. Chick claimed he was no judge of women-folk. Said, "It was not like reading trail signs. Women made queer tracks."

By next year, a lot of people will have made a lot of decisions around here...choices that will deeply, and perhaps permanently, affect their lives and others, too. Maybe the biggest decision of any impact is whether or not the BLM will succumb to the pressures of the whacko environmentalists and rip out the old dam. They want to return the area to "the way things used to be." Yeah, right. Why not clone dinosaurs? Come to think of it, that might be good for tourism, until those ugly lizards got hungry.

Okay, so maybe the dam wasn't a great idea in the first place, but you deal with things the way they are now...today. Over the decades silt and sediment built up behind the dam, trapped from any downstream escape. Even with a controlled removal of the dam, millions of tons of sediment will be released to wash down the river and clog the lower reaches. With the first runoff, after the dam is gone, massive flooding could occur miles downstream. Chester Ratzigg's parlor, along with the village of Towne, could be gone with a lot of good people forced to relocate. It's possible that Chester's bridge could survive, but CR64 would become a road to nowhere. With the Interstate just south, there would be no reason to maintain a road to nowhere. Rufus Jefferson would have to adapt to the four-lane highway to deliver his woodworking projects to Maggie's or his cattle to Big City. That, friends, is a whole lot of coulds *and* woulds*. Oh sure, the river might eventually ream out the muck and return to its original channel, but the Whoosh Watershed would be totally different than it is now...to me, a sad picture.*

Enough. Pray for an end to the drought and, I'll see you all after the spring runoff...God willing and the creek don't rise. Of course, if the creek don't rise, there won't be much of a runoff, and probably no end to the drought.

Go figure.

CHAPTER 31: Laura and the Kayak

Laura stood in the Flies & Lies sports shop looking at a long line of kayaks. As many times as she had been in the store, both as a customer and a guide, she had completely ignored the kayaks, either for sale or rent. In fact, Laura had never been in a kayak.

It was her day off, maybe her last in the Whoosh River Watershed. It was a day for decisions. She had narrowed her options to three: return to Wisconsin to earn a master's degree in ichthyology and then move back to the Whoosh River Watershed; take Professor Russell's offer of a teaching position at Big City Community College and moonlight as a fishing guide; or, throw in with Maggie and in her spare time hang out with Ranger Ted Miller and help with his research. She promised Maggie she would make a decision that day.

Although Maggie hadn't said so, Laura knew she wanted to make her a partner and turn the guiding business over to her. Laura knew money would be no problem. All she had to do was get her father to come out and take him fishing. He would probably offer to be a silent partner, as long as an occasional trip down the Whoosh was part of the deal.

◉◄

Earlier that morning Laura sat on the front step of Cabin #1, her home for the past two years. Drinking coffee, she gazed at the sky, a Rocky Mountain pre-dawn blue. If that's not an official color, it should be. The sun was about to emerge from behind the eastern mountain range through a thin layer of rose-colored clouds. Jet vapor trails divided the sky into three equal parts, one for each of Laura's choices?

Hmmm, was it six of one and half a dozen of another? No, she had three choices. Maybe she needed a three-sided coin to flip. Whatever happened to her Magic '8' Ball she had relied on as a kid?

STOP! Too much sleep last night or too much coffee this morning, probably both. She would make a decision and live with it, at least for now.

◉◄

Laura stared at the kayaks, trying to recall what little she knew about the long, slender watercraft. Brad Hawkins slipped up behind her, grabbed her around the waist, and kissed her left earlobe.

"Bradley, stop it!" She pulled away and turned toward him in mock disgust, "What are you doing?"

"Just greeting my favorite fishing guide...or are you a customer today?"

"What do you know about kayaks?"

"Hmmm, buying or renting?" he asked.

"Renting, I thought I'd do something different today. Brown trout should be schooling at the inlet...up on the reservoir. 'Tis the season to be spawning," she sang. "Of course, you know that?"

"Ms. Menard, I know everything about spawning…only my spawning season is year round."

"My condolences to all your spawning partners…er, sorry, your lady friends."

"Now that was cold…not only cold, but cruel."

"Seriously," Laura said as she turned back to the line of kayaks, "I want to go out on the reservoir and see if I can catch a few fish on flies. That would be something different for me. In a kayak, anyway," she quickly amended.

"Well," Brad stood back pretending to observe her for the first time, "You obviously have the perfect build to handle our trickiest craft."

"Bradley!" Brad knew when to back off, at least around Laura.

"Sorry. You're going out on the reservoir, right?" Laura nodded. "Well, you won't need a whitewater kayak; they're built for maneuvering rapids. If I didn't know how experienced you were in canoes and drift boats, I'd put you in a recreational kayak for the flat water. They're built shorter, with a wider beam, and are quite stable. If you're launching from the dam, and going up to the inlet, you've got a long haul. I'd suggest one of our sea kayaks… some what longer and not as maneuverable or as stable, but they are super fast and easy to paddle. With the shape of their hull, the tracking is excellent."

Laura wrinkled her brow.

"What I mean is, they're easy to keep going in a straight line…a direct course with their foot-controlled rudder. I've got a fifteen-footer out back. It's a one-person kayak, with covered bulkhead to store your fly rod, small cooler and extra clothes.

It has a spray skirt to keep the water out… spray or rain. It weighs less than fifty pounds and is made of ultra-light plastic with a foam core…perfect for open water. Don't be taking it down river. It's not that maneuverable. Anyway, that would be my recommendation."

"How fast can you make these things go?" Laura questioned.

"Never timed one myself, but I've read about an annual race around Manhattan Island; over twenty-seven miles and they do it in less than four hours. What's that, about seven miles an hour? If you get the hang of it, and you're in great shape," he gazed at her again. "Depending on the wind, it should only take you a little over an hour to make it up to the inlet. I'll pack a life jacket and a helmet for you. Use the jacket, but if you stay on the lake, you won't need to wear the helmet. Law says I have to provide you with one and a personal flotation device. If you've got a wet suit, wear it. You'll stay warmer and it helps keep you afloat if you dump. If you do tip over and can't get back into the kayak, don't leave it. Somebody will be along to rescue you. Besides, you wouldn't want to lose the deposit, would you?"

"Thanks Brad. I can see where your priorities are. You're one hell-of-a-salesman. Load it on my truck. I'll give Richard your precious deposit. I'm sure he'll make me sign some sort of waiver." She reached up and gave Brad a brief kiss on the lips.

"For that, you can forget the deposit and the waiver. Hell, forget the rental fee. I'll spring for it. I'll even grab another kayak and go with you…show you how it all works," Brad beamed.

"No you won't," she called back as she headed for the front counter. "Do me a big favor?"

"Anything!"

"Don't forget to throw in the paddle."

On the road to the reservoir, Laura had a close encounter with several mule deer. Not the way to start the trip. When she arrived at the upper eastside campground, overlooking the dam's impoundment, she backed her truck up to the dock.

The stark metallic-yellow kayak overhung her pickup bed by seven feet, but Brad had secured it tightly with bungee cords and tied a red and white bandanna on the grab loop protruding from the bow. She removed the bandana and wrapped it around her neck. Though the kayak was light, its length made it awkward to handle. With some difficulty, Laura was able to wrestle it to the dock and tie it off. She loaded it with fishing gear, a cooler, and her rain jacket. She didn't own a wet suit.

Maggie had packed her two peanut butter sandwiches, a baggy full of carrot sticks, two Snickers Bars, four bottles of water, and two cans of Carling Black Label beer.

"You would make a great mom," Laura had told her. Maggie only gave her a sad little smile.

The single cockpit kayak was tricky to get into, but Laura soon had it under control. It took her less time to master the double-bladed paddle motion and rudder control. With the lake surface smooth as cheap window glass, she quickly moved toward the river inlet.

When Laura left Flies & Lies, the sky was cloudless. By the time she boarded the kayak, the cumulus clouds were building. When she reached the cove, where the upper Whoosh pours into the reservoir, the light was draining from the sky and thunderheads were forming. Not unusual for an afternoon in the Rocky Mountains. A shower, of some variety, could be expected most any day—the later in the summer, the longer the storm lasted.

Laura rigged her fly rod. No bugs in the air, so she chose one of Shirley Wheeler's hand-tied dry fly *specials*, a large yellow and orange stimulator. She knotted it to a heavy #3 tapered leader without tying on the usual length of taper. She hoped to make some fish mad enough to strike the outrageous looking artificial bug. She applied dry fly "floatant" and flipped the bug to where the river current dissipated into the man-made lake, following a six-mile tumble from the upper meadow. With the confluence of the East and Main Branches a couple miles upstream, there was still ample water pouring into the reservoir, even late into the summer. This was true even during drought periods, due to the enormous amount of water held back by the many beaver dams high up in the meadows. The river's current, though invisible, continued gently down to the dam, following the old river's path through the reservoir water, dragged by gravity and the draw from under the dam.

Casting a heavy eight-foot, six weight fly rod wasn't all that easy while Laura sat on her butt, legs stretched out in front of her. She had seen an advertisement for a "fishing" kayak that allowed you to actually stand up and cast. She hadn't read the details, but assumed it was much shorter and wider than other kayaks, possibly built with a platform of sorts.

Laura went through her late-season fly selection with no strikes. She had seen a few dorsal fins extending through the water, but the fish were set on their upstream journey to the spawning waters. The browns showed no interest in any of her offerings.

She reeled her line in and jammed the rod between her thigh and the inner edge of the cockpit. She ate the sandwiches and drained two bottles of water, saving the Black Label for the trip home. "Don't ever drink and drive," she mocked herself. Well, not on that treacherous ride down Canyon Road.

Black Label, where did Maggie come up with that?

Old habits die hard, especially for fly fishermen. The last cast of the season was always with a Hornberg dry fly/streamer. It was a Menard tradition, a tradition she was sure her dad still observed—even if a thousand miles separated the streams they fished.

A "Hornberg" was a fly originally tied in the 30s by a man named, you guessed it, Hornberg. Frank Hornberg. At the time he lived in Wisconsin, so the tradition had extra meaning for the Menards. Besides, the fly was a very productive "attractor." The Hornberg was fished on the surface, downstream, until its progress was halted. A taut line then held it on the surface until it waterlogged and sank. Then it was retrieved, like a wounded baitfish, with short sporadic jerks, varying in distance from two to five inches. This was one of the few exceptions to Laura's personal *dry fly only* rule.

While Laura was casting the Hornberg to the mouth of the inlet, the sky had turned a solid slate color. A fine mist, pushed by a steady breeze, dropped the temperature a good ten degrees. Laura braced the pole between her knees, slipped on a sweatshirt, and pulled her rain parka over her head. She tied the parka at her waist and was ready to retrieve the fly when a huge fish struck. Laura set the hook. She couldn't believe the strength of the creature. Suddenly the kayak was being dragged slowly out of the cove into the main section of the reservoir. Her leader was new and strong enough to hold, as long as she kept the line tight to the reel and the fish didn't grind it against a sunken tree or boulder. She also knew that she had forgotten to ask Brad something:

"Bradley, how do you anchor a kayak?" She had heard of sea anchors, but apparently he had forgotten, or it wasn't included in the rental. How much could a sea anchor cost?

Her reel shrieked. The monster made a long run into the line backing and then took a dive straight for the bottom. Laura retrieved the line, inches at a time, hauling the fish back toward the kayak while it continued to tow the kayak toward the center of the impoundment. If the fish were a "leftover" northern pike, it would have severed her leader long ago with its prehistoric razor-sharp teeth. Failing that, the pike would have given up the struggle by now—at least until it was in sight of the kayak and then it would attempt one last desperate rolling action in hopes of snapping the leader. If the fish was a big bass, or even a rainbow, it would have jumped out of the water several times by now. There was no way it was a Rocky Mountain brook trout. It was much too big. And, it was far too rambunctious for a large whitefish. No, this had to be the largest brown she had ever tied into.

While Laura speculated on the species, the wind, driving directly out of the north, suddenly intensified and began pushing the kayak further out toward the middle of the reservoir. Just as Laura brought the huge brown alongside, a hailstorm hit. Visibility dropped to a few feet and the temperature plunged another ten degrees.

Rather than unhook the fish, she doubled her fly line with one hand and cut the fold with her hunting knife. The fish would drag a few feet of leader and line around the lake until it could rub the fly from the corner of its mouth. No harm done to the fish.

The exhilaration of the battle ended immediately with its release. An eerie calmness overtook Laura. Almost mechanically, she broke down her rod, stuffed it ahead of her and slipped on the life preserver. She settled the helmet on her head, buckled the chinstrap, and double knotted the bandanna. She knew that running before the wind, a very strong wind was the most dangerous way to traverse the lake, but she had no choice. She had no sea anchor to slow and stabilize the kayak. She quickly tightened the spray skirt around her stomach and grabbed the paddle. The wind had become far too powerful. There would be no turning around. No turning back.

Laura immediately set up a rhythmic motion, holding the kayak southeast with her foot-controlled rudder as the wind pushed her directly south. Directly south would drive her into the cliffs of the mountain face, sheer rock that rose from the depths of the reservoir to soar hundreds of feet straight up. It would not be a question of beaching. The question would be how hard the craft would slam into the wall. If she survived, she would have to hit her father up for a loan to replace Richard's kayak.

She could hear him now. "Did they offer you an insurance policy? You should have covered the thing. Oh well, at least the money's for a good purpose, not something frivolous, like a new truck...to get you through the mountains safely." Her father would suppress a grin as he wrote a check, knowing Laura would repay him when she could.

The serenity of the still lake had changed quickly from mirror-like, to gentle but growing swells, to a heavy chop, and finally to whitecap conditions. Hail had reached marble size. Laura was protected from most of the pellet's impact, but without gloves, the tops of her hands were quickly beaten raw. Frozen bullets of water continued to slam, almost horizontally, against her back and helmet. Brad's bandanna gave some protection for her neck. After fifteen minutes, which seemed like hours, she risked a look over her right shoulder. If that direction was northwest, she was still on course and should hit the campground within twenty minutes. Maybe next year she'd cruise around Manhattan Island. "Just for fun," she mocked herself.

The hailstorm ended as abruptly as it started, but the winds continued to build in intensity, bringing a barrage of freezing rain. Thunder rolled in the distant mountains. Did she feel a tingling sensation from the lightning? Tingling or not, her body screamed for an end to the continuous paddling motion, but she never broke rhythm. She had read about athletes hitting a physical wall, or was it a mental wall?

"Think. Think, Menard," she demanded. "Remember your physiology courses, damn it."

Then, straight from a textbook:

When a marathon athlete crosses a point where they have no more glycogen reserves (fuel derived from carbohydrates) the body swaps over to begin using body fat reserves as a source of fuel. This changeover period takes time, and the resultant lack of fuel will affect an athlete's performance. The athlete has **hit the wall.**

Mental, physical, or both, Laura was determined to break through the barrier with the relentless pace she had established. If only she could get to those Snickers bars without slowing the kayak. She didn't dare try. She didn't even dare think about them.

To get her mind off the pain, the near exhaustion, and the out-of-reach candy bars, she recalled sitting at the Roadhouse drinking Margaritas with Maggie. It was Cinco de Mayo. At least it was near enough to May 5th to be drinking tequila and celebrating the Battle of Puebla, whatever the hell that was. In one corner of the Roadhouse, a country-western band attempted to imitate a mariachi band, with little success. Maggie commented how much stronger and healthier Laura looked after three years in the Rockies. "Your upper body has certainly bulked up…driving those drift boats around, I suppose."

"Yeah, big legs, big shoulders, big arms." Laura responded. "Too bad it didn't do anything for my boobs,"

Even the ever-stoic Mike Tapio had to remark. "Not to worry, Ms. Menard. Not to worry at all." His comment was so out of character that the two women stared at him for a second, looked at each other, and cracked up. Maggie ordered two Coronas with limes to chase down their margaritas. The celebration continued.

"Mike. More corn chips, please! And, buy the band a round."

><

With one thunderous clap of thunder, Laura awoke from the hypnotic trance that had engulfed her. She had lost track of time, but had maintained the momentum with her unceasing attack of paddle against water. Her bloodied hands were frozen to the shaft. As suddenly as she had hit the *wall*, she broke through it. No, it wasn't like breaking through anything. Instead, the exhaustion and pain that had pressured her entire body lifted. Her lungs filled with air. Her muscle pain eased. Even more than sudden relief, it was as if the pain had never happened. It was almost blissful. Yet, she still had not interrupted the rhythm of the paddle or the speed of the kayak. She had become the living component of the human-kayak machine set on auto drive.

Laura glanced over her shoulder. Was that a patch of blue sky, a break in the clouds over the mountains? Minutes before, she hadn't been able to see twenty feet in any direction. Now there were hints of the mountain range behind her. With one final gust, the wind abated, the sleet ended, and the thunder rolled on to the south taking with it the acrid scent of ozone. Still, Laura continued to paddle, never slowing. Now she fought the chill, willing herself to not give in to trembling and shivering. What next, hypothermia?

"Think, damn it! Think about something else. You're working too hard to be cold." At least she hadn't broken out in a full-body sweat, another sign of hypothermia.

Over the weekend she had told several people she was going to the reservoir, ostensibly to fish, but really to find a direction for her life. Would she be able to move on without regrets? Of course there would be regrets, but Laura wasn't much for looking back. Was it Yogi Bear or Yogi Berra who said, "If you come to a fork in the road, pick it up?"

A disturbing thought came from nowhere. "Maybe I'm over analyzing everything. Shouldn't I just listen to my heart? Maybe I should pack my truck and head out for California and the Mount Shasta area. I could fish, hike, and ski. Wipe the slate clean. Start all over. Do something I haven't even considered."

"Too late," she told herself. "I've got way too much invested in the Whoosh. Even if I go back to Wisconsin it would only be temporary. My goal would be to come back here, not California. Not anywhere else. My heart? My heart is here with the people, with the river and mountains, even with a village with the simple name, Towne."

Was that the light from a halogen beam breaking through the total grayness scanning the surface of the water? No, it disappeared. She doubted she had seen anything.

Hope is such a creative companion, so often an unfulfilled request.

Where in the world did she pick that up?

There it was again, brighter than before. Could somebody be searching for her? Who knew she was out here on the reservoir? Maggie, Professor Russell, and Ranger Ted Miller knew. Brad and Richard knew—they rented her the kayak. George Otis had heard her tell Maggie her plans. Hell, anyone of them could be looking for her, or not. At this point she'd even appreciate Sheriff Cowdrey showing up. Well, maybe not.

Get real. It was probably just somebody playing with a spotlight. Was she so important that someone would worry enough to come looking for her in this miserable weather?

Through the gently-lifting overcast, Laura continued to paddle. She thought she saw a silhouette of the campground ahead. Campground or not, she was certain of one thing; She was not going to drown in this stunningly beautiful country. Not today—not on the backwater of this majestic river, with the utterly ridiculous name—WHOOSH.

The Whoosh River, for God's sake!!!

CHAPTER 32: Headline

◄●◄

Ruth Ann Ledbetter watched the last of the delivery trucks leave the loading area. She grabbed a copy of the latest addition of the *Buzz* and headed for her office. Settling herself behind her desk, she sighed and looked over the front page.

LOCAL OFFICALS INDICTED

The U.S. Assistant Attorney General today announced that separate Grand Jury indictments have been issued accusing Whoosh County's Sheriff Oscar Cowdrey and County Commissioner Fred Barnes of attempted bribery of an official of the U.S. Department of the Interior. They were arraigned before Judge Elliott T. Elliott and, over the objection of the U.S. Assistant Attorney, were released on their own recognizance. Judge Elliott was quoted as saying; "Where do you think these clowns are going?"

Apparently, Barnes offered money to a government official to expedite a request by a group of East Coast financiers to build a private golf course on 500 acres of government land overlooking the Whoosh River Dam. He was also accused of attempting to influence a pending decision on whether or not to remove the dam. For several years local and national environmentalist groups have been pushing for its demise.

Ironically, Sheriff Cowdrey was attempting to bribe the same official. Cowdrey was representing the local Indian tribe which was seeking permission to build a casino on the same 500 acres. Seemingly, Barnes and Cowdrey, who have worked together on many local projects, were unaware of each others efforts.

An anonymous source said that a Grand Jury was called because of complaints filed with the U.S. Attorney's office by the acting Prosecuting Attorney of Whoosh County, Darwin Caxton Worde. Mr. Worde was not immediately available for comment.

Commissioner Barnes has refused to resign his county seat, vowing to clear his name of "…these scurrilous accusations. I will squash the person who made them. I will fight this to the United States Supreme Court…trust me."

Sheriff Cowdrey resigned his office immediately with no further comment.

Pressed by this reporter, the U.S. Attorney said that further indictments will certainly follow, reaching to the United States Halls of Congress.

In a separate news release from Washington D.C., the Department of the Interior announced the indefinite suspension of any effort by its office to remove the Whoosh River Dam.

Ruth Anne slowly folded the paper without looking at the photos of the accused in the inner pages. She also ignored a special three-page exposé of Commissioner Barnes, Sheriff Cowdrey, and the deceased District Attorney Moore. She had amassed an amazing amount of information about their deals and dealings over their long tenure as elected officials of Whoosh County. She had meticulously documented with names, dates, and locations. Each week she reviewed the file adding incriminating evidence as she uncovered it. Finally, it had become too much for her—much too much. She took the file to the acting District Attorney Darwin Worde. He graciously thanked her and asked only that she hold off publishing the story until he could relay her information, along with his own findings, to the U.S. Attorney General. Darwin assured her that a Grand Jury would be impaneled and indictments certainly would follow. Once they were announced she would be free to print whatever she felt relevant. Not knowing even then whether she was actually going to print the information or destroy it, she readily agreed. Later that same night she realized that if she did not want to question her own integrity for the remainder of her life there was only one option and one option alone.

◖◗

Ruth Anne had just scooped the biggest story in her newspaper's history and she was sad. No, she would not follow the breaking news to the "Halls of Congress." It was all up to the mainstream media now—whatever the hell that is.

Instead, she dialed Melvin and told him to grab his cameras. They were off to cover the opening ceremonies of the Oktoberfest in Big City.

EPILOGUE:

Dear Maggie:

As you well know, Maggie's Corner and Cabin #6 have been my summer home for so many wonderful years. You'll never know how happy I've been out here in "God's Country."

We agreed that you would open this journal only if I failed to return. Apparently the worst has happened (at least for me), or I'd be there again this summer and you would not be reading this. I never told you how much the summers on the Whoosh meant to me, for that, I am truly sorry. Of course, you were the best part—by far the best part.

Remember me and smile. Be glad it all happened, not that it is over. Please look out for our Laurie. She is something very, very special.

With Love Always,

Old Guy in Cabin Six

P.S. You make damn <u>good</u> chop suey.

LAURA'S GRILLED TROUT:

Recipe passed down through the Menard family.

<u>Ingredients:</u>

Fresh trout fillets (boned) with skin left on
Canola oil
½ lb. butter at room temperature
Zest from one large lemon
1 tsp. finely-chopped fresh parsley
Salt & pepper to taste
¼ cup pine nuts, toasted and finely chopped

<u>Directions:</u>

Grate the zest from one large lemon over the butter. Blend with the parsley and set aside.

Rub the trout with canola oil on both sides. Place on grill, skin side down.

Grill until skin is crispy. Turn fish over and cook until done. This should take <u>only</u> a couple of minutes on each side.

Remove trout from the grill and baste the hot-skin side of the fish with the butter mixture that was set aside. Watch it melt. Then sprinkle pine nuts over top.

SHARON MAI'S AMERICAN STYLE CHOP SUEY:

Recipe given to Tony DiMaggio and shared with Maggie.

Ingredients:

1 ½ lbs. chop suey meat
1 small onion - diced
1 cup chopped celery
1 can bean sprouts – drained
1 8oz. can water chestnuts - drained
1 pkg. chow mein noodles
¼ cup soy sauce
Salt and pepper
4 tablespoons flour
Oil for frying
3 cups water
2 cups Minute Rice

Directions:

In Dutch oven heat oil. Mix chop suey meat & 2 tbsp. flour.
Brown meat in hot oil and add onions. Salt and pepper to taste.
When meat and onions are browned, add 3 cups water and
soy sauce.
Cover with lid and cook approx. 1 hour.
Add celery, bean sprouts, & water chestnuts and cook another
15 mins.
Mix 2 tbsp. flour & ½ cup water – add to mixture to thicken.
Make instant rice.
Serve chop suey over rice. Sprinkle noodles on top.
Add more soy sauce if desired.